Soul's Cry

Soul's Cry

Cara Luecht

WhiteFireFire
Publishing

This is a work of fiction. All characters and events portrayed in this novel are either fictitious or used fictitiously.

SOUL'S CRY

WhiteFire Publishing
13607 Bedford Rd NE
Cumberland, MD 21502

ISBN: 978-1-939023-86-5 (digital)
            978-1-939023-85-8 (print)

Chapter I

The rain caught the commuters unprepared with its warm nee-
dle-like cascade. Men in suits rushed by the empty dress shop, ducking
into the doorway alcove for the few seconds it took to shake out their
newspapers, tent them over their hats, and dive back into the afternoon
throng. Women watched from behind glass, not willing to risk the dyed
feathers and crushed velvet adorning their uptown hats.

Ione checked the dime-sized watch she'd pinned just below her
shoulder and shook her head. Nearly noon. The end of Saturday's short
work day always surprised her. If she flipped the closed sign now, she
might miss a late arriving customer. If she didn't, she risked a late arriving customer who wouldn't want to leave, and she didn't want to
skip dinner and an afternoon spent with her sisters at Pastor Whitaker's house.

So she stood, undecided, with the white painted board hanging between her fingers. Even the scroll work on this simple, purposeful item
was more than she'd ever thought she would have. Ione glanced back
to the stacks of fabric and the dusty-pink walls. Heavy curtains draped
across the doorway to the fitting room with the luxury and ripple of excess yardage. Cabinets with glass fronts lined one side of the room, the
contents gleaming in the sparkle of the electric chandeliers, and floor
to ceiling gilt-framed mirrors leaned at strategic angles so ladies could
examine their new gowns.

Ione flipped the sign to read closed and turned off the light in the storefront display window. This morning, like usual, she'd started work in the dark. But with the rain, the day had never brightened. She glanced back toward the wet street and the muffled, constant noise of steel-rimmed wheels against cobbles. At least she was leaving before the streetlamps hissed to life. Ione unpinned her chatelaine from her waist and set it gently on the warm wood counter at the far end of the shop. The set of tools were more like a valued piece of jewelry, a gift from Miriam and Michael on the day her store opened under the simple name of Dressmaker. She spread the delicate chains apart, fingering the tiny scissors, the seam ripper, the cylinder that contained her best needles, and the silver thimble with a single ruby tucked into the filigreed surface. She smiled and opened the drawer under one of the glass cases that held samples of beads and crystals and lace, and pulled out her mother's much simpler version of the piece Ione wore during the day. Her mother, also a seamstress, had died nearly a year past now.

Ione pinned the plain chatelaine at her waist.

The rain continued to fall, its staccato growing in intensity until it sounded like the rush of applause. She remembered that sound. When she sang. Before things got bad and singing wasn't enough—wasn't enough for him.

Clarence.

How long had it been since she'd thought of him? She chewed the inside of her bottom lip. Had it been a week yet? She forced her gaze to the small mirror near the hat stand and concentrated on keeping the bile from rising. No reason existed for him to enter her thoughts. Yet, still, he did. Raising a shaky hand to smooth her tight curls back into submission, Ione studied the play of candlelight against her skin. Her mother had always said how lucky she was to have skin so light. Not light enough to pass as white, of course. And dark enough to earn questioning looks from the women who had heard of her talents but had not

6

been told to expect a negro woman when they crossed the threshold of her shop.

Ione startled. Something scraped against her door. The falling rain had shadowed the entrance, so Ione stood frozen, waiting, listening to the squeal of tiny metal hinges and the clank of the mail slot as it fell closed. On the other side of the window, the crowds still moved fast, still rushed to get home, out of the rain, into the warmth of a fire and the comfort of supper. All except one.

A boy, young, dressed in shabby, too-short trousers rushed out of the darkness, crossing the street, his back to her and his face tilted toward the ground.

He'd dropped something through her door.

A white envelope, face down, glowed against the dark stain of the wood floors. Ione bent and picked up the folded paper. It was wet on the corners but sealed with wax stamped in a nondescript symbol borrowed from a business of some sort. She hadn't seen it before. A payment from one of her ladies would have usually come by messenger. She glanced out the window in a quick search for the boy. The messengers for anyone she knew would have had a much better-dressed household staff member to make runs to the part of town where women wore white and could expect their skirts to stay that way through an afternoon of shopping.

The envelope was soft. Ione slid her fingernail under the smooth edge and popped the seal as she carried the unexpected delivery to the counter. An old kerosene lamp still burned, and the flickering yellow light permeated the folded paper. Heavy green stripes shone through. Ione paused, and then with cold, unfeeling fingers, she teased a scrap of silky fabric from the envelope. The small sample fluttered to the countertop.

Ione stopped breathing.

She didn't want to touch it. Didn't want anything to do with it. It was a cheap piece of her past, mocking her in this boutique, clattering out of her memory into her reality, and reminding her she was a poor black woman in a rich white woman's world, that she had come from nothing—no, worse than nothing.

She lifted the glass off the lamp and took the fabric between her fingers. She needed to burn it. Burn everything that had to do with her past.

A slip of paper slid out of the envelope and fell to the counter. *Not everyone has forgotten who you really are.*

Ione sucked in a shallow breath, choked back a cry that rested somewhere between gasp and sob, and crumpled the sheet in her fist before lifting the frayed corner to the open flame. It caught, the edge curling and turning from orange to fine black embers and then to white ash. Heat swelled and warmed her hand, and she wondered for a second or two what it would feel like to go that way. For everything to be hot and then gone. Dropping the final burning corner of paper into her empty teacup, she added the fabric to the consuming flame. Eventually, the orange glow sputtered and died. Nothing remained to remind her of that horrible year, but she still trembled in the wavering light.

Extinguishing the flame still flickering on the lamp, Ione paused, grabbed her shawl against the sudden chill and her umbrella with its too-delicate lace edge—it probably cost more than her mother had been able to make in her entire lifetime—and closed the door behind her.

Not before checking the street, though. And not before craning her neck to peer into the windows of the apartments overhead, or to watch the dark corners around the alley entrances. She knew what waited there. Oh, how she knew. She remembered hunger and the kind of pain that men so easily inflicted. Suddenly, the warmth of dinner with her sisters and the comfort of her little home above her shop felt miles away. It had been so tempting, so easy to forget. The memories swooped back in, settled into the pit of her stomach. Like everything she'd accomplished had been a dream, and now she'd been slapped awake in a dark room and reminded who she really was.

The rain had shifted into big, lazy drops that trailed down windows and collected on the brims of hats. Still standing in the shelter of the doorway, she shrugged her shawl higher and adjusted the grip on her umbrella, lowering it to shield her face. She thought it had been over, that her new world was safe from her past, and that her secrets had left when he'd disappeared. More than a year separated her from her old life. Ione breathed out heavily, as if she could expel him along with the air from her lungs. More than a year.

She should know better. Nothing was ever that easy. She slipped the key to her store into the lock and turned it, listening for the tumblers to drop, appreciating the secure mechanical sound of metal on metal. She bit back a mirthless chuckle. No. Things had gone too easily. She'd made her way from desperate to rich in less than the time it took most people to rip another year off the calendar. Of course, she had Miriam and Michael to thank for that, for the opportunities, but it hadn't happened without her efforts.

Miriam and Michael. They couldn't know. Rather, they couldn't know the details. They'd always known what she'd been—that was hard to hide—but they hadn't known much of anything about him. Much about the bad decisions she'd made. Much about the fact that she'd loved him, and she'd followed him, given up everything to be with him, and that how Miriam had found her—broken, in the alley—was the result of that ignorant, blind love.

Ione glanced down the street, her mind milking shapes from shadows, until her anger and fear stewed together into something that resembled resolve. But not the kind worn for all to see. More like the kind of resolve a jungle animal makes when they decide that they will not become prey. Not on this day. Ione stepped out of the shelter and onto the cobbles.

She glanced over her shoulder. How had he found her?

And where was he now?

Biting down hard on her bottom lip, Ione breathed in the rain-fresh air and forced back hot tears. She'd been a fool. Whether he watched her from the shadows now or not, she wasn't alone.

Chapter 2

Miriam's fingers ached to paint. She dreamed of the colors, of red and sea-glass blue, and she longed for the familiar scent of her studio. But she hadn't touched her brushes in months.

The last time the paints had spoken so vividly, she'd held the tools and brushed out the fear and the pain. The resulting portraits had led them all into and out of danger. Miriam rested her hand against her swollen stomach and felt a slight kick. She couldn't risk it. Couldn't risk the darkness coming through her hand, not with a baby on the way.

Most of all, she couldn't live with the fear of something going wrong for this new life. When she had lived alone, when no one interrupted her days and she didn't have to be distracted by thoughts of concern or pangs of worry, when she painted strangers and then with a few more strokes of her brush added lines and shadows that spoke of their future, no risk hid in the bristles of her brush. But now, now that she loved and now that new life stirred inside of her, now that she wasn't alone, those predictive brush strokes held more than curiosity—they spoke of her own joys and fears.

Now that she had a future, she had something to lose.

Miriam looked out at the gray drizzle that had persisted all morning and breathed in the familiar scent of the house in which she'd spent her childhood. Her mother's perfume still clung in unexpected corners, and every once in a while, a hint of her father's cigar would float up from a rug that had been kicked or a curtain that had been disturbed. Nothing and everything had changed from the time her mother had died and her father closed the house and moved the two of them to his warehouse offices near the docks.

Miriam sat back in her chair, feeling the give of the cushion, the comfortable spring under the rich upholstery, and glanced up at the self-portrait her mother had completed before her death. It had never been meant for eyes other than her father's, but when Miriam had uncovered the painting, she broke the unspoken confidence and placed the image of her mother—the one that displayed her insecurities and confidence, her fear and joy and love—on the mantle. But the picture lacked sorrow, and that told Miriam her mother probably didn't paint like she did. Her mother probably didn't paint the future.

And that was what stopped her. Miriam shoved her hands into the deep pockets of her skirts and fisted them into the unreasonably soft spring-green velvet. If she picked up the brush, if she turned off her thoughts and let the paint dictate again, if the future turned dark and fear curled in from the edges to invade the faces of the people she loved, what then?

She turned back to the drawings scattered across her morning desk. Sketches for children's clothes—outfits suitable for their customers at the Foundling House—were strewn about, some on the desk, some on the floor, and two hanging from the shelf above her head. Jenny had finished estimating the costs for each item, and Ione had already made small corrections to each of the drawings for last minute cost-saving details. The final step rested with Miriam and with her approval.

Picking up her pen and dipping it into the well, Miriam signed at the bottom of the rows of Jenny's figures and finalized the process.

Another order ready for production.

"Mrs. Farling?" Mrs. Maloney, their housekeeper, opened the door a crack. "Are you still in here?"

Miriam smiled and waved the distinguished-looking woman in. Although given the option to shed the uniform, Mrs. Maloney preferred to wear the severe gray dress and starched white collar and cuffs common to the most formal of houses, even though Miriam had never made an attempt at formality. She needed Mrs. Maloney too much to pretend she lacked dependence on the woman. She had been there from the start, from the point where Miriam had decided to reenter society, and almost from the day Michael had come back into her life. "What do you need?"

Mrs. Maloney stepped in and closed the door behind her. She carried a silver tray with a card adorned with Miriam's name—Mrs. Michael Farling—written in thick swirling lines of black ink on expensive, textured paper. She recognized the handwriting.

"I wonder what Mrs. Penn wants." Miriam glanced at Mrs. Maloney, hoping she would have heard of some approaching event or a likely upcoming social obligation.

"I know of nothing, Mrs. Farling."

Miriam took no comfort in the social expectations that came with the status earned by her father's wealth and her husband's successes. If she'd been raised to drink tea from delicate cups whilst reclining in white wicker furniture, or trained to talk behind the screen of a fan about the newest arrivals from France, maybe then the knots in her stomach wouldn't threaten every time someone handed her an envelope with her name on it.

She hadn't been raised like that, though—gently, and in the arms of a mother. Instead, she'd lived with her father in the tiny apartment above his warehouse, surrounded by the smells and sounds of the docks. Rather than play with teacups and ribbons, her father had placed her mother's brushes into her tiny hands. And under the watchful gaze of her nanny and teacher, she'd painted.

Mrs. Maloney nodded at the paper, and Miriam obeyed, picking up the envelope and slipping the blade of the letter opener under the folded flap.

Mrs. Penn requested her presence this afternoon. An impromptu luncheon.

"This afternoon?" Mrs. Maloney tucked the silver tray under one arm. "Her boy is waiting. What would you like me to tell him?"

"Ask him to let Mrs. Penn know I will arrive as requested by her letter." Miriam shifted her chair back and stood up, allowing time for her pregnant body to adjust to the new position.

Mrs. Maloney nodded and turned to leave. "Is there anything else?"

Miriam glanced at the papers still scattered across her desk and shrugged, accepting the impending interruption to her day. "If I am going out visiting, I may as well drop these off to Jenny at the warehouse so she can get started on this next order." Miriam bent over the table and began stacking the papers in neat piles. "Besides, I want to see how she's doing."

"Should I have the carriage brought around?"

Miriam paused. "Didn't we hire a new driver?"

"Yes."

"I haven't met him yet."

Mrs. Maloney smiled. "I'm sure you will like him."

Miriam frowned at the stacks of papers she now held. "I suppose." She gestured to Mrs. Maloney to lead the way out of the room and then followed her until they reached the bottom of the stairs. "I'm sure he knows where the warehouse is and where Mrs. Penn lives."

"I'm sure he does. I'll check about the warehouse, but I think Mr. Farling has already had him running errands there. And as far as the Penns, well, everyone knows where they live."

Miriam knew she required more handholding than the typical lady of the house. She smiled at Mrs. Maloney, silently thanking her for never reminding her of her faults.

Mrs. Maloney smiled back and reached for the stack of papers. "I'll slip these into your case and let the driver know to ready the horses. Should I send someone up to help you get changed?"

"Yes." Miriam climbed a few stairs before turning back. "What is the name of the driver?"

"Mr. Tamm."

Miriam continued up the stairs. She'd seen Tamm in the gardens behind the house while looking out of one of the small square windows in the hall that connected two of the hidden rooms at the back of the townhouse. He had dark skin and black wavy hair. Their eyes had met, and for a moment, she thought she'd recognized something there, in his gaze. But he'd looked away and ducked into the garden shed to retrieve some tool. Miriam waited, but when Tamm exited he never looked back to check if she still watched.

The Penn mansion ruled the lakefront with dark brick arches and wrought iron authority. Sumptuous landscape carpeted and adorned the square patch of land in the summer, and in the winter, that green gave way to the warmth of well-lit windows that burned against the icy, roiling Lake Michigan backdrop. As if the towering mansion weren't enough to impress the elite, the rooftop ballroom, encased in glass, twinkled in summer evenings with the light of gleaming chandeliers and even brighter society heavyweights. The first time Miriam had visited, she'd expected to be overwhelmed by the enormity of the place and the legend of the woman who commanded it. She'd been surprised to discover, though, that Mrs. Penn turned out to be a fellow lover of art and a valuable friend.

Tamm slowed the carriage and turned into the circle drive in front of the towering home. Mrs. Penn's letter had not hinted at the reasoning behind her request for a visit, but the congregation of other richly appointed carriages foreshadowed the likelihood that Miriam would be joining a large group of others who had also received invitations that morning. Typical etiquette required more than a few hours' notice for a visit, but Mrs. Penn had the prestige to flaunt any number of niceties and the influence to make the invited grateful for her attention.

The carriage rolled to a stop, and Tamm jumped down from his perch above. Opening the door for Miriam, he lowered the stair, offered his hand, and bowed, never making eye contact. Which agreed with Miriam's sensibilities. The less eye contact, the better. She tried to appreciate his evasion, but when their gloved fingers touched, the dead sense of nothing swelled under the fabric and darkened the cloudless sky.

"Thank you." Miriam ripped her hand from his as the tip of her boot hit the cobbles. "I...I'll send for you when I need you."

Tamm nodded once and turned back to the carriage, leaving Miriam to take the stairs under the watchful gaze of the Penn's footmen.

"Good afternoon, Mrs. Farling." The impeccably dressed servant bowed and offered her his arm for the last step into the grand home. "I've been instructed to see you in."

"Thank you, Mr. Jones." Miriam took his arm and followed him into the grand entryway.

He lifted a brow and offered a half-smile at the proof of his remembered name. "Mrs. Penn instructed me to lead you in the back way, if you would like." He leaned in low to whisper as he took her wrap.

Miriam nodded. Mrs. Penn, for all her fierceness, always treated Miriam with unexpected care. It might have been that Michael had previously won Mrs. Penn over so thoroughly, or her friend's love of art and fascination with artists. Miriam could never tell the reason, but she appreciated it.

Mr. Jones handed Miriam's wrap to a waiting maid. "There are about a dozen other women in the room. Mrs. Penn is asking for involvement from all the women who will be attending, but she wanted me to make her desire to have your support clear from the beginning."

Miriam slowed her steps, bringing their progress across the white marble floors to a halt. "Perhaps I should already know, but what is it that she needs?"

Mr. Jones smiled again. "There are some questions about the Women's Pavilion at the Columbian Exposition. From what I hear, there is disagreement over art selections and still some grumbling about the architect chosen to design the exhibit. Mrs. Penn has not said so to me, but I think she is gathering support to maintain control over the artwork and cultural exhibits."

Miriam nodded and together they made their way to one of the parlor's side doors.

He leaned in closer, wise eyes alert and sparking with intent. "There is also some debate over the fashion exhibits."

"I see." Miriam grinned at the servant. Mr. Jones was always a wealth of information. Not the kind that could ever put the Penn family at risk, but rather the sort that smoothed the path for Mrs. Penn's ambitions. He'd been with the family for decades.

He held open the glass-paneled French door. Miriam took a breath, steeling herself for the onslaught of people and conversation, and stepped inside to the swirling kaleidoscope of soft flowers that spilled from crystal vases and vibrating feathers that dangled from brightly colored hats. The ladies, busily smiling and gesturing, leaned in with their heads together, gleaning the most recent bits of gossip. Most of the ladies milling about she remembered from any number of events that had taken place over the past year. Some of them were unfamiliar—likely the new young wives of husbands from prominent local families. But it wasn't the women or the heavily perfumed room or the cacophony of colors that stopped her observations. Rather, it was the wary expression Mrs. Penn leveled at Miriam over the determined shoulder of an unfamiliar lady, and the slight tick of her fingers, calling Miriam to her side, that made Miriam want to turn and run.

She didn't. With one delicately booted foot in front of another, Miriam crossed the room to the now customary accompaniment of low whispers and hushed tones and took her place at Mrs. Penn's side. Her presence, although accepted, was still something of a sensation. The recluse daughter of one of the city's richest men had always been a curiosity.

Not as curious as the expression the strange woman directed toward Mrs. Penn, though. And not nearly as disturbing. Mrs. Penn's steely posture and slightly pink cheeks were enough to make Miriam slide up next to her, despite the low, personal tones of the conversation, and take inventory of the offending woman.

Her dress, with its fashionably large sleeves and narrow skirt, echoed the severe expression she wore.

"I know this will not be a problem," the woman said, the false lilt in her voice at odds with the ice in her eyes. "The agreement was in place long before you stepped in."

Mrs. Penn didn't dignify her statement with a response. Instead, she maintained an uncomfortable stare until the other woman cleared her throat and took a step back. "Good day, Mrs. Black."

Dismissed, Mrs. Black blinked, the heightened color blotching her neck rising to stain her cheeks. With a slight nod, she turned and made her way back through the crowd, past the huge potted ferns, and out the main doors.

"What was that about?" Miriam tore her gaze from the now empty entryway.

Mrs. Penn sniffed, let out a long breath, and then relaxed her posture. "She owns the most prestigious dress shop in town, and she wants to design the uniforms for the women who will work at the Pavilion."

"And why wouldn't she?"

"Because I want Ione to do it."

Miriam couldn't hide her smile. "I suppose that explains it then."

"She may try to cause some trouble, but it won't last long." Mrs. Penn took a step away and nodded to another guest before signaling the maid to ring the bell that would begin the meeting. Glancing back at Miriam, she gestured to the chair in the front row of seats and welcomed everyone to what she introduced as the first of many meetings to decide how the women of Chicago would be represented at the World's Columbian Exposition.

Chapter 3

Ione walked the two blocks it took to get from where she jumped off the trolley to Pastor Whitaker's home. She had stopped looking over her shoulder by the time she'd ridden past businesses and homes and stores of all sorts. Not because she thought the danger had disappeared, but because she refused to be scared. This dinner, once a week, where she joined her sisters with their adoptive family—one who also welcomed her and treated her like she belonged—was the only time she had to spend with them. And she would not arrive looking as if she'd been chased there.

The door of their whitewashed house, snuggled neatly to the fawn-colored brick church, gaped open, and Lucy hopped up and down in the opening, watching for her arrival. Ione waved, and thoughts of the note, of the scrap of fabric, of her past, slid away, insignificant, under the gaze of her littlest sister, who seemed to grow taller every week.

"We're having chicken." Lucy, always enthusiastic, shook her braids with their bright pink ribbons so Ione would notice.

She took her hand. "I see you have more new ribbons." Laughter colored her soft rebuke.

"Yup." Lucy dragged Ione into the front room, where Mrs. Whitaker stood, wiping her hands on her apron and smiling.

"So glad you could come." She sent a playful, chiding glance toward Lucy. "You know, Lucy will start talking about next week's dinner almost as soon as we finish the dishes tonight."

Ione nodded and squeezed Lucy's small fingers.

"Maggie will be coming, but she's running late from an appointment with one of the ladies from church who has some mending that needs to be done. Your sister jumped at the chance to make an extra bit of money."

"Sounds like Maggie." Ione smiled, setting her handbag down in an empty chair next to the door. "I have all the work she could handle, if she wanted it, but she seems determined to do things on her own."

Mrs. Whitaker waved Ione toward the davenport, and then sat down next to her. "I keep reminding her that she can't get so busy that she doesn't finish school this autumn, and she says she plans to leave enough time for her studies. But if you remind her too, it wouldn't hurt."

Ione nodded, appreciating how Mrs. Whitaker watched over her sisters. After their mother had died, Ione had been in too much trouble herself to look after them the way they deserved. Pastor and Mrs. Whitaker stepped in and quickly fell in love with Lucy and Maggie. Ione had been both heartbroken and relieved that they had found this new home. Especially since she'd had none to offer.

She should have had something, but she'd been unwise, and it had cost her more than she'd imagined possible.

And now he was back.

"Is something wrong?" Mrs. Whitaker ducked her chin to look more closely at Ione.

"I'm sorry. Just a busy day, I suppose."

Mrs. Whitaker didn't look convinced. "Maybe we should get you something to drink. Besides, I need to check on the potatoes."

Ione followed Mrs. Whitaker into the humid kitchen, her stomach growling, loudly, at the aroma of roasting meat and fresh bread. She shrugged, embarrassed at her hostess's light laugh.

"Have you eaten anything today?"

"I..." Ione thought for a moment. "Actually, I don't think I did."

"You need to take care of yourself." Mrs. Whitaker cut a slice of bread from a new loaf and slathered it with butter. She handed it to Ione. "Your sisters would be lost without you, you know."

They wouldn't. Ione knew the pastor's wife was being nice. Her sisters had done well without her. They had certainly done better than they would have if Ione had had the responsibility of raising them this past year.

"Oh, and Aaron's brother will join us any minute," Mrs. Whitaker said. It took Ione a couple of moments to register that *Aaron* was Pastor Whitaker's given name.

"Pastor's brother?"

"Yes."

"I don't think anyone has ever mentioned him." Ione frowned.

"His brother, Evan, is quite a bit younger than Aaron. He's just completed his medical training at Howard University." The pride in Mrs. Whitaker's voice rang.

Ione didn't try to hide her surprise. "He's a doctor?"

Mrs. Whitaker nodded, picked up a wooden spoon, and turned to check if the potatoes were done. "He sure is. He's visiting to consider the possibility of opening a practice here in Chicago."

Ione felt the blood rush to her face. She'd come expecting to visit with her sisters, and with the family that had in many ways become hers, but now a stranger would join them. Taking a deep breath, Ione concentrated on shifting her plans from those that she considered comforting to those that would include engaging a stranger in conversation. Disappointment threatened her expression, so she marshaled her face into a smile and picked up a dish towel. "It will be nice to meet someone new. What can I do to help?"

But Mrs. Whitaker didn't answer. Instead, she smiled and waved out the kitchen window, stretching up on the balls of her feet. "He's here." She tapped Ione's cold hand and pointed, as if Ione hadn't seen the broad shoulders and confident stride from where she stood next to her hostess. He was handsome. Ione held her breath. How long had it been since she'd thought a man handsome?

He tipped his hat to a skipping child who dodged neatly out of his way. Ione leaned forward against the counter, following his progress as he turned the corner of the house. Watching the kitchen door, she lifted her free hand to feel for any stray, riotous curls.

Mrs. Whitaker pulled the towel from Ione's other hand and sent a half-smile, topped by the knowing lift of one brow. "Don't worry, he's very nice. And you don't have to do anything but sit there and tell me how your day went."

Ione swallowed, hard. That was the one thing she couldn't discuss.

Miriam left with a list of duties longer than she thought possible. And none of them were simple, like to choose the color for the drapes in the Women's Pavilion or decide on the kinds of pastries that would be served. No. She glanced at the sheet of paper she still held in her gloved hand. Her tasks were to secure the support of community leaders and help to determine how many women would need to be hired to work in the Pavilion during the setup and duration of the fair.

If Mrs. Penn would have only been kind enough to tell Miriam that she had to help Ione choose fabric for dresses or something of that nature. Or better yet, maybe it wasn't too late to offer financial support. Miriam glanced out the carriage window at the lake. Teal blue rippled against the sky, shifting to lighter blue as the water approached shore and shallowed against the sandy bottom. White stripes of waves, their crashing sound delayed by the distance to the road, teased the rocky edge, and gulls screamed overhead, as if they could bully the fish from the water. Miriam folded the paper still in her hands one more time and tucked it into her handbag, frowning at her gloved fingers. She would do as Mrs. Penn asked. But she wouldn't tell Michael—she wouldn't ask him for favors or depend on his connections. Instead, she would do it on her own. She rubbed her expanding belly and leaned back, eyes closed, listening to the waves and breathing in the humid lake air. Mrs. Penn had a way of pressing her into things that she should do anyway.

The fresh scent of the lake became heavier, and Miriam opened her eyes to the more familiar scenery of the approaching docks. Jenny would be waiting for her at the warehouse. And Jeremy. Miriam smiled and returned the wave of a child with a smudged face, balancing on the edge of the gutter, testing fate. Fate, and the standing water and horse muck would likely win, and unfortunately, the boy's mother, who would have to clean him up, would pay the price. Jenny and Jeremy had been married for almost six months now, and Theo, Jenny's adopted son, couldn't be happier.

The carriage slowed and rocked to a stop outside the place Miriam had once called home. Tamm opened the door and held out his hand. Again. Miriam took a breath and grasped the edge of the window, steadying herself for his touch.

But nothing happened. Nothing like the dead jolt she received outside of the Penn mansion.

"There's an alley just down the street. It wraps around the back of the warehouse, where you will find a small stable. I'll send for you when I am ready to go."

Tamm handed Miriam her attaché case and held open the door to the warehouse. "Yes, ma'am."

Miriam nodded and breathed easier as the darkness of the warehouse closed in around her. The scent of boxes and dust and fabric and the outside air, drug in by the skirts of the women who worked there and the daily deliveries, enveloped her. For as much as she loved that she could return to the incredible townhouse where she'd spent the first few years of her childhood, and be surrounded by memories of her parents and the luxuries they'd amassed, it was here, in the warehouse where she'd grown up and learned to paint and spent countless hours in solitude watching the people pass below her windows on the sidewalk, that would always be home.

"I hoped I'd see you before I had to leave." John, the priest from the cathedral across the street, appeared from around a stack of crates. His robes did the best they could to communicate formality but could never quite accomplish the task. The breadth of his shoulders belied his rural upbringing, and his tousled dark hair evidenced his tendency for laughter over reverence. But not at the cost of his ministry. He'd proven time and time again the people he served were his priority. And he'd sacrificed, for her, for Ione and Jenny, and for countless others he'd never mention.

"I've missed you." Miriam placed her small hand against his arm. He covered her fingers with his, his appreciation for her touch evident in the way his eyes closed with her small embrace.

His eyes opened and he met her gaze. "I've been invited to join Pastor Whitaker for dinner tonight. I think Ione will be there too." He took a step back and looked down at Miriam's expanding midsection. Propriety dictated he avoid any mention of her condition, but history had brought them beyond the confines of etiquette. "It won't be long now?"

"I hope not." Miriam relaxed and allowed her exasperation to show. "We still have awhile, but one begins to wonder how such a thing is even possible."

John's large smile did little to hide his obvious fascination. "Remind Michael again for me how lucky he is to have you for a wife, and you take care of that little one." He reached above Miriam's head and plucked his hat from the hook next to the door.

Miriam laughed. "I remind him every day. You don't have to worry."

He opened the door, and the newly-arrived sunshine cascaded in around him, turning his hair into a golden brown and obscuring his features in shadow. She'd painted him what seemed like long ago, and the striking similarity to how the doorway framed him, to how his hair shone, to his hidden expression, took her breath away.

"What is it?" His eyes grew serious.

Miriam shook her head and smiled. "You will join us for dinner next week?"

"Just say when."

"Let's say Tuesday, unless you have other plans?"

"I don't think I have anything else happening. I'll let you know if something comes up. Otherwise, I'll plan to see you then."

With that, he slipped his hat onto his head and ducked out into the light.

Miriam watched the door close, remembering the first time he'd been in her warehouse, remembering how nervous she'd been, and thankful for the transformation of the last year.

She brought her hand to her stomach and felt the slow roll of movement within. The changes she'd been through were nothing compared to what the future held. Again, the desire to paint tempted, made her want things she could feel but not name, but she tightened her grip on the case that held Ione's drawings and Jenny's numbers, and tried to find satisfaction in the worn leather handle and the security of things known.

Chapter 4

Ione woke to the pre-dawn black. Her dreams, a riot of groping hands and faceless men, left her breathless and shaking. She'd been rid of the nightmares for months, but now things had shifted back.

She lifted the quilt and dropped her feet to the thick rug that lined nearly the entire floor of the bedroom in her apartment over her shop. Even with the change that threatened, she couldn't help but smile at the thought of her own storefront. After Jenny married and Jeremy moved into the warehouse to help her, Miriam and Michael brought up the idea of Ione finally opening her own place. She'd wanted it for as long as she could remember.

Ione reached over, struck a match, and lit the lamp on her bedside table. The warm yellow glow illuminated the room that she'd decorated with simple details, and she took a deep breath of the familiarity. It looked nothing like the dressmaker's rooms below, with velvet and lace and opulent trimmings. Instead, she slept under a quilt that had been one of Mrs. Whitaker's, and she cooked in a kettle that had been her mother's. Miriam had given her a set of delicate china with a yellow and pink floral pattern, prettier than anything else in the room. And fashion books strewn about made the place feel like home.

She never, in all her days, thought she would have such a place.

And it was hers.

Miriam and Michael had helped her purchase the store and the apartment, and they'd provided the financing for her inventory, but most of the loans were nearly paid in full, and Ione couldn't help but count the things that she now owned outright. The income she'd made from working at the warehouse, combined with the income she earned for designing and creating the gowns for the city's matrons and their charges, provided more than she'd imagined possible. Still, after nearly six months of having her doors open and serving well-dressed women, it shocked her to list the outrageous prices of fine fabric and crystal trimmings, and watch her customers flick their hand as if the amount—enough to have fed Ione's family for more than a month—was nothing.

Ione felt around for her slippers, slid her toes into the soft warmth, and stood to cross the room. Of the two bedrooms, one she kept closed unless Maggie stayed overnight to help finish a project.

She tied on her robe and smiled at the thought that she'd never have to face a landlord again. She'd never be in a position where a roof over her or her sisters' heads came at a cost that no one should have to pay. She crossed to her kitchen and pulled out the too-fancy teacup and saucer from the shelf above her oven. The delicate porcelain rattled in her grip. She concentrated on holding still, but the trembling wouldn't cease.

He'd found her.

It had been so long since she'd seen him. Ione set the saucer and cup onto the table and leaned against the solid wood, breathing slowly, trying to calm her mind.

But images of that year swam into her consciousness. Pictures of her leaving her mother's home to run off with him. Of him at the piano in the club and her standing by, singing, smiling as the men whistled and called out. She remembered thinking her mother was crazy for mending clothes for the white folks when she could be singing for a living.

And then things got bad.

Ione sank into the kitchen chair and dropped her head to the table.

The club closed, so they'd found a tavern with less light, less money, little food, and dirtier customers. And a bartending owner who wanted to strike a deal to offset the cost of their room.

Clarence thought the idea reasonable, but Ione refused. The fight that ensued had been shameful. She'd returned to her mother bruised, humbled, and sorry.

And the squalor and sickness she'd found when she stepped through her mother's door sucked the breath from her body.

There'd been no food for her sisters. No money to pay the pounding landlord. Lucy lay listless next to their mother, and Maggie did her best to do their mother's mending so they could get something to eat.

Ione shooed them from their mother's bed, sent Maggie for the doctor, and learned of the tumor that crowded and ravaged their mother's insides.

That night, after he left, the doctor sent a basket of food, and her sisters ate for probably the first time in days. That was also the night Ione decided she'd do whatever she had to do to see them through.

So she shook out the dress she'd worn onstage, a cheap striped fabric that looked luxurious from a distance. She'd sewed the places torn during the fight. She'd used a hot iron to straighten her hair so it would cover the bruises on her face, and then she stepped out into the street, and right into the life she'd run from.

Ione took a deep breath and wiped her eyes with still-shaking hands. She missed her mother. She missed her patient understanding and the way she never allowed Ione to blame herself, even when she carried the fault for her actions. And even though Ione knew Miriam and Jenny believed she could do anything, and even though they'd helped one another through so much, Ione missed her mother's gentle kindness and her subtle smile when she approved. Ione looked around the room, longing to show her mother the life she had now.

Part of her also missed having someone to protect her. Because for all that she'd told her friends, and all they'd done to help, and even though she knew they loved her like a sister, and even though they knew what she'd done to feed her sisters, they could never know that she'd been so in love with a man who only wanted her for the money she could earn him.

The decision to sell her body for food humbled and embarrassed her. But that the decision was the result of a love for a man who talked her into betraying what she knew to be right, who convinced her to abandon her own family, and who didn't love her in return—that humiliated her.

She'd sat at dinner with the Whitakers. Watched her sisters eat and laugh. Avoided Mrs. Whitaker's concerned gaze and Pastor Whitaker's brother's obvious charm. That they knew she'd sold herself yet still introduced her to their brother was a testament to a graciousness she didn't deserve.

Sure, they could forgive a fallen woman whose circumstances left her with few options and mouths to feed. It asked too much, though, to expect them to look past the sin when everything had been the result of her own selfish choices.

She couldn't ask them to do that.

So she sat at dinner. Smiled at the appropriate times. Hugged her sisters. Shrugged in agreement when the conversation required it. Pretended like she deserved the honor. And left as soon as politely possible.

From the outside, Dr. Whitaker had been everything a young doctor should be. He'd sat across from her, smiling and asking questions. He bantered back and forth with his brother and with Maggie. Intelligence flickered behind eyes that were lighter than the pastor's, yet that they were brothers was unmistakable. But Ione knew better than to trust her opinion.

And she'd known enough men to never need the complication of a relationship again.

Because her last one still wasn't over. She shifted uncomfortably. It might never be over.

Ione left the still-empty cup on the table and returned to her bed, where she kicked off her slippers and curled under the quilt. Darkness still ruled. She still had time to lie in the warmth and long for sleep to come.

It wouldn't.

"So, Mrs. Penn said she's already asked Ione to design the dresses for the workers in the Women's Pavilion?" Beatrice asked.

Miriam glanced at her friend. She'd stretched out, reclining on the parlor chaise with the *Chicago Tribune* business page suspended above her. With her dark hair worn partially down and curled perfectly over the upholstery, Beatrice looked like some sort of advertisement for skin cream.

"She also tasked me with decisions on staffing for the Pavilion."

Beatrice dropped her arm and let the paper crumple half on the floor next to her. She sat up only far enough to stuff another pillow under her shoulders. "She doesn't waste much time, does she?"

"No, she doesn't." Miriam did nothing to hide her flat tone.

"You do realize she is doing this because she knows you won't try to wrest control from her, right? You are a good, safe choice."

Miriam let her hands and her embroidery fall into her lap. "Now what is that supposed to mean?"

Finally sitting up fully, Beatrice raised a brow and met Miriam's gaze. "You know what I mean. But it's not bad that you are a safe choice. I think the fact that Mrs. Penn is taking control of some of these decisions only makes sense. But she knows that she will have your support when she makes unpopular choices, like asking Ione to design the uniforms instead of the designers at Black's."

Miriam hummed her agreement and frowned at Beatrice. "Why do I feel like everything in society is some sort of trap?"

"Because, m'dear, it is." Beatrice snorted lightly and pointed to the society page that had fallen to the floor. "All you have to do is read that page, and then combine the information there with the tidbits you pick up at balls and concerts and dinners, and a whole new picture emerges."

"I am wholly unfit for this life." Miriam stuffed her embroidery into the basket next to her chair and gazed out the window into the hidden courtyard between her townhouse and the next.

"You are not." Beatrice leaned over and began reordering the paper so it looked like it hadn't been read. "And I'll put this back so Michael will never know I was the first to read it."

"Oh, he'll know. But he won't care. He usually reads the paper at the office." Miriam took a deep breath. The scent of cinnamon and pastries hovered somewhere near. "You smell that?"

"Do I ever." Beatrice smiled. "You suppose we should ring for tea?"

"It's not teatime yet."

"I guess we could wait." Beatrice's disappointed tone didn't communicate patience.

"Or we could go into the kitchen and see what they're doing."

Beatrice smiled and crossed to stand next to Miriam's chair before Miriam had a chance to straighten. "I think I'm moving slower than usual." Miriam scowled down at her expanding midsection.

"I would normally hesitate to agree, considering the delicacy of your condition, but yes. You are slow as molasses."

"Thank you." Miriam leveled the scowl at her friend.

"Well, we'd better get going, or we won't reach the kitchen until teatime, and then they will be up here, and we'll still be hungry."

"I am 'getting going,'" Miriam said. "I'm going to have to stop inviting you over, you know. You make me tired."

"You think I'd wait for an invite?" Beatrice continued her teasing, shaking the wrinkles out of her lavender skirts. "That's charming."

Miriam considered the walk to the kitchens. "You want to take the short cut?"

"You mean through the passageways?" Beatrice went still.

Miriam nodded.

"I've never been through there. I thought you didn't like other people in your rooms."

Miriam shrugged. "I guess I wouldn't mind so much. Besides, it really is beautiful, and one of the exits is just outside the kitchen entrance, so it makes sense."

Beatrice smiled. Words weren't necessary.

Pulling a key from her pocket, Miriam walked to the place between the drapes and the fireplace mantel. She pushed in a wooden knob, engaging the spring mechanism hidden behind the wall. When the knob slid out an inch, Miriam turned it, inserted the key and twisted. The dark wood panel sank into an unlit hall, and Miriam led the way.

Tamm pulled the carriage around back to the stables and waited for the stable boy to lead the horses in. Even the horses in this house lived better than most folks he knew.

Not better than him, though. At least not better than he had lived a while back, until his luck turned and the clubs shut him out. He'd been angry at first, but now that emotion had simmered down to something that resembled determination. He'd get back what he had lost. Somehow he'd manage it, and the past week had brought a gift he hadn't anticipated.

But until everything could return to rights, he worked. And being in the right place at the right time meant he could fill the position in the Farlings' home.

Tamm jumped down from his seat atop the carriage, saluted the skinny white stable boy, and took the stairs two at a time to his room above the stables. The living conditions were better than at some other places, where the men slept in bunks in one large shared room. At least here he had his own space with a bed, dresser, and desk. In the desk, he stored the stationery he'd kept from the fine hotel where he used to live.

He'd stayed there as a paying customer, not as a servant in the servants' quarters. For nearly a year, he had walked with the other rich men, requested services from the concierge same as the other guests, bathed every morning with fresh towels, and slept every evening in crisp linens.

Then his luck at the tables faded and creditors got impatient.

Tamm frowned and pulled the wooden chair from underneath his desk. He sat, leaned back, and eased the middle drawer open, drawing out the stationery. The pen rested against the ink well in a simple stand made more for utility than beauty. He picked up the offending simple tool and vowed to someday again write with pens decorated with silver filigree. Unstopping the ink well, he dipped the pen in and put the tip to the clean sheet of paper. All day, while dragging Mrs. Farling from place to pointless place, he'd been planning what to say.

Finding Ione had been a stroke of luck. He'd lost track of her after she'd left, but it didn't much matter because that was when his streak at the tables began. And even though his luck had run dry, the morning he'd been tossed out of the last den and instructed never to return, that morning, he'd wandered down the street looking in the windows of the shops. Then he'd seen her. Still beautiful, still moving about and working, and apparently well-fed. She'd gained weight since he'd last seen her.

Tamm drew the first letter of her name with a large, loping flourish. He'd always been told his writing was something exceptional, and now he planned to use everything he had.

After all that had happened, he expected she wouldn't want him back without some kind of encouragement, and he'd actually questioned whether or not he should even pursue her. Then he'd overheard the women congregating on the other side of the road. They'd said a negro owned that dress shop. That they were surprised by the quality, and that even though they didn't want to go to a negro dress shop, if they wanted the newest designs in ball gowns for the season, they would go there.

The pieces fell into place.

She'd done well on her own.

She wouldn't welcome him back, with her new business and rich, white clientele, he'd assumed. After all, she'd never tried to contact him. He frowned and smoothed the sheet of paper against the chipped desk. But he was the one who had taught her to stand in front of customers with confidence and poise. He'd showed her how to work an audience and how to charm people out of their hard-earned cash. Tamm smirked, thinking of the sumptuous little storefront. She'd obviously learned well.

Ione owed him. And one way or another, he'd remind her of her debts.

Chapter 5

"I'm not sure the green is for me." The blond woman twisted in the mirror, examining the gown from every direction. "I've always preferred red for the holiday season. This seems plain."

Ione, kneeling on the floor in front of her customer, pulled a pin from her mouth and looked up, careful to hide her surprise at the thought of green velvet as plain. "I think you should give the green a chance. It highlights your complexion."

"But red is so fashionable right now." She crossed her arms over her chest. Ione gestured for her to drop them back to her sides.

"Are you saying you want to look like every other lady at the dance?" Ione shrugged. "I thought the idea was to stand out so your young man might notice you."

The woman's friend snickered and pulled a long ribbon from the box on the counter. She held it up to her friend's fine hair and tucked it into one of the fasteners that held the strands up and off her shoulders. "I think she's right, you know. Green suits you."

The woman allowed her shoulders to relax, examining the way the dress accentuated her long neck, deciding whether her friend's compliment was an honest assessment or one that leveled the competition. "I do like the cut. I have to admit that."

Ione rocked back on her heels and stood. "There." She pointed to the other bank of mirrors across the room. "If you walk over there, you can see how the back looks in these mirrors."

The young woman smiled and stepped down off the low round platform that allowed Ione to perfect hem measurements. She sauntered across the floor, watching how the fabric caught the line of her leg and then released. The nearly invisible bustle accentuated the hollow curve of her back. She stopped and turned to Ione. "Those women were right—you work miracles."

Ione fought to hide her smile. "Thank you, ma'am."

The woman turned one more time in front of her friend. Ione couldn't help but see the slight flash of envy in the eyes of her companion, and knew, before the day's end, she would have yet another client.

"I'll take it. Now, there are no others like this one?"

"None." Ione assured her. "I design unique pieces."

"Good." She walked back behind the curtain.

"I'll call for one of the girls to help you out of the dress," Ione called after her.

She tapped the bell at the counter, and one of her assistants appeared. Grace, a pretty white girl with brown hair and a smile that never faded, stepped out of the back room with a pile of fabric samples. "These just came in from the mill." She dropped them on the counter and slid them to Ione. "Did they send pieces from the wrong bolts?"

"No. These are for some designs I'm working on for the Farlings."

"Oh." The girl's confusion only faded slightly, but Ione didn't feel like explaining her connection with the famous family, especially with two pairs of ears in the dressing room doing all they could to catch even the tiniest bit of gossip.

"She could use some help getting out of that green velvet, if you don't mind." Ione pointed to the closed curtain.

Grace nodded and disappeared behind the fabric that served the need for privacy, careful to fasten the button closures behind her. The fabric samples would need to be assessed for durability and attractiveness, and then weighed against the cost. She would need Jenny's help. Ione slid the fabric aside, revealing the stack of correspondence Grace must have set down first. She never used to get mail. Now her desk cascaded with letters from customers about last minute details, requests for payments from her suppliers, bank drafts from the husbands of the women she served, inquiries from potential clients who desired a meeting, and this time, two others.

Her heart pounded an unnatural rhythm against her ribs, rushing blood to her ears until they rang. Ione sank to one of the upholstered benches where mothers sat to watch their daughters try on new styles.

It had been less than a week since the last one. She held the sealed envelope between her finger and thumb, trying to touch it as lightly as possible. The demanding "I" of her name scrawled into the envelope meant the first letter had not been a mistake. It hadn't been something she'd dreampt. And it wasn't something she could ignore.

She opened it. The envelope fluttered with deceiving levity to the lush carpet under her feet. She stared at the words—the only words—on the clean sheet. *Don't you remember?*

How could she forget? She crushed the thick paper in her fist and stood to pace behind the counter. Oh, she remembered. She remembered the tavern owner's rancid breath and the way Clarence worked to convince her it would all be over soon. She remembered the fists when she'd refused. She remembered the squalor of their apartment, where she would try to bathe the grime away. Oh, she remembered. She remembered everything.

The paper burned against her skin. Setting flame to it wasn't enough. How had he found her?

This time, the trembling started at her knees. Ione fumbled to shove the crumpled paper deep into her pocket before her customers walked back into the main shop. Their conversation behind the changing room curtain swelled and hissed. Ione shook her head to clear away the senseless chatter.

"I'll let Ione know you would like your next fitting to be on a Thursday." Grace held open the curtain for the women, and then tied it to the side with a heavy tassel. "Is there anything else I can do for you while you are here? Did you want to choose a hat or a wrap to go with the dress?"

Ione stood, crossed to stand behind the counter, and offered what she hoped was a casual smile.

The women shook their heads, looking longingly at the rack of hats and other accessories.

The blond pulled her gloves over her fingers, taking time to secure each one with a tiny pearl button at the wrist. "I have to get back home. My mother-in-law is expecting us for dinner, so my husband is coming home early. He will not appreciate it if he has to wait for me because I'm trying on hats."

Grace smiled her understanding and held open the door for the women, thanking them for stopping in and reminding them that she wouldn't forget the Thursday preference. Stepping out from behind the counter, Ione waved her gratitude at the departing pair.

Then Grace closed the door, asked if Ione needed anything, smiled, and returned to the storeroom. Ione collapsed on another bench and tugged the crumpled paper from her pocket. Damp with perspiration, the smudged ink still read, *Don't you remember?*

Ione fought an unexpected wave of nausea, gagging at the imagined feel of his hands around her throat. Burning wasn't enough. She tore a tiny piece off the sheet and let it flutter into her lap.

Then another, and another, until a pile of pea-sized scraps of paper mounded in the hollow between her knees.

"I think I'm done for the day." Grace poked her head around the stockroom curtain. "Do you need anything else before I go?"

"No, thank you." Ione listened to her voice as if from far away.

Grace stared. "Everything is fine?"

Ione forced a nod. "I'm just a bit tired. I'll go upstairs as soon as I lock up."

"Would you like me to do that for you?"

"That's not necessary." Ione folded her skirt over so Grace couldn't see the scraps of paper. "You can go on home to your family."

At first hesitating, Grace finally let the curtain drop, and Ione let out in a rush the breath she'd held in.

She could no longer simply hope he'd give up. She knew what he wanted— the only thing he ever wanted—money.

And for the first time ever, she had it. She also had a budding business and a reputation to protect. More importantly, she had friends with money. Ione felt the pit in her stomach expand. If she had to pay Clarence off to protect Miriam and Michael and everything else they were connected to, then she would do so without question.

Ione gathered the tiny scraps of paper into her fist and searched for the fallen envelope.
Scooping it up, she turned it over, searching for an address or some way in which she might contact him. He had no way of knowing how much money she had—at least, she hoped he didn't—so she might be able to pay him off without much incident.

Not without a way to contact him, though. The envelope revealed nothing.

Which revealed everything about what his intentions really were.

The bell hanging in the hall outside Tamm's room rang. He glanced at the simple clock sitting on the small dresser and frowned. After spending the morning driving the housekeeper to and from stores and shops and all sorts of frivolous places, he thought the afternoon might be quiet. He frowned and tossed to the side the financial section of the paper he'd been reading. The only article of interest had been a discussion of Ms. Beatrice Vaughn's father's involvement in the Fair. She had been to visit Mrs. Farling again this week. It would be nice to have the kind of money that made wasting it building structures for the express purpose of showing off to the world appear to be a good idea.

Not that he'd always had to work for other people. Ione had been worth the investment until she'd gotten uppity and refused legitimate business opportunities. Tamm etched a line deeper into the grain of the table with the edge of his fingernail. He'd bought her a nice dress, or at least the fabric for it, and introduced her to important people, and all she had to do was what every other singer did. She'd had an unusually fine voice, Tamm had to admit, but no one only wanted to hear her sing. Tamm snorted and backed the chair away from the desk. He bent to tie the shoes he hadn't even had the chance to fully take off.

Maybe he would be driving Mrs. Farling to the Penns' again. At least that was an entertaining drive, with the lake on one side and the fine mansions on the other. Or... He frowned. He could be headed back to the docks with the noise and soot from the trains and relentless odor of fish barrels that had known decades of use. Why would someone with legendary wealth want to spend time in a dusty warehouse when they could just pay someone else to tend to things? Tamm buttoned his collar and shrugged on the kind of jacket he swore he would never wear again.

But a simple turn of luck at the tables, and here he was again, working for the kind of people whose games consisted of who could build the tallest building or who could own the largest railroad.

The games were infinitely more interesting than the ones he played now. Tamm closed the door and made his way down to the stables. At least the horse would be hitched and everything ready to go. At least he'd found work driving instead of mucking out the stables and brushing the beasts so the rich folk could ride by, boasting the shining black horseflesh, past other rich folk doing the same thing.

"Everything ready?" Tamm aimed the question at the stable boy, Grayson, while he slapped the horse's shoulder harder than necessary.

There was something satisfying about the quiver of solid muscle beneath the twitching coat.

"She should be waiting. Just drive around front." Grayson watched the ground, refusing to make eye contact.

"Look at me when I ask a question." Tamm stepped up to the carriage and settled on the high seat. "And you don't have to tell me where to go. I am well aware of where I should pick her up."

Grayson turned away, shrugging in agreement. Good. He hadn't looked at Tamm like he'd been told, but at least now he understood his place.

Miriam settled into the carriage seat. The already small space squeezed her even more than usual as each day she continued to expand. She sat back and took in a deep breath, willing the slight nausea that accompanied the lurching start of the journey to stay at bay.

The driver eased out into the light traffic that paraded by the row of townhouses across from the park, and then turned down the main street that led into the area of the city dominated by quaint shops and bustling offices and government buildings where the decisions were made that either cushioned or exposed people to life.

Today, though, her task consisted of nothing essential. Rather, the frivolousness of the endeavor almost made her blush. Today would be the first time she went for a dress fitting at a shop, rather than have the dressmaker visit her at home. That the dressmaker happened to be Ione, and the shop the one Miriam had helped put together seemed to matter little to her scattered nerves.

The trees slowly gave way to rows of homes and shops with doors open to the early summer breezes. The aroma of fresh bread wafted from tiny bakeries, drivers shouted at one another to move out of the way, and young men on bikes rang bells as they weaved in and out of traffic. Miriam waved at a young child flirting with a puddle while his distracted mother chatted with another woman. She smiled. Soon she would be the woman with a child, and soon she would know the feel of her baby's small fingers wrapped around her own. Soon she would feel the child's downy hair against her lips and soon she would watch Michael become a father. She wondered what kind of father he would be.

Miriam's smile faltered. For that matter, what kind of a mother would she be?

The carriage eased around a wagon loaded down with horse manure—an endless problem in a city crammed with people and bustling with business. Miriam brought her handkerchief to her face and breathed slowly. The doctor had promised the nausea would gradually fade. She still anxiously anticipated that miracle.

One street over, a bit past the corner, and they stopped in an available space just beyond Ione's shop.

"Let me help you, ma'am." Tamm again held out his hand and Miriam tried to make her agreement seem less reluctant.

"Thank you, Tamm."

He twitched at the use of his name, almost as if he found it surprising that she would remember.

"I'll be here for at least an hour. If you would like to take the carriage someplace else, please feel free to do so." Miriam watched the expressions flicker across his face. "Or if you would rather, you could walk down to the deli if you haven't yet had lunch."

She tried to imagine how she would paint him if she were to do such a thing, but she couldn't place the color. He was handsome enough to be appealing. His high cheekbones and close-set dark eyes gave him a perpetually interested look, but instead of the kind of interest a close friend might have, his look contained a hawkish quality. He had a friendly sort of face, a face that made her want to like him, but edged with a hardness that called her desire into question.

The color she would use, though. The color stayed out of her reach.

Greens were too natural and blues too calm. Reds and oranges spoke of anger or passion, and while something lurked under the surface, it lacked that kind of dedication. If a color existed that communicated distraction, or dissatisfaction, that might be closer. Miriam picked up her skirts and stepped over the cobbles. If she hadn't been so determined to stop painting, perhaps she'd be more in tune with the kind of hue that would describe the tall man standing next to her. Or not. Maybe she'd have the same problem even if she hadn't abandoned her call.

Tamm knew as soon as the housekeeper handed him the slip of paper with the address of Ione's store. He knew she'd be there, knew he'd have the opportunity to see her, knew he'd have this decision to make.

What he hadn't known was how close Ione and Mrs. Farling were. Watching from the carriage, reins in hand, Tamm mulled over his next move.

The strategic advantage was evident. Ione had never cared much for what happened to her, at least until that one time he'd pushed too hard. And then, it still seemed that her concern hadn't been about how she would reconcile what he'd asked her to do with her own morals. Rather, it had been about the shame she'd bring to her mother, and the example she'd be setting for her sisters. Of course, it made no sense. The damage had already been done, but she didn't see it in the same way he did. Instead, she saw it through the eyes of others. A perspective he hadn't anticipated.

And then he'd lost her.

Fate had carried her back to him, though, and just when he needed her skills. This time, she brought even more value. This time, he didn't have to tend to the ridiculous notion of love in order to win her.

Her care for others would be the opening this time.

Tamm drummed his fingers against his knee, restless with the new information and how to best use it. That he needed to follow her, to discover where she'd hidden her sisters, to learn more of the link that existed between Ione and the Farling family, went without question. How to accomplish it was another matter entirely.

He jumped down from his place in the driver's seat, twisted the reins around the well-worn post at the edge of the road, and pulled his hat lower, covering his eyes as best as possible. Lifting the collar of his jacket, he shoved his hands in his pockets and strolled as casually as possible past the windows to Ione's store.

The pink walls and lush fabrics reminded him of the wealth he'd held for too short a time.

And then he saw her. She stepped out from behind a curtain into a room lit by the glass sconces strategically placed to make the most of the reflection from each crystal bead and mirror and every yard of material laced with silver threads. The lay of her own dress left no doubt the fabric likely cost more than the expensive carpets gracing the floor. Her waist made his fingers itch with the desire to know her again, to shed the charade, to step into the store and remind her of who she was. He took a deep breath in and held it until the blood that pulsed through his veins slowed.

But her expression, the set of her chin, the determined arch of a brow that softened at the sight of someone who obviously held the status of friend, made him stop in the middle of the walkway and stare, earning a shove from the crowd behind.

"Excuse me." A nameless gentleman touched the brim of his hat. Sarcasm dripped from his voice, a reminder that Tamm no longer looked as if he belonged with the gaggle of shoppers who populated the street. Of course, due to the color of his skin, he'd never actually looked the part. Instead, his clothes had been responsible for communicating the privilege of his wealth. Generally, it had been enough to earn him some respect on the street and in the better establishments around town.

Tamm hummed his apology and shifted so he stayed out of view of the women in the store. His clothes no longer helped him blend into this arena. Now he simply waited, another uniformed servant, supposedly content to watch their employers parade their wealth back and forth in front of those whom they considered critical to their desire to step up one more rung.

This diminished status, a servant in a rich household, both marked him and made him invisible. Tamm glanced down the street—at the people who avoided coming into contact with him, diverting their path as if he were another streetlamp, an obstacle to be navigated—and he leaned back, relaxing into the realization that he could probably observe the women without raising alarm. That for him to stand there and stare held no element, no reason for concern. Simply put, his attention to the actions of the woman of the house he served made him solicitous, not suspicious.

He smirked as Ione linked her arm into Mrs. Farling's. Indeed, he would have to determine how close the two had become. Ione couldn't help but care for those around her. It was her weakness, and it was one he could use.

Chapter 6

The idea for a dinner party had expanded to include nearly everyone. Miriam looked up from the delicate slices of jellied citrus fruit that acted as a course between main courses. Whether or not she would ever get used to eating in this fashion was a discussion she and Michael had had on numerous occasions, yet their lovely cook still persisted, claiming that a household like theirs should have food elegant enough to match the furnishings.

John sat across from her. He'd shed his robes in preference for the more casual black trousers and shirt with the white collar he sometimes wore. It always surprised Miriam how broad his shoulders looked when he lacked the concealing effect of the priestly garb. He leaned over, laughing quietly with Jenny and Jeremy. With the proximity of the warehouse to the cathedral, they'd arrived together to dinner.

Beatrice and Dr. Phillips leaned toward one another, appearing to communicate wordlessly in the way they had done ever since they'd met when Jeremy's sister, Rachel, had gone missing. Miriam frowned. Rachel and Winston hadn't been able to make tonight's dinner. But they'd sent their regrets with the excuse that they had already accepted another invitation and asking for forgiveness.

As if they needed to do that. Miriam shook her head at her own thoughts, earning a strange look from Michael that she waved off. She didn't need him thinking she felt ill, or anything else negative. Ever since she'd revealed her condition, he'd taken care to make her life infuriatingly easy.

But Ione concerned her. Miriam lifted her napkin to her lips and dabbed at them, stealing a glance at her obviously distracted friend. Ione's normally calculating gaze and quiet demeanor had shifted inward, and now she wore a haunted expression that stood at odds with what Miriam knew to be a convincingly concealed fierce streak. This time, the downward tilt of her chin, her eyes that never rested on one face too long, and the skittish movement of her fingers as she picked up the fork, then set it down, only to pick it up again, made her appear to be the hunted rather than the hunter who had so far helped orchestrate the fates of them all.

Although small, Ione possessed strength that Miriam—that they all—had come to depend on, and her newfound frailty exposed a need in Miriam that she hadn't realized existed.

"How are the designs coming for the uniforms?" Jenny directed the question to Ione, but her friend didn't seem to hear. Instead, Ione twirled her small butter knife around her first and second fingers, watching the flash of candlelight play against the flawlessly polished silver.

"Yesterday, when I was at the shop, she'd had a few designs out in the back room." Miriam nudged Ione's foot under the table, and Ione nearly dropped the piece of silverware.

"Yes. Oh, yes." Ione took in a quick breath and sat up, forcing her attention back to the conversation. She lightly cleared her throat. "I've completed the general designs."

The room fell silent as Ione's voice, pitched higher than normal, pierced through the low conversational tone of the other guests.

"Will there be several different uniforms?" Miriam attempted to keep the discussion going, earning a strange look from John.

Ione nodded, noticeably relieved by the distraction. "Most of them will be similar, with aprons of different colors—pastels, of course."

"Of course," Michael responded with more hesitation than normal, sharing a concerned look with John.

"What about the shoes? Who will be choosing those?" Rachel, the only one in the group who actually belonged hobnobbing with the city's elite, leaned in, ostensibly caring for little else but the style of the shoes chosen. Miriam could never tell if her distracting additions to conversation were simply because a stray idea popped into her head, demanding to be attended to, or if she was so adept at disarming a tense situation that no one suspected anything more than her desire to know about shoes.

Either way, Miriam appreciated the help. "I don't remember Mrs. Penn saying anything about the shoes."

"She hasn't mentioned them to me." Ione finally shook whatever had been distracting her. "I'll speak with her. I'm almost positive they will be white, or at the very least, light in color."

"That makes the most sense." Rachel speared a long, thin, yellow bean and sliced a perfect inch from the rest of the vegetable. "Everything else in the new city will be white. From what I hear, it is already quite the sight."

The talk of the white city spurred the men's imaginations, and soon debate over the number of electric lights, how the city planned to bring in water, and how they would carry the waste out ruled the far side of the table. Friendly disagreements over whether or not the structure of the buildings could withstand use beyond the duration of the Fair sprung up by the time the desserts arrived.

"At last." Michael smiled and sat back so their newest maid could remove his plate and another could step in, carrying a chocolate soufflé that reminded Miriam there might still be room for a little more.

The dessert, served individually in small, white crockery, always surprised her by its humility. Something she never remembered tasting as a child, the soufflé was her favorite, not because of the flavor, which amazed, or the texture, which comforted, but because it looked like a clump of nothing, flat on top and listing a little to the side. Someone from the kitchen had taken the trouble to dress it up with a sprinkle of sugar, ground until white and powdery. Still, the dessert just sat there, unceremoniously served in the same pot that had known the heat of the oven...but the simplicity lied about the complexity inside. Miriam picked up her spoon and cut into the soft edges, feeling the slight resistance against her pressure and smelling the pungent release of the chocolate-laced steam.

She savored the first bite, admitting she couldn't discount the flavor in her assessment of why this particular sweet held her fascination. But the discrepancy between how it looked and how it tasted held her imagination. She looked around the room at her friends. Most of them she had painted. Most of them she'd gotten right. For Ione, even though she'd been living on the streets when Miriam first saw her, her painting had spoken of potential. Miriam wondered if that painting had not opened a window to hope. If the only thing she had seen was the battered woman she'd tripped over in the dark, would she have even attempted to help her?

Somehow, she doubted she would have.

But that had been the reasoning for everything. Jenny sat with them at their table because Miriam had known her future held promise—a promise that made Miriam question her own apathy and forced her to bring John in to champion Jenny's cause. John was there only because through her paints, Miriam sensed his sincerity. She knew he was safe. Miriam had fallen in love with Michael, but with the assurance that her painting revealed his love for her. She'd believed in Jeremy, Rachel's brother, because what he'd said agreed with what she'd painted.

Miriam wracked through her memories, glancing at each of the faces around the table. Of all her friends, of all the people she considered family, not one of them had joined her based on her ability to love without the assurance and confirmation she felt through the promise inherent in her paintings. Miriam touched the edge of her soufflé again, lifting one crispy edge and peering at the softness within. Did she even have the ability to see someone for who they truly were? For the first time, now that she wasn't painting, she questioned the value of her gift. To think that it helped her see potential in others was easily understood. But did that mean, without her abilities, she would dismiss someone who deserved a chance? Was she as willing to help someone despite how their portrait read?

She met John's interested stare. He would understand her questions. She could talk to him. But Miriam didn't want to. At some point, she had to figure things out for herself. She turned to watch Ione mechanically lift the spoon to her lips and swallow the dessert without apparent thought. First, she would figure out what had Ione so preoccupied. Miriam glanced at her plate again, suddenly unable to take another bite. Then she would concentrate on helping others without the benefit of knowing who they might become. She had to learn to trust outside what her gifts dictated.

A shadow crossed behind the open doorway to the front hall.

Beginning with Tamm, the new driver. There simply was no reason not to trust the man. And although she longed to paint him, she would resist and learn to be content that he lived as a trusted member of their household. He'd done nothing to deserve her suspicion.

Ione couldn't shake the feeling of being watched. Even in Miriam and Michael's home, where the wood paneling in the dining room and rich red carpets blanketed her in a kind of security she'd never before known, her neck prickled and her skin crawled as if the paintings might come to life, might blink down their condemnation, might expose her shame.

She looked around the table. Everyone here loved her. Their smiles and obvious concern when her conversation failed spoke of shared experience and understanding. They knew what she'd done when her mother had grown ill and never held it against her, but they didn't know how she'd betrayed her mother and sisters in the first place.

That, they could never find out.

She shivered and tried to concentrate on the low fire in the hearth at the far end of the room. Burning more for light and mood than warmth, Ione couldn't feel the glow of the flame. Had it been roaring, though, she couldn't guarantee any of it would have registered.

He was back.

And he wanted something.

Ione watched her now pregnant friend from under her lashes. Miriam couldn't find out. The close link they all shared put Miriam and Michael—and really, everyone so closely involved in their group—at risk for extortion or worse.

When he turned angry, no one could predict his next move.

Ione glanced back to the doorway, and then smiled at Miriam when their eyes accidentally met. Ione could see it there, the concern, but she would never let on that there could be a reason for her distraction.

She'd taken precautions, trusting not even her driver. Instead, she'd rented a hack and asked the driver to take a route that wound through the park and through a small shopping district. She'd stopped at a store to buy buttons she didn't need and at the bakery to purchase Miriam's favorite chocolates, all the while checking the small window at the back of the hack to make sure no one followed.

Eventually, they'd stopped in front of the mansion, and the puzzled driver accepted her generous tip with the hint of a question registering in the tilt of his eyebrows. Ione ignored his silent inquiry, checked the street beyond the hack one more time, and hurried to the safety of the door where Mr. Butler had waited to let her in.

And now, here she sat, senses blazing, concentrating on pacing her breathing and holding her trembling fingers steady.

How long he'd been watching, she had no idea. Days? Months?

Nothing in the notes offered evidence for a long search and surveillance or for a simple crossing of their paths. Ione doubted that he'd known about her for long, though. Clarence was not a patient man.

She swallowed the dessert without tasting it and felt her stomach recoil. Dropping her hands into her lap, she glanced up to Miriam, met her watchful gaze, and forced a smile.

"The shop is beautiful." Miriam folded her napkin and set it next to her dessert dish. "I'm not sure if I told you how impressed I am."

"You did, but thank you again." Ione shrugged.

The words Miriam had spoken were soft, quieter than normal, meant only for Ione. And Ione's response had been in kind. There was no doubt Miriam knew something was amiss. Equally clear was the evidence that Miriam hadn't a clue what troubled Ione. Where Miriam often stayed guarded even in the company of her closest friends, today she'd been successful in wrestling her expression into one that spoke of openness. Ione longed to ask her how she was, really, and if the child inside moved much, and to speak of the life they all anticipated. She wondered what colors Miriam had chosen for the child's layette, if they would hire a nurse for the first year or only to get them by the first couple of weeks. Did they plan to have a nanny, as so many of the wealthy families did?

But the questions remained unspoken, and Ione hoped that Miriam could sense her care and know her desire to be that friend. At the moment, though, the reality that Ione needed to protect her friends from any potential consequence of her unresolved relationship with Clarence took precedence over any show of affection.

For over an hour, she'd been sitting in the company of her friends, people who had loved her when she had no one and could offer nothing in return. People who knew she'd done horrible things but thought her still deserving of their time and efforts. John, sitting on the other end of the table, had spent countless hours walking next to her in silence, simply as company while she sorted out the devastation of losing her mother, of being used by men, of the attack that nearly cost her life.

Now, though, the fine hairs on the back of her neck refused to relax. When the feeling became too much, she'd shiver like she'd been doused in the freezing lake. She could fight the feeling back, but the resulting raw nerves meant that she jumped at every sound, every shuffle, every sigh. Ione folded her napkin and set it on the table next to her unfinished dessert. She had to leave.

Mrs. Farling was more than simply a customer to Ione. They were friends. Closer than Tamm had anticipated, even after the visit to the store.

He'd been walking from the kitchen to the cellar steps when he'd heard her laugh and stopped short. Ione never laughed loudly, but the soft sound she made when amused—a breathy exhale with one low pitched syllable resting somewhere between a chuckle and a song—he'd instantly recognized. And the jolt shot clear to his spine, stopping him. He set the bottles of wine he'd been carrying on a hall table and leaned against the wall, listening to the party on the other side.

Twisting closed the top button of his shirt, Tamm looked down the hall for any sign of an alcove or an open doorway that might offer a view into the dining room. No one expected his return. After shelving the wine, he was done for the day. He had time.

The immense and strangely designed house had no shortage of corridors that led to unexpected rooms. Bookshelves glided on silent runners to reveal unanticipated passageways between the spaces and—if he were to believe the bits and pieces from the other servants—led to a network of hidden rooms not accessible from anywhere else in the home. He looked down the quiet hall. The day before, while walking by the pantry door left carelessly ajar, he'd overheard the kitchen maids pondering how Mrs. Farling had strolled into the unlit corner where he now stood and disappeared.

Tamm smiled. Whoever designed the place might have filled it with secret passageways and hidden doorways, but not to obscure movements. Rather, the abundance of secrets did quite the opposite: it could open, expose, and for the right person, allow unusual access and freedom to roam about a house into places that would normally remain a mystery.

Tamm slid along the wall, deeper down the largely unused darkened hallway. He stopped short of the swinging double doors the servants often used. Instead of staying there, listening to the soft glide of Ione's voice, Tamm made his way to the end of the hall where the other servants had noticed Mrs. Farling's unexpected absence. He ran his fingers along the smooth paneling, feeling for any imperfections, any hint that there might be something more to the corridor than a first glance would reveal.

She'd been right to leave him. Perhaps it was that fact that made his neck feel hot and his ears burn. At first, when the winnings flowed in, he didn't consider the chance that he could have been wrong. Now that she sat comfortably in the dining room of one of the wealthiest families in Chicago, and now that she had her own, successful business, and now that he stood on the other side of the wall with the people who served the ones around the table, he had to consider her path had held more promise.

Tamm held in the urge to kick the wall in front of him. He felt nothing. No latch, no handle, no hinges. He exhaled loudly, turned, and leaned against the wall.

That's when he heard it. The soft mechanical click. A magnetic sound. He twisted to feel for anything uneven, any hint that there might be something he missed. The polished wood, cool against his fingers, revealed nothing, until he brushed the edge of a large panel. One piece of trim had lifted. It stood out enough for him to slide his fingernails between, dig in, and pull. There he felt it. The metal rim to a lock.

Dropping to his knees, Tamm studied the mechanism with the tips of his fingers. The lock was elementary. Nothing a piece of wire and a bit of patience couldn't handle. Both, unfortunately, were in short supply for him at the moment.

He stood, brushed off the knees of his uniform, and straightened his waistcoat. Soon, he vowed, soon he could shed the uniform. Soon, Ione would make him another suit. Soon she'd be on her knees in front of him, measuring and pinning. Soon, he would be back where he belonged—seated at the table, instead of carrying the platters for those whose luck hadn't run dry.

Chapter 7

"Do you think everything is going well for Ione?" Michael slipped one sock off and dropped his foot to the oriental carpet that covered nearly the entire hardwood floor.

"Why do you ask?" Miriam stepped up on the footstool and then turned to sit next to him on the edge of the plush mattress. She listened to her husband's breathing as he pulled off his other sock and rubbed his feet against the soft pile. His long legs stretched in front of him, his bare feet reaching the floor. Unlike her, he didn't need to use the footstool to sit comfortably on the side of the bed.

"You know. She's quiet lately."

Miriam nodded. She did know. She'd simply hoped he'd been less observant. It used to be Miriam who asked the questions, who had the sense that things were either going well or had taken an unexpected turn. But she didn't trust her instincts anymore.

"I stopped at the shop today. I needed to go for a fitting. She seemed fine then, but yes, she's quieter than usual."

Michael hummed and stood to untuck his shirt. Miriam watched his now familiar movements. He tugged the fabric out from his waistband, unbuttoned the top three buttons, dropped his cuff links into the crystal bowl on the bedside table, and pulled his shirt over his head, eventually shaking it out and smoothing it over the back of his chair. She never understood the ritual. The shirt needed to be laundered. Why he shook it out, why he smoothed it, why he straightened, placed his fists on his hips, and nodded as if he'd satisfactorily completed a job, she had no idea. Tomorrow morning, the maid would grab the dirty garment and stuff it into a basket with the rest of the laundry.

"I think I may mention something to John." Michael stopped and turned toward Miriam. "Do you think Jenny knows anything?"

"She would have probably said something to me. Well, at least I would hope that she'd say something." Miriam thought back to their recent interactions, trying to mine anything out of the conversations that hadn't been overtly stated. She rubbed her forehead. Right now, though, she wanted to sleep. The baby had spent most of the previous night kicking and turning and in general, refusing to let her relax. Her resulting headache didn't help anything. "I'm going to the warehouse tomorrow. Maybe I'll talk to her then."

Michael nodded, his brow still furrowed with unanswered questions. He pulled off his spectacles, folded them, and set them next to the cuff links.

"Are you sure you want to go to the warehouse?"

She knew the question would surface eventually. So far, Michael hadn't said much to her regarding going about town, and in general keeping the kind of schedule she'd had since living in the townhouse. She took a deep breath and held it. "Do you think I shouldn't be going?"

Michael stopped moving about the room and lowered himself onto the dressing table stool, facing Miriam. "I want you to do only what you feel you can do without putting yourself or the baby in danger."

"And you feel the warehouse may be dangerous?"

"Not especially." Michael rubbed his face and dropped his elbows to his knees, leaning forward.

"But you aren't entirely comfortable with me going there."

Michael clasped his hands together. Miriam watched him study the lay of his fingers. Eventually, he moved one thumb over the other, and then back again. "I want you to be happy. And I want you to be careful."

Miriam nodded. Poor man. He did his best to let her maintain the kind of freedom she'd become used to after her father died. But it wasn't easy for him.

"I'll make sure to take a driver. Besides, it won't be too much longer before I'm not going to want to go anywhere." Miriam slid her palm against her expanding midsection. It seemed to grow daily.

The corner of Michael's lips kicked up in a half-smile. He'd been curious since the beginning, asking questions at night when the house had quieted, content to rest his hand against her stomach simply to feel the movement within. That they could create an entire life was a marvel to them both.

Michael stood, and they climbed in bed together, her back to his chest, his hand over her stomach. Miriam waited to hear his breathing slow, deepen, before sliding from the sheets and tying on her robe.

Slipping down the hall without waking one of the other men who slept in the rooms above the stables was more difficult than he had anticipated. Tamm carefully lifted his jacket from the hook by the door and shrugged it over his shoulders. He flicked open the door latch, listened for any movement behind him, then sank into the shadows and pre-dawn fog.

Tamm hurried across the paved courtyard to the main house, his footfalls sounding like cannons as they echoed off the surrounding brick surfaces. He would have preferred to wear shoes with silent soles, but the risk of being discovered in the house outweighed the risk of being heard outside. At least if he wore the shoes that belonged with his uniform, if someone discovered his presence, he could make some excuse, state some task that had to be completed. Without his uniform, though, his excuse wouldn't ring true. No servant spent time in the main house without being properly dressed. Tamm scowled.

He used his key on the kitchen door, inched it open, and listened. The only entrance he had access to was the service entrance, but it also happened to open to the room where the kitchen help, who had to be up before daybreak, worked.

The deserted room stood silent, the humid air still warm from the previous day's fires. Tamm closed the door as quietly as possible, taking time to lock it again. It wouldn't do for someone to wake and suspect an intruder.

He didn't need light to find the passageway entrance. Feeling his way down the hall, he touched first the fern stand near the opening to the dining room, then the high-backed bench that sat lonely in the corridor, and finally the narrow table next to the entrance. He looked over his shoulder into the inky dark, listening for anyone who might be following, and reached into his pocket to pull out a thin, narrow piece of metal the length of a pen.

Pushing the panel in and feeling it release, he ran his hand along the edge until he could discern the cool metal lock. With a bit of a practiced jiggle, the lock clicked open, and Tamm stepped into the still blackness that smelled of fresh linens and turpentine. He slipped the piece of metal back into his pocket and secured the hidden entrance, being careful to feel the walls so he could recognize it again.

According to the servants—who were largely uncooperative when it came to seeking out information, but talked endlessly with each other when they thought no one else listened—the system of halls and private rooms stretched around most of the house. Tamm frowned. Light would be helpful.

He squinted into the dark, waiting for his eyes to adjust. Frustration unfurled at his predicament. He could light a lamp and risk being caught, or continue on in the dark and see nothing. Tamm chose to take the risk.

An oil lamp sat on the table outside the passageway. Tamm opened the door far enough to grab it as quickly as possible. The matches, he always carried.

With the door secured once again, Tamm struck the match. The rough-hewn floors glowed beneath his feet, their color vibrant compared to the black just seconds before the flame flickered to life. He lifted the glass dome, lit the wick, and replaced it, taking time to lower the flame as far as possible without snuffing out the fire. He shook the match, touched it to his tongue to cool the burnt end, and carefully placed it in his pocket. It wouldn't due to leave evidence behind. Tamm couldn't be sure what he would find or even how he could use the information. Only one thing was certain: information held value all its own. And he needed anything he could get his hands on.

Ione rolled over in her familiar bed in Miriam's house. She'd stayed there for months before her store opened. Even her sisters had spent weekends and holidays in the comfort of what Lucy, her youngest sister, called the sunshine room.

Compared to the way they grew up—sharing a bed under a quilt that was little more than a collection of scraps of clothes too far gone to mend, seeking warmth by sandwiching their thin bodies together, and sometimes trying to fall asleep to the music of hungry bellies—the excess had seemed so foreign. Lush yellow quilts, heavy drapes of creamy brocade splashed with yellow roses, carpets so deep that toes sank into the abundance of tiny pink and yellow wildflowers, rich wood pillars, gold gilt mirrors, armoires full of sleeping clothes in the event that an unprepared guest arrived... Lucy quickly named it for what it felt like the first morning they woke there. The room, the house, their new lives had felt like the gift of sunshine after a lifetime of clouds.

Ione punched her pillow and flopped onto her back. The pillows, the luxury, smothered in the light of a real risk of loss. The risk of people learning just how bad her judgment had been. If the women she served, the society ladies and their mothers and grandmothers, knew of the choices in her past, her business would be finished.

And now he was back.

Part of her couldn't wrap her mind around the shift. He'd returned, but he hadn't done anything to risk her business. Ione sat up and crossed her legs, thinking about the messages. Knowing him, he wouldn't risk the business—a healthy business meant money. One thing Ione knew: he loved money above all else.

Things didn't add up, though. If money existed as the goal, then he should have asked for it by now. Made some sort of demand. Knocked on her door and forced his way into her life.

Ione shivered and pulled the covers up to cover her bare shoulders. This new Clarence, this patient Clarence, made the acid churn in her stomach. She shivered. Tomorrow she would make her excuses, sneak back to her shop, run her store, and stay away from everyone she loved.

It had been stupid for her to come to her friend's home. Her carelessness could have put everyone at risk.

Then Miriam had insisted Ione stay the night. How could she have said no? From now on, she would be more cautious. Countless tasks at the shop vied for her attention anyway. For a while, until she could figure out what he wanted, she could be responsible and stay busy...too busy to place her friends in danger.

Ione found her pillow again. Forced her eyes to close and her mind to stop spinning. Concentrated on her breathing. And fell asleep thinking that the soft shuffling behind the wall at the head of her bed must be mice. She would have to let Miriam know.

Chapter 8

Miriam had stayed longer than she'd planned. She glanced out the window at the still black skies. If she wanted to sleep, she should head back to their room now. She should stop rearranging the dry brushes, stop flipping through the paintings that sat on the floor of her studio, leaning in stacks against the wall. She should pick up the small lamp she'd used to snake her way through the passageways and head back where she belonged.

But she belonged here too. She took a deep breath, ignored her wavering reflection in the bank of windows that boasted a daytime view of a brick wall, and placed a stark white, unpainted canvas on her easel.

Of course, she had no intention of painting anything. She simply missed the focus, missed the feel of her brush as it filled in the rough texture with blues and oranges that she'd invented simply by mixing and stirring and scraping the dyes out of the tubes. She longed for the smell of turpentine, the faint dusty feel of the room, the dried paint splotches on the floor that first dripped off her mother's brushes, and now hers.

Miriam clenched her fists and shoved them into the pockets of her housecoat, quelling a shiver. She should be in bed. *Should*. Everything rested on that one word.

Should could mean anything, though. She *should* be painting, but the responsibility that now grew in the hollow below her heart had introduced a whole new element of meaning to the word. Now, *should* encompassed another human, one whose needs superseded all other obligations.

She only wished the longing would go away.

Miriam crossed to where her lamp burned in the middle of the wood table. There were stacks of papers, preliminary sketches and reference books. She lifted her worn pallet to rest in the comfortable crook between her thumb and finger and held it there, feeling the weight. A smudge of green discolored the edge near her wrist. Miriam glanced at the stack of paintings, trying to recall on which one she'd used that particular shade of green, which canvas would have demanded the dark hues that hid within the leaves of an oak right before a summer storm.

She rolled her head from one side to the other, loosening the tight tendons. The desire to sleep wouldn't be held at bay for long. Setting down the pallet, she needlessly wiped her hands on a stained rag.

Grabbing the lamp, she turned the flame down to barely a flicker, glanced around her room one more time, and slipped into the hidden doorway she'd left open when she'd entered. She was careful to close it when she left, though. No one came into her studio, besides Michael, occasionally, or someone she'd invited. But Mrs. Maloney didn't send in maids to clean, and as the studio was the only room in the attic level on this side of the house, it stayed secluded. She stayed secluded.

But not since she'd become aware of the life growing inside of her.

Miriam made her way across the plank floors, down a set of steps and a short incline, to the door that led to the master bedroom. She dimmed the lamp, eased into the room, and slipped into bed next to Michael. She couldn't resist his warmth, and moved so her body shared the comfortable cocoon his had created. Three breaths later, she closed her eyes to a dreamless sleep.

Tamm watched the light swell in the passageway ahead. He held his breath, turned down his own flame, and sank deeply into the shadows. Whoever carried the light had stepped into a room and closed the door behind themselves. He heard the soft click of a door latch, but there was no way to tell how far away or close the person had been. Tamm calmed his breathing, waited in the dark, and watched for a sign the person might return.

It could have been seconds or minutes before the uneasiness of standing in the dark overpowered his desire not to be discovered. He lit the wick again and continued, dragging his hands along the rumpled back of the lath and plaster walls. The unfinished plaster near the kitchen became rough lumber as he ascended a short stairwell, and by the time he reached the top, the walls, while still wood, were at least smooth. Strangely enough, the place had the feel of being lived in. Tamm couldn't help but relax, even if only slightly.

He had to move quickly. Tamm had no idea if he'd be lucky enough to figure out any of the entrances, or if he would even be able to find his way back out before dawn made his presence known. He picked up the pace, studying the backs of hinges and unlocked doors, smiling at the wealth of access the hidden halls provided. No wonder most of the servants had never been allowed into the dark corridors.

And then he stopped. The hallway ended. One passageway eased up a gradual ramp to the right, and the other stretched into the floors above. A set of stairs, more like a ladder, rose from the rough floor, which here, was covered with a carpet runner. Tamm decided to take the stairs.

It opened to a small room, lined with paintings of people he'd never before seen. Tamm held up the lamp, taking time to study the play of colors and the brush strokes that screamed they were originals. He'd tried to estimate the worth of this family, but now knew even his most generous expectations fell far below their reality.

He frowned and looked around what seemed to be a dead end, until a door-sized painting shifted when he'd pulled ever so slightly on the frame. Tamm shook his head, more disturbed by the lack of time and what he likely missed in his haste to mentally map the passageways than in any of the unexpected things he had come across. He pulled the frame back, and another hall stretched out ahead. By now, he had to be on the second floor near the bedrooms.

Tamm slowed his pace and continued to feel for imperfections in the walls that now felt as luxurious as the real rooms in the house. For a moment, he stopped at the idea that he might have inadvertently stepped into the main residence, but he'd been in nearly every hall in the mansion, and none were as narrow or had ceilings so low. He reached up to touch the smooth unpainted plaster above his head. It was low enough for him to place his palm flat against the cool surface. The farther he penetrated the maze, the more confusing it became.

The hall was at least forty feet long, and as he examined the narrow path, he realized a number of doors exited from the space where he now stood. It had to be the sleeping quarters. Tamm reached out, placed his hand on one heavy wood panel, and then rested his ear against the varnished surface. The silence roared with his own heartbeat so loudly that he wondered if he would be able to hear someone even if they were moving about.

A dozen more steps and he stood in front of another door. While the openings were evident from the hall, he reasoned they must be hidden on the other side. Otherwise, everyone would know how to access the passageways.

This time, he doused the flame again and tempted fate.

The handle turned without a sound, and the night air of the room rushed in around him. He allowed time for his eyes to adjust and quelled a thrill at the slow, methodical, breathing sounds that came from the bed. He took a gamble and stepped in, leaving what appeared from the inside to be just another wood panel, ajar.

The small form of a woman lay under the blankets, her breasts rising and falling with each deep breath. One thin arm wrapped around the scarf she'd worn to protect her hair. The familiarity of the pose stopped Tamm. Ione hadn't gone home as he'd expected.

Tamm tried to calculate the chance that he would have picked the one doorway that Ione slept behind. That in all of his searching, in all of his shifting behind the shadows, his efforts could be rewarded with such a simple solution. Here she was.

He could slip in bed next to her and remind her of what they once meant to each other, of how much they needed each other. A quick glance at the giant four poster bed and the lush furnishings, though, revealed the danger in that approach. Right now, she might not think she needed him. Tamm breathed in the humid night air of the room. She would, though. She would remember.

The desire to climb in next to her nearly made his knees buckle. He wanted to feel the soft skin of her arm as she rested it across his chest. He wanted to know her kisses again, to have her look at him like she did when he'd talked her into leaving her mother to sing for him. His hand trembled. He shoved it deep into his pocket in a tight fist. He couldn't wake her. That much he knew.

But he also couldn't leave this opportunity untouched. He looked around the room for a pen and paper, carefully opening and closing drawers until he finally found a few sheets tucked partially under the desk blotter. While still too dark to do much, the approaching dawn lent enough light for Tamm to see his black letters against the stark white page. He scrawled one sentence, returned the pen to the holder, waved the sheet of paper back and forth to make sure it had completely dried, and folded it in half.

Then he walked to the edge of the bed, resisted the urge to touch her soft cheek, and placed the folded paper on the pillow next to her.

Ione stretched before she opened her eyes. She hadn't slept so soundly since she'd known Clarence wanted back into her life, or at least wanted to make his presence known. Kicking off the blankets, Ione rolled over so that she took up the entire huge bed. At her home, above the shop, she slept in a bed remarkably smaller than any of those in the Farling home. And while she didn't feel the need to sleep like this every night, she wouldn't complain about the luxury every so often.

Eyes still closed, she took a moment to breathe in the new day. She could do it. She didn't want to, but she could. Besides, she had more than enough at the shop that screamed for her attention: dresses for the upcoming season, designs for the mass-produced children's outfits for Jenny at the warehouse, designs and samples for the Women's Pavilion, and the surprise baptismal gown for Miriam's baby. Ione reached down and held in her own flat stomach. She'd never been with child. And she probably never would be. Even the thought of inviting another man into her life made her a tad queasy.

Ione breathed in and out one more time and opened her eyes to the bright room. The drapes still obscured the outside world, but the eastern sun penetrated to the point where it did not matter. Ione smoothed the blankets on the side of the bed she hadn't slept in, stopping when she felt the piece of paper.

She knew, without looking, what it was. Her mind reeled, trying to sort out how he had found her or who he'd paid to get the message so close. She scrambled to sit up and pulled the quilt up to cover her nightgown. He—no, not he, probably someone he'd paid—had been in her room, had watched her sleep. She opened the folded paper and read.

Ione wanted to pound her fists into the mattress. She wanted to scream, to throw things, to knock over tables and chairs. She wanted to yell out the windows at passersby that she was not who she once was, that she had changed, and that she didn't deserve this monster back in her life.

But she did deserve it. She deserved it all. The people who didn't were her friends who had nursed her back to health, who had made her remember she still had talents, who had helped her build a business.

Ione unfolded the sheet of paper. The trembling had stopped, had been replaced by a steady rage. She could feel the blood rush to her face, to her arms, to her feet. She jumped from the bed, with the note crumpled in her fist, and threw it into the cold fireplace. Fumbling overhead, she located the matches with numb fingers and set flame to the hated thing.

Like the other messages, this one had been short. A single sentence. Another question. *Do you miss me?* She'd almost laughed aloud. Miss him? Miss the cold nights and the hunger, singing for a meal, and always the feeling that it was never enough for him? Miss him? Not in the least.

Ione crossed to the armoire and pulled out one of the spare dresses she kept at Miriam's. The color didn't matter; the fabric didn't matter. Only one thing mattered. She needed to get out of this house, back to her own place, and deal with the mess that had suddenly become her life.

Had it been only days since she'd gone to sleep in her own bed in her own apartment, thinking of potential colors for Beatrice's ball gowns? She nearly laughed aloud. A few scraps of paper, and everything she had worked for could be gone.

But maybe he'd forgotten a few things about her. She ripped the corset from the drawer, did her best to tie it over her underthings, and stepped into the full skirts. When she had laced her shoes, she opened the curtains to a still morning and a silent street. Good. She could get out before everyone woke.

The house had been built like a fort. The floorboards never creaked and the door hinges opened without protest. The only noise was her footfalls as she crossed the hardwood once she'd reached the first floor. That, and Mr. Butler asking if she needed anything. She had forgotten how quiet he could be.

"I'm fine." Ione pulled on her gloves and settled her hat over what she knew looked like a mess. Securing it with two expertly placed pins, she lied. "I'd forgotten that I have an early morning appointment I need to get ready for."

He smiled, accepting the lie, and Ione ignored the tightening in her gut at the realization she was now lying to the people she loved in order to hide the truth of the one she feared. She paused. "You have always been so kind to me."

"Of course, ma'am. What else could I be to such a wonderful woman?" His slight bow and questioning eyes had Ione nearly blinking back tears. "Should I call for the driver?"

"No. It's too early. I'll walk the couple of blocks and catch a streetcar."

"If you are sure." His tone left the statement open for Ione to change her mind.

"Oh, I almost forgot." Ione reached inside her handbag. "Would you please give this to Miriam?"

"Absolutely." He took the folded piece of paper from her hand and placed it on the silver tray with the other correspondence.

She smiled, and he opened the door for her. Ione could feel his eyes on her as she walked toward the street and as she turned right and made her way past the other townhouses. It wasn't that she didn't appreciate his concern, but she breathed a sigh of relief as the hedges and fences blocked his view.

The fully leafed trees canopied the streets and paths that wound through the park. Ione longed to walk amongst the green, to become lost on one of the paths as they curved between the massive trunks. But she didn't. Caution reigned now.

Ione glanced back down the street, checking for any signs someone might be following her. She had to make a plan. She couldn't simply wait for him to make his desires known while risking her family and friends' welfare. She'd been selfish once by leaving behind those she loved. Ione shifted a bit to the right to make room for a few pedestrians who had joined her on the sidewalk. Now, the definition of selfish had changed. Now, the act of staying meant she was only thinking of herself.

She wouldn't make that mistake twice.

Chapter 9

Tamm swirled the last sip of cold coffee in the bottom of the mug and stared at the few left behind grounds of the hastily brewed beverage. Across the street, Ione bustled around her shop, stooping to measure the hems for her customers, reaching for fabric samples, smiling at doting mothers, and offering reassuring nods to nervous daughters.

A production, created to impress.

He frowned and looked back to the kitchen door, wondering where the waitress had gone off to. When he'd come in, he could tell the woman would have preferred he take a seat near the rear of the restaurant, out of sight of the pedestrians. He ignored the wordless directive, instead choosing one of the tables that looked out over the street. The vantage was enough to ruffle the portly waitress, with the added advantage of a perfect view of Ione's shop.

He set the mug down with a hollow thud. With Ione moving around the shop, displayed in the large panes of glass and framed by luxurious curtains on either side, he felt as if he were staring at a stage performance. And if he ignored the stomping waitress and the streetcars and the carriages, well then, the show she put on was just for him.

"Want more?" The waitress scowled, one hand on her hip, the other clutching a steaming pot of coffee.

Tamm nodded, not bothering to look at the woman. She muttered something under her breath as she walked back, but he didn't care to hear it. Not with Ione acting in the show she so obviously orchestrated.

He leaned forward, both elbows on the table, and willed her to look up.

She played coy. She was so good at it too.

She would pay for it though. He had all the time it took.

That last note might have been too much. Tamm reached for the sugar and poured it into the steaming cup. The decision to leave the message had been one of impulse. He silently cursed his own rash decision. Impulse always made for trouble—at the tables or in life. He should know that by now.

He dropped the spoon back onto the saucer and turned the mug so it lined up with the checkerboard pattern on the tablecloth. He'd made no plans for how long he would sit there, and it being late morning, he was the only one left of the early rush. Fighting the urge to sit back and lift his feet to an empty chair—after all, he didn't need to be rude—Tamm instead watched the people stream past the window. Men in suits, tipping hats to women dressed in every color imaginable. The crowd surged and ebbed, the flow opposite to the charge of horse-driven carriages and the challenge of the lumbering streetcars.

And then someone different. A colored man, dressed as nicely as any white man, walked right into the front door of the shop.

Tamm sat up, craning his neck to get a better look, but the ever-increasing traffic obscured almost everything. He fished a few coins out of his pocket, dropped them on the table, and left the still steaming cup behind.

The noise of the street assaulted him as soon as he opened the door and stepped into the throng. Horse dung, perfume, sweat, and tobacco all mixed, creating an aroma as thick as the traffic. The clank of metal wheel rims against the cobbles was only outdone by the roar of conversation and the call of a newsboy. Tamm watched for an opening, and then dove across the street.

The man had disappeared. From the outside window, there was no telling where he could be. Tamm cursed under his breath and tried to find a place where he could observe unnoticed for a while. Women still milled about amongst the dresses and stands of hats and other fripperies, but Ione had also vanished.

He'd considered the possibility before—that she might have met another man, that she could have someone else in her life. But he'd dismissed it. After all, he knew she would always come back to him if he wanted her after she'd so selfishly abandoned their dream. Once was all he'd asked at the time. Just once to help make the rent that month.

The anger settled, unwieldy and burdensome. She knew better.

He'd only wanted her back, only wanted what had been stolen from him. The cascade of losses, the debt, his entrance back into the life of a servant, for as much as he'd wanted to ignore it, it had all started with one event: the night she left.

He fought to keep the sneer off his face. She didn't need him anymore, that much was certain.

It didn't have to stay that way, though. Tamm considered his advantage. She'd come back...but if she didn't, he could still make her pay.

Ione had been holding the pins in her teeth when he'd stepped into the shop. She'd nearly swallowed them.

"How can I help you?" She stood up, confused, brushing loose threads from her skirts. It being nearly noon, a few things were a given: her hair no longer laid smooth against her head, her dress was undoubtedly crumpled, and she'd probably been perspiring. None of it added up to happily welcoming a well-dressed man whom she'd only met once but had definitely called to visit.

He removed his hat and twisted it nervously, as if looking for someplace to set it but not really wanting to commit to staying that long. "I thought..." He cleared his throat and offered the young lady on the pedestal half of a heart-stopping smile. "...that you may allow me to escort you for a walk during your lunch hour."

Ione couldn't help but stare.

Pastor Whitaker's younger brother looked down. The only time she'd ever spoken with him had been at the last family dinner. "Of course, if you are otherwise occupied, I could try back later maybe."

Her lack of response had embarrassed him. Ione immediately regretted her silence. He deserved better.

The young woman whose dress she'd been marking for hem length caught Ione's gaze with a sly one of her own. "We have to get going anyway." She glanced at the clock on top the cabinet. "We have plans for lunch as well." Holding the dress, she stepped down and toward the curtains that allowed for privacy. "We could take a break, and maybe stop back in this afternoon?"

Clearly, she wanted Ione to abandon her post and join Dr. Whitaker. They had no idea.

"I... It would be nice to go for a walk." Ione tried not to drown in response to the deluge of problems flooding her mind. She had no interest in men...in fact, she figured she'd had enough of men to last a lifetime. Even if she could be interested, Clarence had come back, and she had no idea what he wanted. Beyond that, how could she ever be honest with Evan about her past? He deserved more. He was a doctor, for pity's sake, and the brother of the minister who had adopted her sisters. Hadn't Pastor Whitaker had the sense to set him straight about her?

He smiled at her response. A whole, honest smile. One without guile or any intention other than a walk on a beautiful day. At once, Ione wondered how her life had suddenly become so complex.

She also wondered how it was that his smile made the complications feel like they could float away. She mentally shook her head, making sure to keep her smile pasted on. "If you would like to step into the back room, I think Grace is there. She can show you where you can wait for me." One thing was certain—nothing could be fixed standing in front of exceedingly curious customers.

"Thank you. Good." He nodded, awkwardly, and made his way to the storeroom, stepping around counters and dress stands, and ducking under the curtain. The room was too small for his black-suited presence.

Ione's customer raised a knowing brow and didn't even try to hide her smug smile. She thought she knew.

But no one did. And Ione would sacrifice everything to make sure it stayed that way.

"Her responses have been cryptic." Miriam sat up to the small table in what was now Jenny's apartment above the warehouse. Jenny and Jeremy's, she supposed. Miriam smiled into her cup. She could have never imagined how quickly life changed. Less than two years had passed since she'd lived here, painting and doing her best to keep people away and out of her life.

"I sent her a note yesterday and haven't heard back from her yet." Jenny stood and placed her empty plate next to the wash basin. "I thought I may see what John thinks."

"What should John think?" John took the last couple of steps to the landing outside the open doorway, looking both welcoming and formidable in his black robes.

Jenny smiled and waved him in.

"I didn't even hear you." Miriam tried to keep the surprise out of her voice, but as always, she failed. John was one of those people who required honesty.

"You talking about Ione?"

Miriam frowned. He was also one of those people who, infuriatingly enough, didn't need you to tell him much in order to gain access to the honest answers he sought. There was no point in easing into the conversation. "Did you notice how quiet she was during dinner?"

John pulled out a kitchen chair that had been tucked under the end of the table and sat. Jenny held up the teapot, and John nodded his agreement to her offer. "I did notice. That's why I stopped over when I saw you were here." He looked at Miriam. "Do you know what the problem is?"

"I haven't a clue. Everything with the business is going well, and as far as I know, her sisters are doing well—better than well." Miriam picked up a spoon and stirred her cooling tea. "She spent the night at my house after dinner but left before everyone was up. Mr. Butler gave me the message that she'd had an early appointment."

"Did she mention it the night before?"

Miriam and John both looked to Jenny as she joined them. "I didn't hear anything." She shrugged.

"Maybe I should stop in for a visit." John picked up the cup Jenny had placed in front of him and sipped the steaming brew before setting it down on the saucer. "I haven't had much of a chance to spend any time with her since she opened the shop. She's been so busy."

"Maybe that's the problem," Miriam suggested weakly.

"How are you?" John shifted the focus.

Miriam stiffened at the abrupt change. "Fine. Everything is great." She tried to send a convincing smile.

"I don't believe you."

Miriam took a deep breath. Over the past year, she'd become accustomed to closer physical proximity with this group, and she'd even grow used to having people in her home. More difficult, though, was the relational breach of her carefully constructed boundaries. Sometimes, usually when she least expected it, the invasion caught her unaware. She glanced down to her hands, folded tight against her skirts, and willed the tension to leave her body.

"I'm sorry." John sat back to put a little space between them.

"Don't…" Miriam unfolded her hands and wiped each finger with the napkin she'd had crumpled in her lap.

"It wasn't my place to say that." John leaned back in and held out his hand, waiting for her to respond.

"You are concerned. That's what friends do. They show concern." Miriam said the short sentences as if she were reading them from a children's book. She took a deep breath in and lifted her hand to John's, feeling his large fingers close over hers.

Last year, the contact would have necessitated days of seclusion to recover. Now, it grounded her. The warmth of his touch, the rough texture of his fingers, the jagged edge of an imperfect nail, reminded her they shared this experience—that his happiness depended on hers, and hers on his, and that with all of them together, their little hodgepodge of a family had everything they needed.

He released her hand, and cool air rushed around her fingers.

"I think I'll stop by Ione's sometime this week and see how she's getting along." John scraped his chair back and stood. "Things look busy downstairs." He nodded to Jenny.

"They are. We received a larger than expected order, so some of the ladies are working extra hours to get it done by the end of the week."

John stopped before he reached the door. "These jobs for the women, they've made all the difference."

Jenny tried to hide the pride evident in her smile. "We just keep busy. Down here by the docks, life is hard."

"That being said…" Miriam slid her empty cup across the table. "…we should probably get to work. I have fabric measurements from Ione. There's a rush on this one, so I thought I might help at least get the order in."

Jenny set Miriam's cup near the other dirty dishes, and they followed John down the steps, accompanied by the whir of sewing machines and the fast snip of scissors. John picked his hat off the rack and ducked out onto the street with a smile. Fifteen women were working. Miriam tried to find satisfaction in that number. Fifteen women in their community now had food for their tables and a safe place to work. Fifteen women didn't have to wrestle with the kinds of decisions Jenny and Ione had had to make. Fifteen women were no longer completely dependent on their husbands for their livelihoods. Miriam shoved her hands into her apron pockets and watched as they concentrated on each tiny stitch. Why then could she not shake the feeling that something had gone dreadfully wrong?

Chapter 10

Tamm paced the floor of his tiny room.

She'd cost him money. He, of course, still wanted what she owed him. But now, now he wanted more.

Watching her that morning, how she moved as if she knew he'd observed, every sway of her hips, every turn of her long neck, every smile, he had to wonder if she'd done it just for him. Had she sensed his nearness? Had she felt the same jolt he'd been surprised to discover still jabbed every time she looked his way?

And no doubt, she looked his way.

Tamm sat on the edge of his unmade bed and kicked off his shoes. Replaying the morning, her movements, he didn't doubt that even if she hadn't seen him, even if she hadn't known for sure how close he stood by, at the very least, she felt his presence.

Shoes off, Tamm fell back to lie down and stare at the ceiling. She wanted him. Why else would she have invited that other man if not to spur his jealousy? Tamm smiled.

If she wanted to play, then he could oblige. Rolling to the edge of the bed, Tamm stood and crossed to the desk to sit down and write his next letter.

Soon, she would be back. Soon, he would no longer be called on to serve and cart around her friends. The thought still chafed. Tamm concentrated on keeping the stroke of his pen light. Soon, very soon, she would invite him back.

It felt good, knowing that she felt the same way he did, that he wouldn't have to prove to her that they should be together. Tamm waved the note back and forth to dry the ink, and then he sealed it.

The fully leafed trees overhead created a canopy of green. Ione looked up, ignoring the guilt of her deception but unsure how best to deal with the handsome, smart, and completely oblivious man at her side.

They walked, her head only reaching to his shoulder. The sun that made it through the leaves fell in carefree spots on his face and hat and back and on her hand, balanced lightly against his arm. He glanced down, catching her assessment, and Ione pretended to be interested in the play of light on the trees. After a while, they turned the corner, stopped at a lunch cart, and he purchased two pastries filled with roast beef and vegetables. Then he set to prove how much she didn't remember—or, she suspected, didn't know—about men.

She never thought about it much, but she'd never before been courted. Not like how he seemed intent on doing it. Prior to the time she'd run off with Clarence, there had been no men in her world, and then he'd entered her life like a force of nature, crowding out everything that was not him. Somehow, he'd made everything else fade away. Her mother's wisdom no longer held value, her sister's amusing playfulness deteriorated to irritating, and when she looked in a mirror, unless she stood next to him, her own reflection lost its vibrancy. Without him, she stood, simple, dull, a typical poor black woman in a neighborhood of other typical poor black women, everyone looking at the same, prescribed future of taking the trolley to a rich, white woman's house to scrub the floors.

She'd wanted more, and he'd been more than willing to help her see the future she'd desired.

She glanced from under the rim of her hat at the man walking next to her. Dr. Whitaker noticed the small movement and met her shadowed gaze with the half-smile she quickly recognized as the expression he offered when words weren't necessary.

She breathed in the fresh air and closed her eyes for a second, willing her nerves to cease firing at every slight movement or sound that he made. It wasn't so bad—this quiet walk. The way he'd tucked her gloved hand in the crook of his arm and led the way through the trees in the city park.

"Would you like to sit over there?" He pointed to an empty stone bench that overlooked a large grassy area.

"That should do." She had no idea what kind of conversation to have with the man. Things popped into mind—warnings she wanted to give him, like *you might want to step back*, or *you'd run if you knew what I used to do for money*. Neither seemed appropriate, and while she wouldn't typically approve of Pastor Whitaker offering such personal information, the man who now wanted to sit and eat a meal with her should have had some sort of counsel.

They sat, and he dug into the bag, retrieving their lunches, each wrapped separately in yesterday's newsprint. Ione pulled off her gloves and took the pastry from him. For the briefest of moments, his fingers brushed the back of hers.

Sound stopped. The rush of the breeze through the leaves, the call of pigeons, horses' hooves, and the quiet roar of a city filled with people and their conversations all faded to nothing. Instead, she heard the hitch in his breath, her own heartbeat, and noticed the way his jaw twitched. For the first time in over a year, Ione remembered what it had been about men that had made her love Clarence in the first place: they were so foreign, so different from the safe female world she'd created. And then she'd learned the danger in those differences. But something had changed in the past year. This time, the opposites—his strength where she was weak, the roughness of his hands where hers were soft—instead of opening a chasm of fear, laid bare the empty place that had so long been filled by instinct and mistrust and simple despair.

Dr. Whitaker was the first to recover from the brief physical connection. "I hope these taste good." He pulled the newspaper back to reveal his, and then took a bite. Tearing her eyes away from the stubble on his jaw and from the realization that she felt no fear, no foreboding, she followed his lead and bit into the tender pastry.

The flavors bloomed. Roasted meat, carrots, spices; each one she tasted in turn. She chewed slowly, concentrating on the movement, on swallowing, and on the reality that she hadn't tasted her food in longer than she could remember.

"My brother said that you recently opened the shop. How long has it been?" He dove in for another bite, waiting for Ione to answer.

She swallowed again. "Only a few months. Before that, I worked at the warehouse with Jenny."

"I think I remember Aaron saying something about the warehouse and how you are working to make low-cost clothes for the Foundling House." He cleared his throat. "That's admirable work."

Ione blinked, not expecting the compliment and not sure how to respond. *Thank you* seemed like a lie. If she spoke of gratitude, she ignored what had come before, what had led to the need for the business. To skip over the compliment in favor of elaborating on the current success or struggles rang of evasion, but in the scheme of things, ignoring the problem would be preferable to lying about it.

Or she could change the subject. "Not compared to what you've done."

Dr. Whitaker nodded, taking her cue. "When is the last time you walked along the lake?"

Ione dropped her hands to her lap, still firmly wrapped around her lunch. "What is it that you want?" She couldn't let this go any further. She wasn't suitable, and she wasn't willing to tell him why.

He mirrored her movements but not her expression. Where she'd wrestled her expression into one that would communicate determination, his remained open. "I'm hoping to finish my lunch."

"But why did you stop at the shop? Why did you invite me?"

Dr. Whitaker looked up at the sky long enough to compel Ione to do the same. A lazy cloud ambled across the expanse of blue. So often, the haze from coal furnaces and the dust from thousands of horses whipped up to block the view. But on a day when the wind stopped, when no rain threatened, the sky in Chicago took on the endless blue of the lake that touched the eastern horizon.

"Because..." Dr. Whitaker dropped his gaze to rest on hers. In the sun, his light brown eyes had flecks of green. "Because I was hungry, and a walk sounded nice."

Ione ran up the stairs to her apartment above the shop. She needed to get changed, to hurry over and see Mrs. Whitaker, to find out what they had said to Dr. Whitaker, and to beg they discourage the man.

She didn't bother to light another lamp. Instead, she carried the one she already had with her to her bedroom and swung open the armoire. While she designed and sewed dresses for the city's richest women, she rarely had time to create her own wardrobe. Until recently, today really, the modest selection had not bothered her. But now, running her fingers over her conservative options of primarily grays, navies, greens, and a lavender, she suddenly realized that over the course of the last year, most of her dresses had been made to serve some need, and always with the purpose of revealing as little skin as possible.

Reaching to the back of the armoire, Ione pulled out a dress she'd yet to wear. She shook it out and laid it over the end of her bed. Like most of what she wore, its gray color at first glance did not call attention. She had chosen it for exactly that reason—it looked plain. Ione opened another shutter on the lamp she'd carried into the room and tipped it toward the dress. Like Ione, the dress spoke in secrets.

The gray fabric shifted in the flickering, yellow light. It turned first a deep purple, and then gave way to a pearl that shimmered with movement.

She took a step back and considered. She'd ordered the fabric for an evening gown because of its ability to change with subtle shifts of light. Unfortunately, when it arrived, the feel of the fabric, far too heavy for ballroom wear, meant she had to do something else with it.

Ione ran her fingers over the dress. Pearl buttons—fake, of course—rose from mid hip to chin. Not in a straight line, though. The buttons began off center, almost in line with her right hip bone, and snaked toward the center as they worked up. The tight sleeves ran past her wrists, then flared in the middle of her hand, so that the slight and severe curve of the fabric above her wrists accentuated the detail of her fingers. From where she stood, the effect was both stern and feminine. Absolutely circumspect, without descending into the fashion sensibility of a grandmother. The dress invited nothing but respect.

Ione unfastened the work dress she wore, wriggled it down over her hips, and let it fall to the rug at the end of her bed. She longed to loosen her stays, to let her lungs fully expand, to stretch and scratch and lie down after working all day, but she ignored the desire and instead lifted the dress she'd unearthed from the back of the armoire over her head.

The rich fabric smelled of linen and the lavender sachet she'd hung between the garments. Perhaps if she turned down the lamp, buried her nose in the soft skirt, and sunk to the floor, she might sleep. Unconsciousness might take over, and she might forget the task at hand. Ione flirted with the thought, with the temptation to do nothing. To ignore the letters. To pretend her past was not hers. To masquerade as a woman deserving of a man like Dr. Whitaker.

No. She'd done things she regretted, made horrible decisions, been the kind of woman to abandon her own family, but she'd never been a liar. She shoved her arms through the narrow sleeves, ignoring the guilt that came with the knowledge that this luxury, this whisper of fine fabric over her sinful skin, was never meant for her.

With dress gaping open, she crossed to her dressing table, grabbed the button hook, and concentrated on not looking at her reflection during the endless process of securing the dress onto her body and then her ankle boots to her feet.

The opulence of the matching cape nearly embarrassed Ione back out of the dress. Instead, she grabbed it, tied it at the collar, doused the lamp, and descended the back steps to the alley.

She looked up between the buildings to a sky aflame. Orange and lavender shot up toward the approaching night in a nameless plea her confused soul echoed: *please*. Please, keep the darkness away.

Clarence, her past, her future. Ione lifted her skirts and stepped into the street. People rushed back and forth. She'd miscalculated the effect of her dress. Approaching women hushed. She'd never been shy, but under the scrutiny of a multitude of eyes—she could feel them—she wanted to sink between the cobbles.

It was too late to change. She needed to get to the Whitakers', to make sure they understood, to dissuade Dr. Whitaker before he visited again.

Ione shivered. She needed to get out of the street, to step into the warm home her sisters shared, to remember, even for a minute, that at least the people she most cared about were safe.

But her thoughts drifted to Dr. Whitaker again. His eyes, and his hands, and the gentle way he asked a question and waited for her answer, as if he really wanted to know. Ione shook her head, trying to clear her mind.

He probably wasn't interested in her anyway. Ione smiled at a passing child holding tightly to her mother's hand. Why would he be? He needed a wife, someone who could be a good mother. She would be wholly unsuitable.

Ione sucked in a breath and held it.

She needed to be honest. This visit was more to convince Mrs. Whitaker to make sure her brother-in-law knew he couldn't be interested. Because if he was, it would be up to Ione to dissuade him.

Until their walk, Ione thought she'd learned to be impervious to men. But she was weak.

Tamm leaned against the fencepost, waiting for a sign she'd gone upstairs so he could drop the note into the mail slot of the shop. Even after she'd turned down the shop lamps, the upper windows stayed dark. He shifted his weight from the right to the left and back to the right before examining the dirt encrusted path with the toe of his shoe. She certainly knew how to tease. He kicked a pebble. It bounced twice and splashed into a puddle at the edge of the street. She'd always know how to do that.

Tamm tried to keep a pleasant expression on his face. It wouldn't do to stand in the street, scowling at a dress shop. That was another of her powers: making him forget his goals.

A news sheet from that morning swirled between the buildings with a gust of wind off the lake. Tamm waited, scooped it out of the air, and shook out the wrinkles. At least now he could look like any other person, reading to pass the time.

The curtains in her window hung, lifeless and dark. Tamm sucked in a deep breath of humid city air and held it. She had to turn on a light sometime. It made no sense that she wouldn't.

A woman dressed in shimmering gray slipped from the alley. Her hair piled high under the back of a matching hat, the tilt of her chin, and her high cheekbones left no mystery to her identity. Ione had places to be.

Jealousy stabbed him. He should be escorting her to whatever function she planned to attend. She glanced back, and her narrow shoulders turned. A gust of wind toyed with the cape, flipping it over to ride against her back. Her handbag hung from her wrist by a string.

It wasn't the fact that he had stood outside waiting or that the letter he'd penned crackled against his chest in his jacket pocket. It wasn't that she looked beautiful or that she obviously had plans that he, in his current financial situation, would never be invited to. It wasn't the way the fabric hugged her thighs as the wind plastered her skirts to her small frame, or the way she lifted one delicate hand to cover the tasteful plumage on her hat. Simply put, her fragility angered him.

He fought the urge to stomp into traffic, to cross the street, to come up behind her, and to remind her that she needed protection. How dare she risk herself like this? How dare she walk unaccompanied, dressed in clothes that invited men to want? Tamm's normally steady grip shook with the efforts to stay put. To watch.

He looked down the street, checking for men who might be following. Who knew? She certainly moved carelessly through the evening streets. Finding no one of concern, Tamm let the wind take the newspaper again and stepped into the traffic.

When she turned the corner, Tamm darted across the street.

Someone had to look after the foolish woman. He wanted her back. The thought settled firmly in his mind. He wanted her back. He deserved the kind of rewards she could bring, and despite her mistakes, she deserved someone who wanted to look after her, to keep her from endangering herself with poor decisions and even worse choices in friends, by the looks of the dandy that had called that afternoon.

It wasn't about him simply needing her money or about her owing him. It was so much more. They belonged together.

It might take convincing, but he'd have her back again. Somehow. Of that, there was no doubt.

Chapter 11

Ione knocked on the Whitakers' door and immediately regretted her haste. Of course they wouldn't be expecting her. She should have sent a messenger. Frowning, she adjusted the string of her handbag so it didn't cut into her wrist. She should have just forgotten the whole thing.

The streetlamps stood like sticks against what had become a deep purple sky. Ione wished she could describe color the way Miriam did. Miriam knew names for hues Ione had never heard of, but when she spoke them, Ione knew exactly the color she described. The color at the horizon wouldn't be red, it would be rubies, or raspberry, or blood.

No sound came from behind the door. She looked down the street to the dark windows of the empty church and back to the stoop where she stood waiting for a family she was both a part of and not. Her sisters had found family, a mother and a father, in Mrs. Whitaker and Pastor. While Ione couldn't be anything but happy for them, it meant that Ione couldn't be the first person they turned to in trouble.

Likewise, they shouldn't be the first for her.

Ione closed her eyes for just a second. A second where she could stand on the porch and pretend that she belonged. She needed to warn Mrs. Whitaker to advise her brother-in-law against pursuing a friendship that could only lead to disappointment. But now she could see herself in the foolish light of an evening, alone and dressed far too nicely to have arrived anywhere uninvited. She bit her bottom lip until she tasted metal, and then turned to leave before anyone noticed her.

"Ione?" Mrs. Whitaker stepped out from behind the house. "Lucy thought she'd heard someone knocking, but we didn't believe her."

"I thought I might stop by and speak with you for a moment. But I didn't want to intrude."

"Oh goodness, no intrusion at all." Mrs. Whitaker waved her hand, signaling Ione to step off the porch and into the side yard. The quaint house the Whitakers lived in was the picture of perfection. A white-washed fence surrounded the flower gardens, completing a picture that reminded Ione of how much she didn't belong. Miriam and Michael's wealth, while intimidating, held nothing that she could compare to her own life. She'd never walked those streets as a child, never dreamed of having servants or of eating meals with too many courses to count. Growing up, she had no idea people slept on piles of down, that there were larger collections of art in some folks' homes than in her teacher's picture book, and that a whole part of town existed where the people who cleaned up after the horses were dressed in better clothes than her everyday ones.

But the Whitakers, with their pantry stocked with preserves in every color, their cleanly swept floors, and even more pristine souls, reminded her of how different they were. She'd grown up looking into the picture windows of families like theirs, wondering why she didn't always have a warm fire, a laughing father, and a calm, unworried mother. The Whitaker family exposed the raw nerve that was her childhood, and it took all Ione had to sit quietly some days and marvel at the memories her sisters would be able to treasure. It wasn't that she wanted less for them—quite the opposite. She wanted them to be part of that scene in the windows. She wanted them to grow up never knowing that areas of the city existed where people would do anything for money—where she had done anything for money.

"Everyone is here tonight." Mrs. Whitaker had been talking the whole time that Ione's mind had been wandering, so when they rounded the corner to where the family sat on the back porch and both Pastor

Whitaker and Dr. Whitaker stood to welcome her, Ione could hardly catch her breath.

"I'm so sorry." Ione took a step back. "I didn't realize you were all visiting." She raised her hands, waving away their objections. "I can come over later, when you don't have plans. I should have sent a note before I decided to stop by."

"Nonsense." Mrs. Whitaker's brows furrowed in protest. "You aren't company. Family stops by whenever they like."

Under the pressure of everyone's eyes on her, Ione fought the urge to run. Dr. Whitaker touched her arm, bringing her senses back to the present in a rush of confusion. "I..." she hesitated, unsure how to explain.

"Sit down and have some lemonade." Dr. Whitaker took her arm and led her to the empty seat next to his. He leaned in as he held her chair. "I'm glad you stopped by." The words were meant only for her ears.

She felt his every syllable, every exhale, every change in tone at the nape of her neck. She tried to breathe evenly, to not look stricken when she met Mrs. Whitaker's unhindered smile. Although the Whitakers didn't know everything, they knew enough to discourage any kind of interest.

But here Maggie was, sitting in front of her, grinning like a Cheshire cat. Had everyone lost their minds?

Ione took a deep breath in and folded her hands in her lap. Obviously, she would not be communicating her troubles with Mrs. Whitaker tonight. In truth, by the looks of things, her unanticipated visit likely set her mission back a few paces. Like always, she would make do.

She looked out from under her lashes at the handsome man seated next to her, trying to ascertain what it was about Dr. Whitaker that drew her.

It, his presence, changed everything. And nothing.

Tamm followed her to a white clapboard house snugged up cozily to the church next door. The sunset had cleaned the city of the dirty details and left only the warm, reflective colors of the approaching night. He almost considered stepping out from between the buildings and rescuing Ione from her lonely perch when a woman he'd never met rounded the corner and called out to her, as if she were family. That they knew each other was not in doubt. How they knew each other, another matter entirely.

She followed the woman through the neat beds of flowers and around back. Tamm lifted the collar of his jacket and trailed along on the other side of the street. He stopped short when the men stood to greet Ione. The same man who had interrupted his plans for the morning.

The letter in his pocket burned. He knew now. She wasn't playing coy. She was out to humiliate him, to replace him. She knew he watched— there was no way she couldn't have felt his gaze as he followed her. He backed into an alley and punched the brick wall until blood oozed out of his hand and onto the hard surface.

The message had been clear. He'd been a fool to think she might have changed, that she might be sorry for the way she'd abandoned him. No. Her visit, the way she'd dressed so he could remember how she felt when pressed against him, the way she walked as if she'd wanted him to follow, and now the way she'd greeted the man with the shy lie of a smile that had fooled him too. Clearly, she refused to acknowledge him. Refused to help him. And now—he looked down at his damaged knuckles—she paraded her new life as if to rub salt in the wound.

But she didn't know he still had power. Even if she wanted to think her money and her friends could protect her, she'd find out right quick how wrong she'd been.

Tamm pulled the letter out of his pocket and tore it slowly in half, letting the sound punctuate the finality of his mission.

She'd left him the first time to return to her family. Now she'd done it again.

She would pay. One way or another, she would pay in the way most dear to her.

Miriam fastened the loop on the portfolio of drawings for the Women's Pavilion. Tomorrow she would have to meet with Mrs. Penn to hand them off. Ione, busy with too many evening gown orders to count, had passed the duty to her. Miriam slid the folder next to the others on the shelves above her desk and eased out of the chair. The task became more difficult with each day.

"You need help?" Michael, seated at his desk behind his own stack of papers, smiled and looked at her above the rim of the spectacles that had slid down the bridge of his nose.

"Am I entertaining you?" Miriam snapped back, only partly joking. She stood fully, stretched a stray ache out of her back, and frowned. "Are you ready to be done for the night?"

Michael hummed and placed his pencil in the middle of the pile of correspondence, so as not to lose his place.

The large room where they both worked served the dual purpose of a parlor with multiple seating areas. Not that they both didn't have other offices tucked into quiet corners of the main floor, but since they'd been married, they'd both migrated to this room that Miriam knew so well, even after night robbed them of light.

Miriam turned down the lamp that still burned near her desk and made her way across the room. She stopped at the sparkling row of glass doors that looked out over their private gardens. Tucked between their townhouse and the next, it was a gift from her father to her mother. A corner of nature in the city. A secret place for only the two of them. The neighbors were unaware of the hollow between their homes, and the only windows that looked down on the expanse of green and growing trees was the entrance she now stood at and the windows in her studio at the very top of the house.

"It must be a full moon tonight." Miriam craned her neck to see if the orb hung between the buildings, but from her vantage she could see little but the reflected silver light.

"I think it is." Michael stood, extinguished his desk lamp, and made his way to stand next to Miriam.

She looked out over the shimmering grass to the now fully leafed-out tree. A family of cardinals had found their way into the sanctuary, as well as one of the squirrels. Somehow, despite the huge brick walls and the buildings, the animals had found a place to belong, away from the dangers of carriage wheels, soot-spewing chimneys, and housewives with brooms.

"It's a bit like us, you know." Miriam leaned back into Michael. "This place. We hide away as best we can, and we bring our friends who like to hide too."

"I, for one, am glad of your father's foresight. I like it." The smile in Michael's voice came through, and Miriam couldn't help but smile in response.

But when he dropped a kiss onto the side of her neck, she also couldn't help but wonder if it was enough.

"What's troubling you?" Michael pulled back. She could feel his gaze on her profile, wondered what he saw there. Her love, her gratefulness, or the growing sense that the safety they reveled in was all an illusion?

Miriam shrugged. "Nothing. Just thoughtful."

"You haven't painted in a while."

"I know. I thought I would take a break from it for the time being."

Michael slowly spun Miriam so that she looked up at him. His eyes, normally blue, looked gray in the lack of light. He pulled her closer, and she responded by pressing her ear to his chest. His heart pounded a rhythm faster than hers. "I worry that you aren't painting because you're afraid of something. But I can't place what it might be." He whispered the words against the hair at the top of her head.

"You don't have to worry." She pulled back enough so she could put space between herself and the truth in the words he spoke, but not so much as to let him feel an echo of the lack in her own being. "Let's get to bed. We have a lot to do tomorrow."

Chapter 12

Ione didn't hesitate to turn on the lights once she returned home. In fact, she turned on every gas light as she entered the back of her shop, the electric lights that Michael had insisted on installing even though they'd all thought the addition frivolous, and the lamps in every room of her upstairs apartments.

Now she sat, alone, at her table. She unfastened a few of the buttons under her chin and dropped her head back, relishing the feel of the air on her neck. The dress, while beautiful and interesting, was styled in the convention that covered nearly every inch of skin. And while that convention had been slowly slipping from popularity—no doubt due to the lack of comfort in summertime—it still persisted, and Ione often still fell victim to its subtler charms. One of those being that no one could fault her for a lack of modesty. The other: she'd shown far too much skin for far too long. She could cover from head to toe every day for the rest of her life, and she doubted she'd be back to even footing with propriety.

Ione stood, walked to her windows, and pulled the parlor drapes closed. Then she did the same in every room of the apartment. She couldn't help but feel safe with the Whitakers, but she couldn't shake the feeling that she was being watched.

And she was probably right.

The thought sent a shiver through her entire body. Ione made her way into the kitchen and stoked to life the nearly dead embers in her

103

small stove. A few sticks of kindling, and the flame roared to life against the sharp evening chill that had overtaken the room. She filled the teapot next, set it on the warming surface, and found her way back into her bedroom, where she continued to unfasten the now obviously inadvisable number of buttons. What had she been thinking?

And then, the sound of shattering glass tore through the brittle air. The crash had been both expected and unexpected. In the moments after the rock rolled out from under the bedroom drapes, and the broken pane of glass tinkled to the floor in countless tiny shards, she'd had the benefit of reflection. If it hadn't been expected, if she hadn't known some kind of retaliation would be aimed at her, then she wouldn't have turned on every lamp in the house. She wouldn't have a pot of tea brewing even though the clock had ticked well past the time she normally turned in. She wouldn't have closed every curtain and worn a dress nearly impossible to remove on her own.

She'd erected walls the best she knew how. Ione sucked in a breath and walked to the place where the rock lay, impotently wrapped with a piece of torn paper. She let the breath out slowly and bent to pick it up.

The twine fell away, the rock tumbled back to the floor, and she smoothed the paper against the palm of her shaking hand.

You will pay.

Tamm felt the dead thud of his heart against the wall of his chest. It pounded, slow, insistent, forceful. He would have what he wanted.

Unlike the last note, the rock had not been an impulse. He'd planned it from the time he'd finally understood Ione's purpose in walking to that minister's house. The letter, much nicer, really, that he'd been burning to give to her had been long forgotten by the time he'd realized what he needed to do. Tamm sneered at his reflection in the small mirror in his room. She needed to be taught a lesson. Typically, that wasn't something he would have looked forward to. But her relationship with the Farlings, the way she paraded her wealth—wealth she was not entitled to—around for him to see, the way she welcomed new men into her life...

Tamm pulled the unused letter from the jacket and tore it in half—everything she'd done meant that she needed to learn her place.

He laid the one half over the other and ripped again. Everything she'd become since she'd left she owed to his teaching, to the way he'd shown her how to work with people, how to get what she wanted. She'd been a child when he'd found her. Tamm tore the paper again and watched the pieces flutter onto the desktop.

Miriam rolled over and slid out of bed again. Michael still slept. The house offered nothing but the creaks and groans of aging, drying lumber. The floor felt cold against her toes.

She ignored the shock, preferring instead how the chill brought her body to life in a way that grew more precious by the day. Michael would protest if he knew. He would chastise her for risking illness, for ignoring the needs of her body, for choosing the danger of a chill over the comfort of house slippers, but Miriam needed *something*.

Anything. She couldn't paint, couldn't trust herself to pick up the brushes and tubes of color. The life inside rolled in agreement. Maybe after the child was born, maybe after she came out with ten toes and ten fingers and ate well and slept well and looked around the room with bright eyes, maybe then Miriam could trust herself enough to paint a future of hope. Because if fear, if pain, if death dripped off her brush and onto her canvas—Miriam placed her hand over her swollen belly—if her paintings spoke of destruction for the life inside her belly, it would kill her.

Having something to lose was new, unsettling.

Miriam walked out of their room and into the sitting room that separated their two suites. She never slept in her own room—rather, she used it more as a dressing room—but the sitting room reminded her of the few memories she had of her mother and father together.

Her mother had died when Miriam had been young. Her father, heartbroken, had moved them both out of the home they'd shared and into the apartments above the warehouse. There, she'd stayed, even after her father's death, until helping Ione meant that she had to let go of her own fears of the outside world.

Now her fears had turned inward.

Miriam avoided the passageways and opened the door to the hallway that stretched the length of the second floor of their townhouse. The oriental rug, made specifically for the space, filled the hall nearly from edge to edge. Miriam rubbed her cold toes against the warm wool and then made her way through the dark to the steps. She could choose to go up, to her studio, or down, to the parlor. Instead, she wandered into the rooms where guests sometime stayed.

Jenny's pink room—the room Miriam had had as a child—was filled with ruffles and lace and everything a girl should have; everything Jenny, who had been put to work on the streets by her father, had been denied.

She closed the door as silently as possible and crossed the hall to the room where Ione preferred to stay when she visited.

The door opened silently. Miriam slipped into the dark room and breathed in the cool air. Even in the summer, with the breezes off the lake and the multitude of windows, their home rarely became hot. But on this side of the house, where the sunlight only burned during the morning hours, the room needed a fire almost nightly to keep the chill out.

Miriam wandered to the bed. She missed her friend. Something had changed, and while Michael and John had discussed if Ione might need some help, if her schedule had become too much, Miriam knew that was simply a man's explanation. They liked problems that could be fixed with a small adjustment in schedule or with an intervention of the male sort. Miriam knew better. A simple schedule overload wouldn't even be a stumble for Ione. That woman was made of a resilient kind of material Miriam could only wish she shared.

She pulled out the dressing table stool and slowly lowered herself down to sit. Moving had become a thoughtful process. Miriam smiled. She still had a way to go. In some respects, the changes were unnerving, but the sheer number of adjustments her body made were more a source of curiosity than one of concern.

Mrs. Maloney had the maids go around and pull drapes closed in the evening and open in the morning, regardless of whether or not someone stayed for the night. But the room's bright pallet couldn't be subdued, especially with the cool light of the full moon illuminating the curtains so they glowed.

Miriam looked around. The armoire cast a deep shadow against the wall behind, and Miriam stared into the void, trying to make out the edge of the painting she knew hung there.

But nothing looked right. The black shadow did more than conceal—it distorted the line of the wall. It made an opening where none existed, a void that should not have been there.

Miriam raised a shaky hand to her chest, and then let it fall to hang limp at her side. An opening did exist. She'd almost forgotten the secret door to the passageway behind. She levered herself back up, using the dressing table for support, and crossed to the other side of a room that seemingly stretched out in front of her.

The suck of air that plastered her nightdress to the back of her calves was the first confirmation that the door had been left ajar. Miriam reached the wood panel and pushed until it clicked closed, a sound that echoed throughout the unoccupied space. Suddenly, Miriam wished she had not left the safety of her own bed, Michael, her space that smelled like him, that called with its warmth and its comfort and its security.

Miriam reached out again and pressed her hand against the cool wood. No one knew of this opening. No one. Even she had forgotten about it. She rarely came down the passageway that ran along the sleeping quarters. There was no need. And of the servants, Mrs. Maloney was the only one who knew any details of the hidden hallways, staircases, ramps, and secret rooms. And even the housekeeper hadn't actually walked through them.

Even Michael typically avoided the winding halls.

For the first time, Miriam wished for locks on the doors. But whether they should be placed in the rooms to protect from someone hiding, or in the hiding place, to protect Miriam, she couldn't say.

She backed away, increasing the distance between her and the door. Looking around the room, staring into each shadow and over any place someone could hide, eventually the backs of her thighs brushed against the edge of the mattress. She sat, feeling the give and spring of the soft surface. It should have made her want to sleep. It should have reminded her that she was exhausted, that she needed to close her eyes, to rest her head on the down-stuffed pillow. She glanced over to the head of the bed, where the pillow next to her still held its round impression.

She jumped up and pulled her robe tighter, closing the gap at her neck. Someone had been here. She backed up toward the main door, keeping the disturbed pillow in sight.

While she might have convinced herself that the unreliable drafts that sometimes swept through the rooms could have opened the passageway, or while she might have believed a servant had accidentally found the space, what was without doubt was that someone had been here, lay down, and left. Perhaps only when they heard Miriam enter.

She fought against the shiver that swept along every nerve in her body and opened the door to the main hall.

Feeling her way along the corridor, Miriam counted her steps. It wasn't that she couldn't see, or that she needed to measure any kind of distance—it was purely instinct. Every fourth step she inhaled, four more, she exhaled. The pace, an echo of her nighttime walks when she'd lived alone, comforted her. They reminded her of the feel of the carpet, of the caress of air swirling around her feet, of the grain in the wood paneling, of her paints upstairs.

Before she'd married Michael, Miriam walked the fog-enshrouded streets at night, moving from one circle of light to the next, but never stepping into the glowing orbs that pulsed from the lamppost's gas flames. When she had tired, she would find the warmth of her apartment above the warehouse, have a cup of tea, and fall asleep as the first streaks of sun burned up and over the lake.

When she'd woken, she would paint what she'd felt as she'd walked. She'd paint the happiness, the pain, the successes. And then she would paint what persisted: an unhappy child sometimes became a satisfied adult, the future of a beaten boy often remained dark, the adult face of a girl who lived in fear usually stayed both childlike and fearful. Everything she'd felt at night, everything she'd watched from her windows above the street during the day, melted onto the canvas. And from the jumble and confusion she'd felt at the first streak of paint came the portrait of something she could name. Even if that expression turned dark, she could at least label it as dark and understand it as so. Sometimes, though, the dark turned to light, and a portrait of grace emerged; one of hope, of determination, surfaced. It was for those moments that Miriam touched paint to canvas.

Ione's portrait had been like that. The distress Miriam had seen and painted of Ione when they were children of nearly the same age transformed to an expression of courage and tranquility. Miriam smiled at the memory, and the hollow inside opened a bit further.

She slipped into the shared sitting room between her room and Michael's, and then into the room where Michael lay, snoring softly.

The urge to paint nearly made her turn from the luxury of their bed, nearly made her ignore her cold toes and the uncertainty of someone in the house. But she fought it and won.

Miriam slid in next to her husband, closed her eyes, recited the possibility that she'd only imagined the impression on the pillow, that the passageway could have swung open on its own, that she'd imagined it all.

And when the sun began to illuminate the lifeless drapes, Miriam closed her eyes, and finally sleep came.

Chapter 13

The night before had been a failure, but Ione didn't have time to think about it. She rushed from the storeroom into the shop and glanced at the clock that ticked the seconds away from its perch above at the very top of a shelf full of fabric samples. Ten minutes until she would unlock the doors. Ten minutes until the arrival of her first fitting, and every line of the appointment book for the day had been filled in.

She slipped her hand into her pocket and felt the cold weight of the stone from the night before. She'd destroyed the note, but the stone she'd kept as a reminder that the lunch from the previous day, the conversation and laughter of that evening, and the smiles she'd shared with Dr. Whitaker were only temporary. The knowing glances from Mrs. Whitaker, Lucy's excitement at having her whole family to witness her little-girl antics, and Ione's own bliss-filled thoughts could never be her reality. They were stolen from another woman's future—someone who could have a husband and a family of her own. Ione rubbed her thumb along the edge of the smooth, flat rock, nearly the size of her palm. He must have picked it up on the beach with the intention of breaking through one of the literal barriers between them. If any man was ever capable of walking along the shore, absorbing the breathtaking view of water bluer than any of her fabrics and sand as clear as glass, and think only of how to use a piece of nature to destroy her world, it was Clarence.

"These came in late yesterday."

Ione startled at the interruption.

Grace, her face nearly concealed behind a new armload of samples, elbowed her way past the half-closed curtain and dropped the stack on the counter. She glanced at the clock. "Ten minutes? How is that even possible?"

"I think we need to plan to get in earlier on Wednesdays." Ione wasted a fraction of a second to recover. She frowned at the samples and picked them up, one at a time, reds first, from the metal rings riveted to the corners. The rack, something Michael had designed and ordered to be built, allowed customers to see how the fabric draped and feel it run between their fingers without the inconvenience of taking down an entire bolt. Grace followed Ione's movements, beginning with the greens, so that they weren't tripping over each other to get the fabrics hung in the few minutes they had left.

"Who was that man who stopped by yesterday?"

"Which one?" Ione knew perfectly well which one.

Grace gave her a withering look. It wasn't every day that a well-dressed man stopped into to the shop, at least without a wife or sister at his side. And it couldn't be overlooked that he was negro, and professional, in a city where most negro men worked in the service of others and didn't dress nearly as nicely as Dr. Whitaker. Being in the clothing industry, Ione knew that the quality of the doctor's clothes wouldn't be lost on Grace.

"He seems nice." Grace placed the last sample—a leaf-colored silk— on the rack and twisted to grab another handful from the counter. "Did you go to lunch?"

Ione took a deep breath and bit the inside of her bottom lip, trying not to smile at the memory she wasn't worthy of having. The thought of the two of them walking in the park, her gloved hand tucked into the crook of his arm, him supporting her and smiling as she took a seat on the stone bench, and how he'd handed her the paper-wrapped lunch— it felt like she had the memories of watching another couple, a pair of strangers. Never had she anticipated being courted. In all her plans for the future, visions of family meant dinners with her sisters at the Whitakers', or sharing a silent joke with Miriam at the Farlings' table. There had never been a table of her own in her dreams, and absolutely never a man to sit next to her.

"We walked in the park and purchased lunch from a vendor." Ione kept the explanation simple.

Grace hummed a sound that communicated something between agreement and interest.

"I'll get the rest." Ione escaped to the back room, the stone in her pocket riding heavily against her thigh. Another thing to add to the list: find someone no one knew to repair the glass. She didn't need those questions.

Michael, dressed for the day, stood next to the bed and watched his sleeping wife. Curled on her side, with one hand tucked under her cheek and the other placed protectively over her stomach, she looked completely at peace. He watched her chest expand with every breath in. Carefully, so carefully, he bent to place his hand next to hers. What had once been flutters she'd happily shared had changed to outright kicks and rolls that made him wonder at how everything even fit together. He'd seen pregnant women before, and while they usually went into seclusion for the last couple of months, he wasn't completely ignorant regarding the female form. What caught him off guard was the burgeoning sense that what grew inside his wife was his to safeguard. He took in a shaky breath at the resulting surge of protectiveness that had his hand trembling against her warm nightdress. He lifted his palm, severing himself from the feel of his child's movements, and took a step back.

Michael adjusted his tie and quietly stepped out of the room, careful to close the door behind him. He had to get to the office early.

"Would you like some breakfast?" Mrs. Maloney met him at the base of the stairs.

"No, thank you, though."

The request had been more out of politeness than an expectation that he might accept the offer. Michael took the morning's paper that Mrs. Maloney handed him, secured it under his arm, and grabbed his hat off the coat tree. He'd have breakfast later at his office. For now, he needed to be on his way.

"Tamm has the carriage pulled around already."

"Thank you." Michael reached for the door latch but paused. "Could you look in on Miriam after a while? She's still sleeping."

Mrs. Maloney pursed her lips and shook her head. She was a tall woman, and her high cheekbones, intelligent eyes, and the pile of gray hair that always sat perfectly atop her head gave her a look of authority that no man or woman in their right mind would doubt. She'd been with Miriam since she had decided to open the house.

"Was she walking around for most of the night again?" Mrs. Maloney slid one hand into the slit of a pocket on the side of the straight gray skirt.

Michael nodded, wondering exactly how many of the same skirt she must own. He'd rarely seen her in anything else. "How long has it been since you've been on a holiday?"

Mrs. Maloney blinked, the question obviously catching her off guard—a rare occurrence. "I'm not sure." She shrugged, the casual movement appearing incongruous with her typically stiff work demeanor.

It wasn't that she was cold—much the opposite, she'd been like the mother Miriam had needed as she moved back into her family's townhouse. Rather, Mrs. Maloney simply defined proper. "I think you should plan to take a week, maybe before the baby arrives." Michael glanced up the silent staircase. "We've never had a baby before. We may need a fair deal more help than we think."

"That you will." Mrs. Maloney nodded. "I'm not sure I have ever taken much of a holiday before. I'll think about it."

"Good." Michael opened the door and stepped out onto the front stoop. The morning air still held the damp of the night. Tamm, sitting atop the carriage, jumped down and held open the small black door. Michael glanced back to Mrs. Maloney. In the seconds before she secured the door, her eyes had taken on a dark but veiled look of displeasure, and Michael hoped he had not offended her by suggesting the holiday.

Miriam sat on the edge of the bed, waiting for her lady's maid. She never used to need help getting her dresses on. She frowned at her reflection in the dressing mirror. Now, with the constrictive corsets, the popular additions of trimmings and lace and buttons and who knew what all else, and the multiple layers of fabric, she was hopeless to make sense of any of it. Add to that the undeniable truth that she could barely fit into anything, that her belly seemed to grow larger and tighter by the day, she broke into sweat even thinking about trying to wriggle into the layers.

"Are you decent?" Sally's voice called from the hall. "Mrs. Maloney sent me up."

"Come in." Miriam leaned to stretch her back. "I'm not sure if I can claim decency, but it's as good as it's going to get."

The young woman hid a smile behind her hand and stepped into the room with a small curtsy.

"How long have you been here now?" Miriam squirmed until she reached the edge of the bed, preparing to stand. Sally rushed forward.

"A couple of months." She took Miriam by the elbow and helped her stand.

Miriam felt foolish. "Do you like working here?"

"Of course, ma'am."

Now she felt even more foolish. If she could only be like Ione, who never struggled for the right words, or Jenny, who typically didn't care, tasks like this one would be so much easier.

"I need to get the corset on so I can have any hope of fitting into my dress." Miriam pointed at the peach pile of fabric next to her. Although not her favorite color, it at least had an empire waist.

Sally immediately picked it up and shook it out, laying it flat on the bed.

"I wanted to get dressed myself, and last week, I could have, but you are going to have to help me lace this thing tightly if I want to go anywhere today." Miriam grabbed the corset and lifted it for Sally to see.

"Are you sure, ma'am?"

"Why?" Miriam examined the garment for a flaw that she'd missed.

"My momma says you shouldn't use corsets on a baby, and if you do, you should only wear them loose."

Miriam frowned. "I think I would like your mother, but I have to go out this morning, and I can't go anywhere like this." She gestured to her nightdress.

"That's true, ma'am." Sally picked up the corset and gestured for Miriam to spin. Then she reached around and hooked the top hook-and-eye closure at the back.

Miriam made the mistake of glancing down at her protruding stomach and the corset that, while intended for a pregnant woman, Miriam suspected had most likely been designed by a man. "This is hopeless."

"Let's see what we can do."

The girl started lacing the back, working from the top to the bottom so that when she was done, while Miriam felt the pressure, she wasn't uncomfortable.

"Why don't you try to sit and see if you can do it."

Miriam hadn't thought of that. She grasped the edge of her dressing table and lowered her now ample body to the bench, being careful to breathe out on the way down.

Slowly, she looked up at Sally. "I think this will do." She offered a tentative smile.

Sally didn't look as convinced. "Are you going alone? Do you want me to send someone with you?"

"No. I'll be fine. Besides, I think this will be my last trip out until the baby comes. I'm not sure I can do this any longer. I have no idea how some women work until their children are born." Miriam's thoughts floated to the women who worked at the warehouse. They preferred to keep busy until their time came, and then were back at work in a matter of days, at the most.

"Pardon me, ma'am, but some women carry their babies smaller than others." Sally shrugged a tiny apology.

Miriam concentrated on not being offended. It was true. She was enormous.

"I'm sorry. I shouldn't have said that." Sally looked longingly at the door.

"No. You are right." Miriam sighed. "Help me into the dress, please. The faster I can get this thing on, the faster I can leave and get today's task list crossed off."

Sally lifted the fabric over Miriam's head and let it cascade down. The process of buttoning and fastening and tying ribbons was accomplished with efficiency, and soon Miriam stood in front of the mirror examining her reflection.

"Maybe this will help." Sally laid the matching jacket over Miriam's shoulders.

"I look like a trussed-up hippopotamus at the circus."

Sally quickly covered her mouth to stifle a laugh, but only succeeded in causing a snort to escape.

Miriam smiled. "Maybe you could just follow me, making that noise, and then the picture will be complete."

At that, they both had to sit for a minute to recover. Miriam wiped away the stray tears from her cheeks. "Thank you for helping. This can't be fun."

"Not at all, ma'am. Glad I could be of assistance." Sally stood up to leave. "I'll tell Mrs. Maloney to let me know when you get back so I can help you out of that"—she pointed at Miriam's dress—"thing."

"Absolutely." Miriam glanced down at the mounds of peach covering her protruding belly. "Besides, I think my only other option would be to stay in it forever."

Chapter 14

"Someone is at the delivery door." Grace peeked around the curtain to the front of the store.

"Good. I'll be right there." Ione waved her back and then locked the front door behind her last customer. More than anything, she wanted to kick her shoes off, shrug out of her clothes, and fall into bed. Tired didn't even begin to describe how she felt.

"He says he's here to fix your window." Grace pointed at a plain-looking man in dirty trousers and a clean shirt. His mustache kicked up on the sides, waxed into tight curls.

"I think a lady, a Ms. Smith, requested my services." He directed the statement to Grace.

"I am Ms. Smith." Ione took a step forward, finally earning his attention.

"Oh, pardon." His tone cooled, and he sent a disapproving, fatherly stare to Grace, but he directed his next question to the correct person.

"You sent a note that said you had some broken glass?"

"Yes. It's upstairs."

"Do you have a husband I should be speaking with?"

"No. But I can take you to see it."

He *hmphed* his objections to being forced to work for a woman. The fact that she was negro didn't help matters.

"I'll go too." Grace sent the man a look that was every bit the match for his.

"If you'll follow me, please." Ione led the way, with the repairman and Grace in tow.

Once in the apartment, Ione pointed to the window, and she and Grace stood by the stove, waiting for him to finish. Ione had to remind Grace to uncross her arms and correct the obvious frown.

"He's rude," Grace said through her teeth, crossing her arms again.

Ione smiled. "He's like most other men who come in here to find an unmarried black woman owns this shop."

"That's ridiculous." Grace's furrowed brows and the rising angry blotches on her neck left no doubt as to her loyalties. "You're the most talented designer and seamstress in the city. He should be honored to be asked to fix your glass."

Ione covered her mouth, fighting the smile at the ludicrous statement despite the threat of the rock in her pocket and the angry man in her apartment. "I bet when you woke up this morning, you didn't think you'd be saying 'he should be honored to fix your glass.'" Ione mimicked her hushed tones and crossed arms and finally succeeded in cooling Grace's temper.

"I've got the measurements. Who's going to be paying? I'll need it upfront." The man set his case of tools on the kitchen table with a thud and worked on spinning his measuring tape around his hand so that the material fit back in his shirt pocket.

Grace moved to point at the offending use of the table, but Ione touched her arm to let the girl know she didn't mind.

"Since when do you need payment before the new pane is installed?" Grace traded her folded arm stance for one with fists on hips.

"That's fine. I'll pay for the materials upfront." Ione lifted a brow, waiting for the man to challenge the slight change of terms.

She didn't have to wait long. "Whole thing, or I don't do it."

Grace took a step forward. "Since when—"

"Then you don't have to do it." Ione offered a chilly smile. "I am prepared to pay you for the materials, but I will not pay for labor I haven't seen."

"Are you questioning my honesty?" The man took a step toward Ione. A dribble of sweat made its way down out of his greased hair and hovered for a moment over his eyebrow before falling onto the floor.

"Just good business practice, sir." Ione pandered to his need for authority. Whether it was women he had a problem with or blacks who owned businesses that troubled him, Ione didn't know. Nor did she care. She just needed the window fixed.

She lowered her tone so it took on a submissive hue. "Sir, if I paid everyone up front for everything I had done, I would not have a business. Surely you wouldn't deny me the security of my policy?"

He took a step back and fished a blank bill of sale from his tool box. The dirty pad of paper likely served a multitude of purposes, but Ione only cared about the receipt and his agreement to come back and fix her window. His pencil scratched loudly against the paper in the silent room. "I should be back in two days with the glass." He handed Ione the slip.

"This appears agreeable. If you would like to follow me downstairs, I'll pay you before you leave."

The three of them filed back down the stairs, Ione in front and the repairman followed by Grace.

Ione slid the bills across the counter so she didn't have to touch his hands, and Grace glared him out of the building.

Miriam stretched to rid her back of the stiffness that had built for most of the day. After Tamm had dropped her off at the Penns' mansion, and after she'd followed Mrs. Penn as she'd made her rounds—dodging waiters in tuxedos as they carried trays laden with tiny cucumber sandwiches, fruits and vegetables cut to look like different fruits and vegetables, and passing on desserts too numerous to count—Miriam wanted nothing more than to be at home. And the day wasn't close to being done.

She took the small plate someone handed her and filled it with the offerings. Then she stood with a plate full of food and no desire to eat it. She took a bite, swallowed the lump, and set the dish down on a table with an empty corner.

"Have you been to see the Women's Pavilion yet?" Beatrice popped a cracker, covered in some paste-like substance with a red berry balanced on top, into her mouth in one delicate motion.

"No."

She shrugged. "Well, there's not much to look at yet, but I think it will be amazing."

"Do you have the agenda for the meeting?"

Beatrice juggled the plate and her handbag for a moment before shoving the dish in Miriam's direction and digging until she found a folded piece of paper with the day's plans. She smoothed it out and leaned in. "Did you know that a couple of the international delegations are here today?"

Miriam glanced around the room. "Where?"

"I'm not sure, but France and Spain are here now, and I think they expect England to join soon. I heard that Spain will be displaying some of the crown jewels."

They scanned the crowd, looking for anyone who might be wearing a different fabric or whose hat might be of a different shape.

Beatrice frowned. "It sure is crowded."

"I know." Miriam pushed the plate back toward her friend and grabbed the paper to fan herself with.

"Are you feeling ill?"

Miriam shook her head, looking for a place to sit down. "It's just warm in here."

Beatrice leveled a critical eye at Miriam's midsection. "Let's find you a chair." She took her arm and led Miriam farther away from the crowd.

"I have to honestly say I didn't expect this to be so hard." Miriam followed her friend, grateful Beatrice was making the decisions. "When I think I still have over a month to go, well, it makes me want to go hide somewhere."

"I can't see how you could get any bigger." Beatrice frowned at Miriam, as if she had a choice in the matter. "I think your doctor is crazy."

"Beatrice..." Miriam chided her friend.

"It doesn't take much in the department of brains to look at you and notice there's little to no room left."

"Thanks." Miriam shot Beatrice a wooden look, intending to make light of the situation.

Beatrice laughed lightly. It was a sound at once trained and refined, yet free enough to be contagious. Her formal upbringing, quite the opposite of Miriam's, had given her the ability to not only influence a crowd with her wit and charm, but also—and this was the rarer quality—made her approachable. It all came with a streak of brutal honesty, though. They'd learned to appreciate that too.

"I think you are reaching the end, young lady." Mrs. Penn came up behind the two of them and placed her wrinkled hand on Miriam's shoulder. "I know you want to help, but you do not look comfortable."

"I'm fine." Miriam protested the potential restriction. "I still have better than a month to go. I can't sit at home that long."

"There are more than enough tasks to attend to that require nothing more than sitting at a desk with a lamp and a pencil. Those will be yours. Besides, we need to put together our recommendation for the artists whose work will be on display." Mrs. Penn pulled a chair close to the bench Beatrice had found for Miriam and sat. She moved closer. "I've been watching for your application."

Miriam fanned faster with the folded paper she'd yet to return to Beatrice. "I had not planned..."

"I know, dear. But think about it."

Miriam opened her mouth to continue in the excuses, but clamped it closed at the wordless signal from Mrs. Penn.

"I'm calling your driver back around. I'll collect a few things for you to work on at home, and then we can discuss your thoughts later. Right now, I think you should rest."

Miriam wanted to argue, but she knew Mrs. Penn was right. Beatrice helped her to her feet and walked her through the crowd to the door where they could see Tamm waiting by the carriage.

Beatrice looked at the man, measuring him the same way Miriam always felt inclined to do. She wanted to ask her friend what she thought—did he make her uneasy too? But there was no time to do so before Tamm came to gather her.

Dr. Evan Whitaker signed his name to the bottom of the lease and set the pen on the desk. "Is that all?"

The man who owned the building he would rent for his office and home nodded his balding head and grunted in agreement. That he hadn't been happy about renting to a colored man had been obvious. But those hesitations tended to fade as the opportunity to make money emerged.

The building had been sitting empty for some time, that much was unmistakable. And it needed work. But Evan wasn't afraid of work. He'd worked all his life. Just because he had finished his schooling and his residency didn't mean the work stopped. Quite the opposite—he shook the prematurely aging man's limp hand—now the work began.

The man set two keys on the table: one for the back door and one for the front. Evan folded his copy of the completed contract, slid it into his jacket pocket, and picked up the keys. "Good doing business with you." Evan nodded, earning a grunt from the man whom Evan suspected hadn't spent a day in his life satisfied.

Stepping out onto the street without a glance back, the man left, leaving Evan to explore the place that would be his for the next five years.

Much like any of the other buildings in the crowded, less-than-affluent part of town, the new doctor's offices were small but convenient. The downstairs consisted of a main entrance, three private rooms—two that would work for examinations and one for his study—and a small powder room with working facilities. He'd been surprised to find the luxury in this part of town, but the convenience had been added for the previous lessee.

He opened the door to the stairs that led to his apartment. Evan fought to control the smile that spread without his permission, but eventually he gave in and enjoyed the reality that he finally, finally had his own practice. And not just a practice. Because the Provident Hospital had recently opened its doors and agreed to welcome him, he was not just a doctor—he was a doctor with admitting privileges to a functional, respected facility.

At the top of the steps, Evan turned down a small hallway into an open parlor. Not exactly a parlor yet, he thought, as he considered the peeling wall paper and the scuffed floors. But it would be soon. Two rooms split off the main area. He walked through the first one into his tiny kitchen. One cabinet, missing a foot, listed at a precarious angle, and the small stove... Well, he'd have someone come in and check the flue before he tried to light it. It didn't really matter; he couldn't cook. The other door led to his sleeping quarters. No furniture graced the empty space, but that was fine. Aaron and Evangeline had offered an extra bed, and he'd made do before by hanging a string between hooks to keep his clothes up off the floor.

He ran his hands down his vest and let his thumb catch in the pocket for his watch and rest there while he took in the sight of his apartment above his office in the city he'd hoped to practice in.

He couldn't help but wonder what Miss Smith would think of the place. She served a clientele who would not welcome him as their physician. But her talents with fabric and design and wrapping other women in silks and satins in a way that made the men in the room take notice had been enough of an incentive for the mamas to look beyond the color of her skin. Evan hoped someday he'd have a similar reputation.

He took one last look around his new apartment and made his way downstairs. Running his hand along the imperfect plaster wall, he walked the perimeter of what would serve as the waiting room, counting the paces, figuring the length of benches he would have to order.

He tried to envision how it would all look when he hung his shingle above the door and began seeing patients. He would stand there, in his white coat, usher patients into the examining room, smile at the children and mothers, and stitch up the fathers. For now, though, he'd stop by the church to see Aaron and tell him the news, then maybe the house if Evangeline was home. She would have some suggestions for how to fix up the place. Then, maybe, he would drop in and see Miss Smith. *Ione*, he'd heard his family call her, but he hadn't yet asked permission. And she seemed to be quite dedicated to maintaining a formality between them.

He hadn't experienced that particular challenge before. In truth, most women were agreeable when he showed interest. Most women giggled and fanned and stole sideways glances when they thought his attention drifted. Not Ione—Miss Smith, he corrected himself. Not her. He thought of the grave set of her chin and her serious demeanor. When they'd been alone, she'd answered his questions clearly and honestly. Her hand had felt confident tucked into the crook of his arm, and it spoke of a straightforward approach that she likely applied to everything in her life. She would have to be confident and bold in order to accomplish what she had, but he couldn't help but feel like even when her expression read as open, something hidden stayed shuttered behind her eyes.

He pulled the key from his pocket, stepped onto the busy street, and turned to secure the door to his practice. *His practice.* He let the words tumble through his mind, liking the way they sounded. He secured his hat so the persistent Chicago winds didn't whip it down the road, and put effort into walking, not jogging, to his brother's office.

Chapter 15

Miriam made her way up to her room. She needed to take a short nap. The day, despite that it had been cut short by Mrs. Penn and Beatrice, had worn her out.

No wonder women secluded themselves for the last month or so. She paused on the bottom step, and for the first time ever, actually considered counting how many there were.

It wasn't like she was facing the Himalayas. And the typical baby weighed what? About seven pounds? Miriam frowned, grasped the handrail, and heaved herself up the stairs, determined not to look like a fat, old, rheumatic lady who couldn't move on her own.

"Do you need help?" Mrs. Maloney called from below. Not really that far below—Miriam turned around to look. Only a few steps. But it felt like it had taken her an entire flight's worth of effort. Actually, all things considered, if reality echoed effort, the world would be a better place. Miriam hid the scowl that wanted to take over her whole body.

"I'll be fine. I'm afraid I'm moving a bit slower than normal."

"Nonsense." Mrs. Maloney rushed the few steps to take her elbow and wrap her arm around her waist. "You just keep hold on that rail, and we'll get you upstairs."

Miriam nodded, grateful for the support.

"If you ask me, that doctor of yours is a fool."

Miriam looked at the frown that had worked its way from Mrs. Maloney's mouth to her typically sophisticated eyebrows. They didn't speak of sophistication now, though. Now they were bunched up and frustrated.

"There's no way you still have better than a month to go. I've had babies myself, you know, and I've attended more laboring mothers than I can count. You, young lady, do not have a month until this baby arrives."

Miriam looked down. While an early birth had been top on her list of fears, suddenly it seemed a perk to think the doctor could be wrong.

"You are going to be tucked into bed, and you are not going to move until that baby comes out."

Miriam opened her mouth to protest but was interrupted.

"Or..." The housekeeper paused to help Miriam up the last stair. "Or I'm going to tell Mr. Farling that I think you should have a nurse attending you."

"Oh...that's not..."

"If you think that's not necessary, then you will do as I say. You can't have a healthy baby if you are exhausted."

Miriam frowned at the woman despite the relief she felt.

"I will have a dinner tray brought up to you in an hour or so. It's Mr. Farling's late night at the office, anyway. You should take the opportunity to rest."

She tried not to relish the idea of lying in bed and waking only to read or eat a piece of toast, but she couldn't. It sounded wonderful.

Miriam nodded, and Mrs. Maloney helped her to the side of her bed where Sally waited to untie her boots and assist her in shedding the brutal corset. She couldn't even imagine the stripes it had left on her skin this time.

Ione paced behind the CLOSED sign in her front window. She tried to look busy, flitting from here to there while Grace finished tidying up from the day's traffic. But once Grace had waved her good-bye, Ione gave up the ruse, turned down the lights, and watched for any sign of him on the street.

He hadn't sent another note after the one that'd accompanied the rock through her window. Ione frowned at her own ability to label a rock coming through the window as Clarence sending a note. She'd always excused his eccentricities—again, even to herself, she made it sound nice. Ione picked a loose string off her sleeve. Correction: she'd always excused his abuse. She paused at the harsh word, allowing time for the truth to settle.

A light rap at the door jarred her back to where she stood, at the window, looking for signs of him...or the next rock to come sailing by.

Instead, Dr. Whitaker stood with his hand over his eyes peering into the glass like a child scoping a Christmas display with fake snow and porcelain dolls. Their eyes met. She couldn't pretend she wasn't here after he'd seen her. Ione tried to frown but had trouble doing so, considering the way all the blood seemed to abandon her extremities to concentrate on the double-time her heart suddenly demanded.

This was getting out of hand.

Ione acknowledged him with a nod and flipped the bolt on the door. "Come in." She held it open and then quickly closed the door behind him and backed away from their unintentionally close stance. She darted back and pulled the dangling string of the green roll-up shade.

He turned to watch the action, a curious half-smile making him seem younger than she knew he was. Some people were like that—young forever. Ione felt old, became aware of the weight of her own body. The feel of her own worries as the closed shade stood in stark contrast to the force of his optimism.

He cleared his throat and shifted, casting a questioning glance at the now covered window. "I thought I might stop by. I have some good news..." He let the sentence trail off.

"Oh." Ione realized the mistake she'd made in pulling the shade, but it was too late, and the last thing she could do was offer an explanation. "Oh…" She fumbled for words. "I'm just closing up."

He nodded, as if what she had done, effectively isolating them inside her store, made perfect sense. Did this man overlook every flaw he saw in everyone he met, or was it only her?

"I just came from Aaron's place, and they invited us both over for a celebratory dinner."

Ione looked down at her plain dress and instinctively lifted a hand to smooth her hair. "I'm still in my work clothes." The excuse sounded weak even to her ears.

"I can wait down here if you want to walk together." The thought that she might not want to go, or possibly had other plans, must not have occurred to him.

He was persistent.

Ione glanced back toward the street, now blocked from view, and then back to him. He smiled at her indecision. But she wasn't indecisive, she wanted to tell him. She knew what she wanted, and she made it happen. He held out his hand in a questioning gesture. Ione wanted to let him know that she didn't flirt and didn't patter on about simple matters. That she used conversation to get things done, and when necessary gave up sleep or food to meet a deadline.

But here she was, looking like a simpleton, and here he was, smiling like he didn't mind. Ione wasn't sure if the most disturbing part was that he would accept this kind of incompetence or that she felt such a need to disabuse him from the idea that she couldn't do everything on her own. Or, the nagging sense that his acceptance intrigued her.

There was no way he could accept everything in her past, though. That much she knew. No man could. Except, of course, Jenny's husband. But he was different. There couldn't be two men like him out there.

And, Ione reminded herself, she didn't want that kind of complication anyway. Her life was confusing enough. "I'll be down in a bit. You can have a seat if you would like." She looked over to the small settee, upholstered in pink velvet, and stepped into the stairwell, closing the door behind her. She leaned against the cool wood and concentrated on the smell of paint and dust and that morning's coffee.

At least she wouldn't be sitting around, waiting for Clarence to throw another rock through her window. Or worse. Ione crossed her arms and rubbed warmth into her shoulders. She should wait for him. She should watch and find out exactly what he wanted. She should protect her friends and her sisters by not risking Clarence finding out about them.

Ione stepped quickly toward her apartment and then crossed to her sleeping chambers. She whipped open the armoire and chose a light lavender affair that concealed every inch of skin from wrist to chin. The thin fabric, comfortable for a summer evening, didn't cling or caress in any way. If she worked in the church, the cut of the dress would be above reproach. She unfastened the hidden buttons of her work dress that ran from under her right arm to her waist and with a wiggle, shed the garment.

The lavender dress went on quickly. Ione tucked under her matching hat the parts of her hair that threatened to fly away with a few more pins than it should have taken, splashed a bit of water against her face, and made her way back downstairs.

She eased the door open to the sight of Dr. Whitaker sitting on the pink settee, a beaded piece of sheer fabric stretched across his knees. Still hanging from a long thread, the needle dangled in the air between his feet.

He looked up. "Do you do this?"

"Sometimes." Ione watched as he trailed his finger along the glimmering line of glass beads. "That one is Grace's work."

He shrugged and folded the delicate fabric back into the same shape Grace had left it and dropped it into the basket.

"You like it?" Ione closed the door behind her. With the mixture of his masculine frame dwarfing the pink overstuffed seat, and his fascination with the part of the world reserved for women, Ione found it difficult to decide on her next move. Was this man a friend of her friends? Did he want more? Had they told him she wouldn't be, couldn't be interested? Were all doctors curious about details, even those most men found dull or lacking in importance?

"It's beautiful." Dr. Whitaker stood and took a step closer to Ione.

Instinctively, she backed away.

Unfortunately, he noticed. "Is everything okay?" He left the question to hang in the air like overripe fruit.

Ione scrambled for a suitable answer. "Of course." She pulled one glove over her bare fingers. "Are you ready?"

He nodded, but his expression made it apparent that he would have rather pressed for information. "You do have an amazing place here." They wormed their way through the storage room and out the service door into the alley.

Ignoring the compliment, Ione locked the door and pulled on the latch to make sure it was secure before turning to face him. She followed him out onto the street, where other workers pushed by in a rush to return home to dinner and family after a long day. "What did you say we were celebrating, anyway?"

"My new practice." The smile that spread across his face communicated everything, and Ione couldn't help but mirror back a bit of the overwhelming emotion.

She smiled up at him, and he stopped in the middle of the sidewalk, earning scowls from the woman who had been following behind them and probably trying to get on the next streetcar.

"You have the most beautiful smile I've ever seen." His face had gone serious, contemplative. An expression Ione hadn't seen before from him. A dimple formed in his left cheek, also something Ione hadn't noticed.

She shook her head, as much to break the spell as to disagree with his assessment of her smile. She had a normal smile, a normal face. She was neither beautiful nor ugly, but somewhere in between. She possessed nothing to distinguish her from the next woman, other than her abilities with a needle...and a past that made anything between them impossible.

And the feeling that if he reached down and pulled her to him, if he wanted her lips, if he took a step closer, closed the distance between them, she wouldn't back away.

Oh God, Ione prayed. *Oh God. I can't.*

Chapter 16

Miriam woke to a darkened room. Someone shuffled about. She tried to organize her thoughts, but with the naps she'd been taking, breakfast in bed, and enforced seclusion at the hands of Mrs. Maloney, her days and nights had scrambled. She waited for her eyes to adjust to the dark, watching for a shadow to appear, hoping it was Michael.

"I'm sorry." He carefully set an overnight bag on the edge of their bed. "I didn't want to wake you."

"Where are you going?" Miriam rolled to her back, her belly looming large under the blankets, and struggled up to a sitting position. "What time is it?"

"It's about nine o'clock." Michael sat on the edge of the bed and placed his hand over the baby. The quilt had slipped and Miriam could feel the warmth of his palm spread beneath the simple shift she fell asleep in. "Tomorrow I need to go away for a couple of days, but I'll be back as soon as I can."

"What's happened?" Embarrassed at being found sleeping without even the proper nightclothes, Miriam lifted a sheet to cover herself as much as possible.

"You don't have to do that on my account." Michael raised a brow.

Miriam sent him a withering look. "I'm as big as a house."

He shrugged and turned to untie his shoes.

"So, what's happened to make you have to go so suddenly?"

"Nothing major, but there is a problem with one of the rail lines moving south. I keep getting conflicting reports, and the board decided the best decision would be for me to take a look. I'll be going with a couple of the other members tomorrow by train." He dropped one shoe to the floor with a thud.

Miriam didn't want to be the pregnant, needy wife. She looked around the room, and her eyes fell to the book she'd finished that afternoon. "I'm going to need another book."

"I'll miss you too." Michael turned and met her gaze. "And there is no way you have a month left. In another month, you will explode."

"Thank you." Miriam frowned and crossed her arms. The movement held less threat than it should, considering the adjustment she had to make due to the lack of space in the front of her body. She dropped the attempt at mock irritation. "I think you're right. Do you think it's possible to explode? Have you ever heard of that happening?"

Michael chuckled but stopped short. "You know, I've never heard of it, but I have no idea. Not for sure, anyway." The look of horror he leveled at her midsection shifted their roles.

"I'm sure it can't happen." Miriam reached over their bed and touched his arm. "Everything will be fine. You will go and come back, and in a month's time, we'll call the doctor and I'll give birth to your daughter."

"You mean my son," Michael teased. He stood and walked over to his dresser to pull out a few necessities for the next day.

Miriam tried to remember if she had eaten dinner. She thought Sally had brought a tray, but it no longer sat on the end table. She wasn't hungry. "Did you eat dinner yet?"

Michael stopped for a second or two and then nodded. "Yes. At the office. Mrs. Maloney sent enough for everyone to eat. We knew it would be a long night."

"What did you have?" Miriam still couldn't recall what she'd eaten. She hoped Mrs. Maloney had sent the same thing over and that the reminder would encourage her foggy mind to engage.

"I imagine the same thing you had."

Miriam looked down at the leaves climbing across the fabric of her quilt. The various shades of green, the branches that looked almost real, and the tiniest of white cherry blossoms broke up the background of woven greens and blues. She touched the pink tip of the flower bud she'd watched as she'd dozed off with the sun still high overhead. "Did the others enjoy their dinner?"

"They especially liked Mrs. Cook's roast beef. The way she slices it thin, and there's something about her gravy... We even discussed it." He dropped a pair of socks into his bag. "She must have some spice that we couldn't name. But like always, she exceeded any of our expectations."

Now she remembered. The beef gravy had been remarkable. Suddenly Miriam's stomach growled, and she wondered if it had all been eaten.

"How long has it been since she's worked here? More than a year, I know that much."

Miriam nodded, still thinking about the tender beef and the soft roasted carrots with the honey glaze that had also adorned her plate.

"In fact, I think most of the staff has been here more than a year. It's time to look at their pay and adjust it if need be."

"Sally hasn't yet." Miriam glanced at the ceiling, trying to dedicate a larger portion of her brain to something other than food. "But she is wonderful. I'm sure she could use a little extra, especially with the additional tasks she's had to help me with."

"Anyone else you can think of?"

"I think the last person we hired was Tamm. The driver."

"Yes." Michael turned and checked the contents of his bag. "Tamm." He mulled the name over while mindlessly picking up a pressed and folded white shirt. "Tamm."

Miriam watched him for any signs her husband might feel the same way she did about the driver. Signs that her hesitation, that the near-revulsion she felt when Tamm stepped a little too close, or moved away a bit too fast, or watched the other pedestrians as a tiger might assess a gazelle, might be unjustified. But Michael turned before Miriam could divine the information she desired.

If only she could paint Tamm, sort out the jumble of emotions he brought with him every time he stood in front of her, his expression masked and serious. But it wasn't the lack of levity that concerned her. Miriam picked a piece of lint off the blanket. Because when he smiled— Miriam tried to find the word—when he smiled, a darkness opened possibilities that she felt should never see light.

John jumped down from the rented hack, tossed a coin to the driver, and took the steps to the Farlings' front door two at a time. He'd promised Michael he would look in on Miriam while his friend was gone.

The door opened before he had the chance to knock, and Mr. Butler stood on the other side, his expression typically dour, but his eyes communicating his generally gay humor. "Good afternoon, Father. To what do we owe the pleasure?" Ducking his head, the man took a step back, making room for John to come into the cool foyer.

John smiled and handed him his hat. His persistence in calling John by his title reflected his own Catholic heritage. Something none of the other friends in their circle had in common. John had thought long and hard about the oddity that none of his closest friends shared his specific beliefs, nor did they attend his church, but had decided no one was perfect. John smiled at his own joke.

"Something funny, Father?"

John felt his face flush. Mr. Butler had caught him being entertained by his own thoughts. "No." He changed the subject. "How is Mrs. Farling?"

"I'd have to get Mrs. Maloney to give you any specific information, but I haven't heard anything to cause concern." He hung John's hat on the tree next to the door. "In fact, I believe she's sitting out in the garden for a while. I'll let her know you are here."

"No need." John waved him away. "I'll let myself in."

John took the double doors to the right of the entryway. The panels of glass that opened out to the hidden garden nestled between the townhouses were open. The sheer curtains billowed into the room on the edge of a breeze. Miriam sat on the single stone bench under the flowering tree that now absorbed more than a quarter of the available sky view. The gardener had tended to the area, fighting back the vines and weeds that had taken over during the years of neglect after Miriam's mother passed, and now the stone path met the grass with a curved, well-defined boundary; the flowers, chosen for bright color and lush petals, made the brick walls that surrounded the garden all but disappear.

Miriam sat, her butter-yellow dress secured above the growing babe and flowing loosely around her hips, falling to the ground in gauzy waves. The scene was at once so perfect and so serene that John felt as if he were treading on sacred ground, like his footfalls would do the same work as one who trampled graves. Before he could turn away, though, Miriam lifted her gaze to his, and the perfection of the scene shattered.

In three strides, he made his way to the garden, and then rushed to her side. Her pale complexion fairly glowed blue against the stunning color of her dress. "What happened?" John dropped to the bench next to her and pulled her into the protection of his arms. This woman, the woman he'd watched as she'd wandered the streets around his cathedral, this woman he loved as a friend. Had he not been a priest, he could have loved her more.

Yet to make a sound, she shuddered and turned her face into his robes, and John looked up at the square patch of sky, willing her to open up, to let him in, to tell him what had happened. Miriam was a contradiction—soft but stubborn; scared but brave; solitary, but it was she who had connected them all. So he waited until she was ready.

"I miss him." Three tiny words, and John could glimpse into her world.

"He should be back soon." John pulled back a bit, surprised by Miriam's sudden need for her husband. While the two were close, and their connection undoubtedly strong, her tangible dependence on him didn't fit John's perception of his friend.

"No." Miriam shook her head and straightened, pressing her handkerchief tightly over her eyes. "I miss my father."

John held his breath. How long had it been since he'd died? At least a couple of years. "What... I mean..."

"He did everything to keep me safe."

John pulled her away and stared into her eyes. "Did something happen?"

"No. Well, I don't think so."

"What do you mean?" He purposefully held a tight grip on her shoulders. This fear, this hesitation, had nothing in common with the Miriam he knew.

She broke eye contact to stare at something just out of reach.

"Did something happen? This isn't like you." John forced her attention back to his face.

She took a deep breath and held it, frowning, and then inched back enough to make conversation possible but not so much that John felt she shrank away from his question. "When I lived at the warehouse, every day was the same. The sun rose in the same way, I walked the same paths, the people who passed by were familiar faces... I could predict everything. So even after he died, everything stayed familiar and safe."

"And now it isn't."

Miriam pushed off the bench and wobbled for a second before she walked around to stand under the tree. She picked off a small piece of bark and studied it. "It's more than just that. When it was only me, then

I didn't mind so much. I painted until I felt I had an answer or I simply waited. But now I have more to worry about."

"So, you are worried about the baby?"

"I guess." She dropped the piece of bark into the grass and then leaned against the tree. "Maybe I'm simply being unreasonable." She let out a harsh laugh that John hadn't before heard from her. "The doctor says that women in their last months—well, to hear him describe it, we are little more than nesting animals."

John snorted. "Is this the same doctor who claims you still have a month to go?"

Miriam answered him with one raised brow.

"Not sure I would trust his assessment of your situation." John patted the bench, signaling Miriam to sit again. "What brought this on?"

Miriam looked back to the house, scanning the windows in the parlor, and then drifting up to the studio windows high overhead. "It's nothing. I'm sure I'm simply making something bigger than what it needs to be." She suddenly stood, careful to watch her balance, and then nodded toward the house. "It's almost teatime. Let's see what Mrs. Maloney has."

John followed her in. Something had happened to put her in such a strange state, and obviously, she didn't want to discuss it.

John made a mental note to call on her more often.

Ione walked down the street, back toward her shop that had remained free of disturbing notes for the past week. Dinner with the Whitakers had again included Dr. Whitaker as well as her sisters with their suspiciously conspiratorial glances.

He'd asked her to call him Evan.

Her reflection flickered past in the store windows, now closed. The sky grew darker by the minute. She picked up her pace and watched the alleys for shadows. This part of town boasted very little in the way of crime, and policemen stood under the lights at nearly every corner. That didn't mean they'd be willing to help her, though.

She tucked her handbag tighter under her arm and felt in her pocket for the keys to her store. She would go in the front door, rather than the rear. No need to walk through the alley.

Mrs. Whitaker had clucked her tongue at Ione's concerns. They'd stood together in the kitchen, washing the plates from dinner, accompanied by the light buzz of conversation from the parlor and the occasional chuckle when someone told an amusing story. That Maggie and Lucy liked him, they left no doubt. That Pastor and Mrs. Whitaker thought Ione made a suitable potential partner for Evan, they had also done little to hide.

And when Ione reminded Mrs. Whitaker, as she took the wet glass and ran the flour sack over it to dry and shine it, of how unsuitable she really was, Mrs. Whitaker looked at Ione like she'd grown another head.

"You are a new person." She'd let the next plate sink under the suds and stared at Ione until she looked up and met her gaze. "You listen to me. You had a bad run. You did what you had to do to survive."

"But I also made some bad decisions on my own." The sentence had been stuck in her throat for days. Not everything had to do with luck, or the lack thereof. Not everything was the result of poverty. She'd also been stupid and rebellious, had ignored her mother's advice because she thought she knew better.

"Who hasn't?"

The simplicity of that statement had caught Ione off guard. She'd let the towel drop onto the counter, and then used it to cover her face, shaking her head. *No.* She couldn't do that to a man who'd done things right. One who went to school, worked hard, became a doctor in a world that fought his decision every step of the way. He was an honorable man. She'd forgotten they existed, and she absolutely didn't deserve one.

"Yes." Mrs. Whitaker took her by the arm and forced her over to the kitchen table to sit. "He knows that unusual circumstances led you to us. He knows of the trouble, of the danger. We've shared enough with him to make him aware that, like everyone else in the world, you will both have to learn about each other. We didn't break confidences, but he's prepared if you feel you should be honest with him."

Ione had studied her fingers, folded against her skirts, wishing, for the first time since she'd thought she'd been in love with Clarence, that someone else could make this easier.

Outside her store, Ione pulled the key from her pocket, inserted it into the lock, and twisted it until the tumblers fell into place. Then she stepped into the dark room, closed the door behind her, took in the familiar scent of fabric and coffee and perfume, and dropped into the pink settee where Evan had earlier sat.

She needed to think. To sort things out.

The Whitakers had already done so much for her, for her sisters. They'd given Maggie and Lucy a home and welcomed them into the family. And now they were willing to overlook character flaws Ione couldn't possibly ignore. She'd sold herself to men. She'd allowed herself to be used for the price of food for her and her sisters.

And she'd promised herself never to be dependent like that again.

Ione reached down and hefted up her skirt, revealing one shining boot. She pulled the lace, watched it unravel in the low light, and then twisted her ankle until the ties loosened.

Dependent looked different now. Now that she had money and a thriving business, now that her sisters weren't in danger of going hungry, dependence shifted from one of physical needs to one of emotional needs.

All the money in the world couldn't repair her heart if she let it be broken again.

Ione kicked off her shoes and leaned back into the cushions. Dr. Whitaker—Evan—was nothing like Clarence.

She hadn't heard from him in a week. Ione sent up a quick prayer that by some miracle something had distracted Clarence, or he had traveled to someplace different, or, well, something. But a week with no notes, no broken glass, no news of any kind made for a good week.

If she removed Clarence from consideration, if she ignored the possible threats and focused solely on what she wanted, could she consider continuing to spend time with Evan?

Even the thought made the blood rush to her face. Never, never had she dreamed she would want another man near her. And now, not only did her heart nearly stop when Evan looked down at her, but also she couldn't stop thinking of him, of remembering what it felt like not to be alone, of wondering what it would be like to look up at a man who might be able to love her more than his own ambitions.

Ione felt around for the pins in her hat, found one round end, and pulled it out. Another, and another followed, and soon she tossed the hat onto the nearby counter. He liked her, that much she knew.

And, heaven help her, she liked him too.

The temptation to believe Mrs. Whitaker, to think Evan might be able to overlook her past, burned in her mind.

Ione stood, grabbed her shoes and hat, and made her way to the stairs.

After dinner had been cleaned up, they'd all taken the streetcar to the part of town where Evan's new office sat, empty, waiting for his patients. Also, they'd laughed, waiting for furniture, some paint, and a good cleaning. But it would be perfect. They could all see him there, taking in sick people, tending to children and old folks, and making that part of town a better place.

And as they walked through together and as his hand brushed protectively against the small of her back, Ione couldn't help but envision how she could help him. How they could help each other. How she didn't have to do everything alone, even though, up until the past few days, she thought that had been exactly what she'd wanted.

They'd left together, dropping Ione off at the corner of her block. She'd assured them all, especially Evan, that she could handle walking the few doors down to her own shop unaccompanied. Until today, it had never occurred to her that a man might not want her to walk alone.

Ione dropped her shoes at the end of her bed. More accurately, when Clarence hadn't wanted her to walk alone it was because he had wanted to parade her down the street for his friends to see her, or because he'd wanted to keep an eye on her. Never out of any sort of need to protect her.

She shed her dress, slipped her nightgown over her head, and fell into bed.

Chapter 17

Darkness fell, and Miriam woke to a silent house. She lay there alone, tucked into the warm covers, listening for the chime of the grandfather clock in the hall until it rang the quarter hour.

Seeing as how she'd missed the hour, the chime was of little use. She frowned and kicked off the covers, marveling at the swell of her belly.

She'd had no idea her body had been capable of this kind of transformation.

Miriam struggled to sit up, slid her feet over the side, searched for the step, and then climbed down. Michael would be away for one more night, but it didn't matter. It wasn't like she could sleep anyway.

But she missed his warmth.

She sat at her dressing table and opened the small watch she usually pinned under her shoulder. A quarter after one. Again.

She sighed and glanced at the place her hairbrush used to sit.

After this morning, she'd hid it in her skirts, went around to the kitchen entrance at the back of the house, and stuffed it deep in the trash bin.

She hadn't wanted to tell anyone what had happened. Her irrational response to the long hairs so much darker, coarser than her own, wound around the bristles felt at once a sanity-questioning overreaction and a dangerous underreaction. Hair couldn't hurt her.

But Sally had light hair. Jenny, even though she hadn't visited in a while, had brown hair. Ione's curly tresses, although dark, were nothing like the hairs in the brush. Miriam again listed off all the people she knew worked in the house: Mrs. Maloney and Mrs. Cook had gray hair.

No one had hair like she'd found. But someone had used her brush. Miriam examined her comb for any stray strands. Nothing.

Rubbing her upper arms, she fought off the chill that had nothing to do with being cold and sat up straight to work out the ache that had been building for most of the day.

If Michael noticed the missing brush, she had no idea how she could explain it. Stray hairs had disturbed her enough to throw away a perfectly good brush? She hadn't even told John when he stopped by to visit. Her reaction made no sense, even to her.

But that didn't mean she could ever use it again. So instead, she'd thrown it out with the rubbish.

Miriam stood, hand to her lower back. She pressed to see if pressure might help the pain. It didn't.

Michael would be back in the morning, and then maybe she could forget about the brush and her reaction to it. Besides, a maid likely borrowed it—someone new, maybe, with black hair. No other explanation existed that made sense.

The pain that had started in her back radiated around, and a light moan escaped her dry lips. Miriam walked over to the glass of water she'd set out earlier and took a long drink. For a minute, she thought she spilled it. But the warm, spreading puddle at her feet had nothing to do with the water in her hand.

The baby was coming.

Ione rolled over in bed, willing sleep to take her but knowing it wouldn't. The sun had yet to lend light to the backside of the drapes. She groped in the dark for the matches.

Clutching the tiny wooden box, she struck the match with shaking fingers and lit the bedside lamp. Light swelled, filling the space around her but leaving the corners in shadow. Ione turned the flame up as far as she could, coaxing comfort from the false life in the fire. She had no reason to toss about, no cause for her heart to keep racing and for every noise to send her bolting from the bed.

She concentrated on breathing in and out, on fighting the urge to turn up every gas lamp in the apartment until they hissed in frustration. She let out an exasperated huff and kicked off her blankets. If she had to be awake, she might as well get something done.

Ione abandoned her room in favor of the kitchen, where she sat at the table to wait for the coffee to percolate. She smiled at the thought of the smooth, hot brew and forced her thoughts to what she needed to do that day. A hat that should have arrived the day before didn't, and no news came to explain the delay. Ione made a mental note to send a message of apology to the woman who had ordered it, but first she needed to have Grace find out when they should expect the item.

The coffee began bubbling. Hot little explosions doing everything they could to release steam under the pressure of glass. Ione stood to collect her cup and saucer, when a pool of cool air swirled around her bare ankles.

A chill ran up her calves and caressed her knees before disappearing again. Ione set the cup down on the saucer, clinking one piece of delicate china against another and threatening to shatter the porcelain. She turned to face the window, where the sheer curtain that hung over the closed shade settled back into place.

Something had disturbed the soft fabric.

Ione tied her robe tighter and picked up the knife that still had a smear of butter from the toast she'd prepared before she'd gone to bed. She fisted it in her hand and listened for any sound, any hint that someone had concealed themselves within the walls of her apartment.

Her breathing, in and out, fast, uneven, crowded out any other noise.

Ione took a step toward the window, and then another. The last few came in a rush. She jerked the curtain to the side, exposing nothing but floor and wall and a fluttering shade. She pulled it up, exposing the night sky and the city streets behind the cloth. The window had been left open.

Only a couple of inches.

Ione racked her memory. When had she opened it? Before meeting with the Whitakers? After?

Maybe she'd sent Grace up for something and she'd opened the window. Ione settled uneasily with that possibility. It could have happened. Maybe when she'd stepped into the back room for something.

The coffee fought against the glass dome, frantic to get out. Ione dropped the knife on the table and turned to the stove. She removed the pot from the heat and set it to the side.

She hadn't sent Grace up to her apartment, though. She knew she hadn't.

Ione ignored the fragrant brew and frowned at the stairs that led to the shop below. If she didn't check, she'd never be able to relax.

She made her way down, stopping to listen every few steps, hoping to hear nothing but the sound of her own ragged breath. Once at the bottom, she opened the door to the cool still air.

Nothing. No one mulled about. The shadows didn't shift unexpectedly, the room appeared exactly as she had left it.

She walked the perimeter, checking for anything out of place, jiggling door knobs and refastening locks. Eventually, she frowned. The thought of a hot cup of coffee won over the obviously unwarranted concern, and she returned to her rooms upstairs.

She had so many things to do. A life to get on with. She couldn't be obsessed with thoughts of broken windows or threatening notes. She had better ways to spend her time.

Miriam lay on her back in accordance with the doctor's orders. He claimed the baby would be early, that because her water had broken, they would all have to wait, and that she should give the baby the best chance possible by staying as still and calm as possible.

"He's gone." Mrs. Maloney stepped into the bedroom and closed the door.

Miriam glanced to the woman who always had every answer. The one who had ignored her eccentricities, met her needs, and never asked questions. If Miriam's mother were alive, she imagined she would be somewhat like Mrs. Maloney.

But Mrs. Maloney was the housekeeper, not the midwife, and Miriam had no right to rely on her in this circumstance.

"He said that it could be a day or two yet. That just because my water broke, it didn't mean that the baby would be coming soon."

"Oh, that baby will make its way into the world when it is darn good and ready. And if you ask me, it's not a bit too early. I know that doctor has the backing of many of the families around here, but I can look at you and see that this baby is ready to come out." Mrs. Maloney fussed with the water glass, and then frowned at the closed drapes. "And this requirement for a dark, stuffy room...nonsense." She walked over to the window, ripped the curtains open, and lifted the window sashes. Sounds of the city floated into the room: carts and horses and the hum of conversations soared in with the clean, tree-scrubbed air from the park across the street.

"But that's not what the doctor said." Miriam struggled to sit.

Mrs. Maloney grabbed an extra pillow from the chaise that sat at the end of the bed and stuffed it behind Miriam. "When your contractions start for real, then you might want the sound to stop. Or you might want more. But the important thing is you can have whatever you want. Your body knows what's best, and some stuffy old man has no business telling you how to give birth to your own baby." She straightened the blankets and tucked them around Miriam's legs. "Nonsense. It's just plain nonsense if you ask me."

Miriam had to stifle a smile. It wasn't like Mrs. Maloney to be so adamant about anything. Normally, she nodded acceptance for just about any idea and simply did what needed to be done. But somehow, the doctor had gotten under her skin in a way that Miriam hadn't before seen.

"And Michael should be here soon. Mr. Butler sent a message to his office. They expect him later today."

"I feel fine." Miriam ran her hand over her belly and frowned. "I mean, I know this is going to get worse, but I'm fine right now."

Mrs. Maloney paused her ruffling and fluffing and stuffing to meet Miriam's gaze. "You will do marvelously. We are all here for you."

"I've never been good at waiting."

"So don't." Mrs. Maloney sent a meaningful glance toward the door. "I won't tell the doctor. He isn't here. Besides, the labor will be faster if you walk around a bit at first."

Miriam shook her head. "I haven't done this before. I think I better mind the instructions."

Mrs. Maloney patted her knee tucked tight under the blankets. "You do whatever you want. Sally will be in and out, and if you need anything when she isn't here, just ring the kitchen bell and someone will run up."

Miriam nodded her understanding, feeling very much like a child who had been snuggled into bed for having nothing more than a sore throat.

But it did take the pressure off. The desire to paint, to work through with color the parts of her world that refused to make sense, had to be tamped down.

She had no choice. Right now, only one duty filled her thoughts: give birth to a healthy baby.

Maybe then, when things were right, she could pick up the brush, feel the paint dry on her fingers, filling the ridges and lines, hardening under her nails in a multitude of colors that spoke to her.

She missed the staining. How the paint would turn one nail blue and the other orange, and how her fingers would smell like turpentine on the days where she needed to clean them for an evening party.

The child inside gave one emphatic kick to her rib cage, and her stomach tightened into a hard ball. It didn't hurt much, yet.

Maybe after she gave birth and held her baby, cuddled her and fed her, maybe then she would be free to paint again.

Chapter 18

Michael flew out of his office, jumped into the carriage his secretary had had enough sense to have waiting for him, and willed the horses to move faster through the interminable traffic of downtown Chicago.

The blasted city could be a wretched place at five o'clock in the evening.

He'd known, known that he shouldn't have left this far into her pregnancy. Even though the doctor said they still had time, with the help of a few medical volumes borrowed from the library, Michael had done his own math—math that pointed to a different date, one closer to now.

Of course he hadn't let on to Miriam. That wouldn't have been exactly a delicate conversation. But he'd suspected, and then been enough of a dolt to take off on a business trip despite his worries.

He glanced out the window. They were stopped. Dead stopped. By the time he arrived at home, the child would be preparing for grammar school. Michael frowned, pulled his handkerchief from his pocket, whipped his spectacles off his face, and wiped the glass lenses with a vengeance.

He hadn't told Miriam about his fears, not only because the conversation would have been a bit awkward, but also because she'd had that lost look about the corners of her eyes that harkened back to when he'd first answered her summons to meet him at the townhouse.

His post as her father's solicitor had been his first real employment. And when her father, a man who in many ways had been like his own father, died unexpectedly, and when Miriam made her wish to remain in the warehouse apartment known, Michael had done as he'd been told.

But he'd also taken the lessons he'd learned from her father and continued to apply them to both her inherited fortune as well as his growing investments.

Michael returned his spectacles to their perch on his nose and tucked the metal hooks behind his ears. He glanced out the window again at the unmoving landscape of buildings and the constant, river-like flow of the pedestrians.

And then she'd decided she loved him too. He'd always loved her—from afar, of course—but that she returned his feelings... Well, he still couldn't think about it without sporting a humiliatingly transparent grin.

It hadn't been easy at first. Her fear—not fear, her distrust of her own abilities while being surrounded by the society that couldn't get enough of her story—had been difficult to manage. After all, a beautiful, reclusive heiress coming back into society for mysterious reasons sounded more like the plot to a dime novel than something that happened in Chicago society. But that was exactly what had happened. Although no one knew of the real reasons for her return.

The carriage lurched forward, the driver finally forcing his way into the line of other well-appointed carriages filled with impatient employers. Michael sat back, feeling the vibration of the cobbles under the wheels. He closed his eyes and concentrated on the red that flashed whenever the low sun made its way between the tall buildings.

Their marriage had started off strangely. She wandered at night, painting and thinking, and whatever else she'd always done while living alone. Michael pretended not to mind. But then slowly her wandering lessened. And more and more often he would wake to find her still lying next to him, snuggled against his chest. He'd breathe in the scent of her hair, concentrate on the warmth of her limbs intertwined with his, and know that whatever happened, they would always have this. Them. Together.

But she'd changed recently. Started wandering again. Often times, he would wake up alone again, her pillow cool to the touch, her space next to him enormously empty. And while he wanted to believe that everything was fine, that it all had to do with expecting a child, that everything would go back to normal once the baby was born, part of him feared the experience of carrying his child had changed her forever.

She'd stopped painting. Not that she'd shared the information with him. But he'd noticed. Her hands were no longer stained, and she didn't disappear for long stretches of time in the middle of the afternoon. He didn't have to remind her of social obligations, and then enjoy the inevitable panic when she realized just how much time she'd spent at the easel.

With the pause in her painting, she'd grown quiet. Contemplative. As if the thinking she'd always done at the easel still held her hostage.

Finally, on their street, the buildings sped by. Once in front of their home, the carriage came to a fast stop, the horses grunting in response to the tight pull of the reins. Michael hopped down before Tamm had a chance to open the door for him and took the steps to the front door two at a time. Mr. Butler had been waiting.

"She's in bed resting. The doctor has been here and gone already. He said to send for him when things get moving a bit more."

Michael nodded and sprinted up the stairs, screeching to a halt outside the door to their room. He bent over, placed his hands on his knees, and caught his breath before bursting into the room. He didn't want to frighten her.

"How are you doing?" he spoke as he opened the door to their room and peered around the edge of the doorway. The empty bed looked like it hadn't been used in days.

Michael looked around the room, checking the chair by the fireplace and the chaise at the end of the bed. Nothing. He closed the door quietly and stood staring down the hall. Where would she be?

"Ah, Mr. Farling." Mrs. Maloney stepped around the corner while carrying an armful of newly bleached linens. "She's in her room."

Michael scrunched his brows in confusion but decided to leave the questioning for later. They'd always shared a room. He knew childbirth could be a messy business, but not so much that it would bother him. After all, she was giving birth to his child.

He crossed through the parlor that connected their rooms and opened the door to hers, this time without knocking.

"Why aren't you in our room?"

Miriam smiled and waved him over. Michael felt his heart slow to a more normal rhythm. Everything was going to be fine.

She patted the empty spot on the bed next to her. "The doctor says first babies can take a while. The contractions haven't even begun in earnest. This will probably be a long night. You will want somewhere to sleep."

Michael tried not to look at her like she'd sprouted another head, but heaven help him, how in the world did she think he could sleep in a bed by himself when she would be in a separate room laboring away? "I'm not sure how you think this will all go, but I have no intention of leaving your side."

Mrs. Maloney cleared her throat. "We'll leave that decision for later." The stern set of her frown communicated exactly how she felt about men in the birthing room.

"I'll at least be here as long as the doctor will let me." Michael scowled at Mrs. Maloney, earning a smile in return.

"We'll see."

Miriam rested her hand against his forearm and took a deep breath. Her expression locked, and she hissed the breath out through her teeth.

"Was that a contraction?" Michael couldn't help but be alarmed at the transformation in his wife's features. "Shouldn't someone fetch the doctor?" He directed the question to Mrs. Maloney, pointing to Miriam's stomach. He knew the gesture was that of a demanding child, but he couldn't help it.

"Not yet." Mrs. Maloney shook her head. "She's got a long way to go."

Evan paced across the empty floor of his new office, waiting for the arrival of the furniture he'd ordered the day before. He'd woken early, knowing it would be his last night in his rented room. Tonight, he'd be sleeping in the apartment above the space where he would soon begin seeing patients.

He wondered briefly if the colors he'd chosen were colors that Ione would like.

Not that it mattered. Except it did. For some reason, it did.

He opened the door, stuck his head out to look down the street, first one way, then the other, and closed the door again.

She'd agreed to call him Evan. They hadn't known each other for long, but because in many ways she already belonged to the family, using their given names felt natural.

At least that's what he thought until he heard his name gently escape her lips for the first time while sitting around the table with his brother, sister-in-law, and their adopted daughters. Then he simply wished they'd been alone, that she would stand facing him, whisper his name for only the two of them to hear. When he reciprocated, when he breathed her name in response, under the scrutiny of his family, the moment had been almost too intimate to bear. He'd wanted to intertwine his fingers with hers, to stroll along the twilight streets, to know so much more.

The door banged open, the glass panes shuttering in surprise. Evan shot to his feet and rushed toward the delivery men. They balanced a high cabinet between them.

"Where you want it?" The second man to enter shouted over the top of the piece as if the inside of the building must be as loud as the street outside. His thick Irish accent reminded Evan of being back east, and he felt a commonality with the man that had no reasoning behind it.

"Over here." Evan pointed to an imaginary spot on the floor where he hoped one day his nurse might stand.

The loud man grunted his understanding, and with a nod, the men lined up and set down the heavy piece with a thud.

"We got more to bring in." The second man, presumably the one in charge, nodded toward the loaded wagon sitting at the edge of the street. "You want it all brought through this here door?"

Evan took a step to look at the pile of furniture neatly wrapped in blankets and tied down. "This is probably the best entrance. Some of the things will have to go upstairs, but most of it will be down here."

The men hurried back out to heave chairs and tables and benches off the back of the wagon. If they moved quickly, he might have time to meet Ione and escort her for a walk during her lunch hour. He checked his pocket watch.

"Did you hear?" John burst into Ione's shop, his robes billowing behind him.

The woman at the counter deciding on ribbons dropped the spool. It rolled lazily toward the edge of the counter. Ione caught it and sent John a censorious glare.

He did make quite a scene. Long ago, Ione had decided that his robes played tricks. Where for some priests, the black floor-length garments did nothing, turning the men into almost non-men, for John, they hid his size. Until he burst into a room, filling the doorway, bringing his dark presence into a place of pink and lace and floral upholstery, the robes simply were what he wore. But once inside, they magnified his size and made him look—at least to Ione—as she imagined a guardian angel would appear if they entered a room with protection in mind.

She felt safer with him around.

"Hear what?" She rolled the ribbon back onto the spool, ignoring the wordless questions dashing off between her customers.

John looked around the room, seemingly noticing for the first time that they were not alone. He kicked his head to the side, signaling that Ione should follow him to the back room. Ione caught the raised eyebrows. That little ploy did nothing to satisfy the curiosity of her customers. If anything, it would get their tongues wagging faster than ever.

"You'll have to excuse me." Ione slid out from behind the counter. "Grace can help you if you make any decisions. Otherwise, I'll be back shortly." She followed John's disappearing robes into the room where she kept stock and worked to put the pieces of the gowns together.

"What's happened?" Ione shook out her skirts, hoping to rid the fabric of a few of the loose threads she collected every time she helped a customer.

"Miriam is in labor."

Ione looked up. She couldn't keep the concern off her face. "Isn't it early? Is she...is the baby...?" She let the words trail off, hopeless to and unwilling to give voice to her concerns.

"Have you seen her lately?"

Ione glanced down. How long had it been? A couple of weeks? "No. I can't say that I have."

"The doctor still says she's early, but not so early that the baby shouldn't be fine. I just left there. Michael appears confident that all will be well."

"You'll wait here?" Ione unpinned her chatelaine and set it on the work counter. "I'll be right back down with a few things for the night."

"They didn't say they expected you to come," Ione heard John say as she made her way up to her apartment.

She paused. "Are you going to stay?"

"Of course," John conceded.

"Of the two of us, who do you think will be more useful?"

A half-chuckle escaped. "That's not fair."

"I don't play fair," Ione shot back, sinking into the shadows of the stairwell. "You know that."

The contractions were infuriatingly regular. Miriam tried not to hold her breath, tried to do as the midwife instructed, tried not to snarl at the doctor when he said everything progressed as he expected it would. How any of the teeth-grinding, gut-twisting pains could fall under the category of "as expected" was simply beyond her comprehension.

She'd always thought that women must have been exaggerating. That the ones who complained about the pain were also the ones who commonly fell into long sicknesses caused by mysterious headaches or the ones who fainted at the slightest provocation. Right now, Miriam wanted to tell every one of them she was sorry. So, so sorry. Dear Lord.

"It will be over in a bit." The midwife gripped Miriam's sweat-slick hand and urged her to breathe until her muscles unclenched and her body remembered how to breathe out again on its own.

A soft knock at the door, and Ione came rushing in, followed by Jenny. Michael had long since been exiled to his office to smoke what Miriam was sure was pipe after pipe whilst pacing next to John.

"Where's Theo?" Miriam tried to sit up, only to be pushed back by the midwife.

"You need to relax during contractions. No talking."

"He's at home with Jeremy." Jenny ignored the strange woman and sent Miriam a cross-eyed stare to communicate exactly how she felt about her interference.

Miriam almost giggled, but the next contraction whisked away any thought other than the pain as her body attempted to expel the life it had created.

"It's time for you ladies to leave, now."

Ione ignored the midwife and walked over to stand next to the bed. Miriam felt her friend's presence as waited for the pains to subside and her eyes to open, and for her focus to return. "If you need anything, I mean anything—" She glanced quickly in the midwife's direction— "you send someone down."

"Or just holler," Jenny added. "We'll be listening for you."

Miriam would have told them how much she appreciated them, how much she never imagined she'd have friends, how they'd changed her life, how much she loved them both, but another contraction, fast on the heels of the last, stole her breath, and the next time she opened her eyes, they were gone.

Chapter 19

The house had calmed. Miriam held her newborn daughter to her breast, and the perfectly healthy infant nuzzled closer. The marvel of her delicate fingers, the tiny pink fingernails, the softness of her skin... Miriam held her breath at the wonder of it all.

She'd never been around babies, so every jerky movement, every whiff of the whisper-soft hair, every yawn, blink, and twitch held her fascination. The impossibility of it all—that she and Michael could create a whole human—had her reeling with the magnitude of the event.

Michael rolled over and stared at them in the dim of the evening light. "I can't believe she's here. Finally." He reached out his hand and watched as her tiny fingers wrapped around his much larger one, smiling at their daughter's tight grip. "She's so strong." He sat up and twisted so he faced Miriam on the bed, sitting cross-legged and leaning over the baby. "I'm not sure what I expected, but I can't stop looking at her."

"I know." Miriam watched her daughter's impossibly delicate eyelashes brush her cheeks. The doctor had been wrong. She wasn't an early baby; not so much that it made a difference, anyway. Her even breathing and the pink of her toes and fingers, the alert eyes, and the way she'd fought her way into the world all pointed to a healthy, full-term child.

"I think she looks like an Ava." Michael met Miriam's gaze and smiled.

Her mother's name. They'd discussed using it if they had a girl but had decided to wait until after she was born to see if the name fit.

Miriam agreed.

The nurse eased into the room. Miriam watched her gentle approach and knew they'd picked the right woman to help her in the first few weeks. Although, at this point, Miriam couldn't imagine handing over the baby to anyone, let alone someone they barely knew.

"I think I'll hold her for a while longer." Miriam glanced up to the nurse's tight, professional hairstyle and clean uniform.

"Do you need anything, then?" The nurse straightened the blankets in the small, white wicker bassinet and slid it over closer to the edge of the bed.

Michael shook his head, his attention fixed on his daughter. Miriam dismissed the nurse with a half-smile. She left, closing the door quietly behind, and leaving them to marvel at the miracle they finally held.

Ione tried not to drag her feet as she stepped off the streetcar and made her way down the block back to her shop. No one had slept much during the night, watching Michael pace with John not far behind, and waiting to hear the promise of a cry.

The little bundle had held out until midafternoon. By that time, the four of them, clustered in the parlor, had attempted to play games, struggled with the first paragraphs of numerous books, bitten their fingernails to their quicks, and finally settled on watching Michael puff pipe after pipe.

When the gusty cry finally made its way down to them, Michael jumped up, nearly tossed his pipe to John, and ran up the stairs. John laughed, tapped the long dead tobacco ash out of the pipe, and followed to wait at the bottom of the steps. They knew enough to give Michael and Miriam some time, but it had not been easy.

Ione sighed, watching the people pass by in their rush to get home after a long day. The sun glinted off the windows on one side of the street, lending a golden glow to the typically unremarkable thoroughfare.

Grace was just turning the sign to say closed as Ione stepped up to the door.

"How did it go? Is everything all right?"

Ione nodded and smiled, aware of the softness in her features borrowed from the time spent looking down at a child who would undoubtedly grow with the love of two parents and an entire gaggle of honorary and enthusiastic aunts and uncles. "They had a girl. Her name is Ava."

"That's a beautiful name." Grace's wistful expression belied her youth and the hope that so often paired with it.

Ione pulled the pins from her hat and dropped it onto the counter. "I think I am going to bed now, and I will sleep until tomorrow." She glanced around the tidy room. "Is there anything I need to look at before you go home?"

"No. Nothing that can't wait until tomorrow."

"Good. If you're ready to go, I'll follow you and lock up."

Grace picked up her hat off the coat tree, gathered the things she had carried with her that morning, and stepped into the alley. "Oh." She stopped. "I almost forgot. That young doctor stopped by again. He was hoping to escort you for a walk during lunch."

"Evan?" Ione immediately regretted the question. How many other young doctors were there to choose from?

Grace raised a brow and ignored any potential comment about how many suitors Ione might be considering. "Evan?" She parroted Ione's use of his given name, smiling as if to conspire against her. "If you mean Dr. Whitaker, then yes, I suppose Evan did stop by."

Ione felt the blood rush to her face. She gave Grace a sidelong glance and frowned to cover the smile she could barely contain at the thought of him dropping in again. "See you tomorrow, Grace." She cut the conversation, closed the door, locked it, and then leaned there for a while.

He'd come back. It wouldn't be long before she had to tell him the truth. Come clean about what she had done, had been. She pressed her hands to her hot face. It was apparent, despite her efforts not to encourage the man, that he was interested in her.

And heaven help her, she was interested too.

She let the knowledge wash over her, ready for the fear to creep into the pit of her stomach, for the pulse to pound the blood into her legs so that all she wanted to do was run. But it didn't. Her heart beat steadily along.

She kicked up from her leaning position and made her way up to her rooms, running her fingers along the textured wallpaper and the smooth wood as her mind wandered to possibilities. Hope had to be held at bay. He had no idea of her past, and he might want nothing to do with her. Ione knew, though, she couldn't afford hope, couldn't let the fluttering in her chest turn to anything more before she'd exposed her secrets, before he knew.

Because if she did, if she let him in and he rejected her after he found out...Ione didn't want to think about it.

It was a race against the clock. Tell him before she cared enough to worry what he would think.

Ione ignored the hitch in her breathing that evidenced it was already too late for that.

Tamm watched the people come and go from the birthing room through the pin hole he'd drilled into the wall. The passageways he'd come to know quite well. Over the past few nights, with Mrs. Farling confined to bed, he'd been able to map the tunnels, halls, and much to his surprise, the secret rooms. He hadn't expected those. And with Mrs.

Farling now occupied with the infant and recovering from her child's birth, he had free access to nearly the entire house without the fear of an unanticipated meeting.

Ione had been there. She'd waited with the rest of them and then fussed over the newborn for the appropriate amount of time before heading home. She'd decided to walk to the streetcar rather than accept Mrs. Maloney's offer of their carriage. Tamm had almost choked as he'd heard the words slip from the old housekeeper's mouth. That would have destroyed everything. If this was going to work, Ione couldn't know that Tamm had access here.

So he'd watched, and waited, and now, as Mr. Farling stepped out of the room for a second and Mrs. Farling dozed in bed, her hand resting protectively against the side of the bassinet, another opportunity had been revealed.

He eased the passageway open and inched out onto the soft carpets. The memory of similar luxuries, of the comfortable rooms he had before the run of bad luck, made the current lack burn deep.

Slow, deep breaths. In and out, pause, in and out... His body longed for the sleep he'd gone without that night. But the opportunity, laid out in the bassinet, was worth the sacrifice of his comfort.

Tamm shrank through the opening, holding his breath, timing his footsteps with Mrs. Farling's every exhale, until he stood at the edge of the infant's bed. The baby's lips moved as if she suckled in her dreams. Her fists, bunched over her head, twitched in the foreign, cool air as they became accustomed to the empty space of the outside world. Tamm marveled at how weak the new bundle of flesh made the parents.

Reaching in, he felt the baby's warm breath against the back of his knuckles. The quiet squeaks, the sounds of rest coming from the infant in silky swaddling, flaunted the luxury of it all. Tamm drew his fingers along the edge of the white linens, his heart racing. Mr. Farling could come back any second. He could walk into the room and see him standing over his wife and child. Tamm shook his head. Seeing that expression of weakness, of victim-hood, on the man's face would almost be worth getting caught.

Instead, he reached in, tested the soft weight, balanced the head on the tips of his fingers and the baby's bottom on the palm of his hand. Endless options stretched in front of him.

He glanced toward the door, then the open passageway, and then looked at the pink infant one more time before turning her the opposite way Mrs. Farling had placed her in the crib.

Tamm straightened, turned, and left the room, careful to close the secret panel behind him.

Chapter 20

Michael dropped the book. It landed on his toe, but he didn't register the pain.

"Did you hear that?" He met Mrs. Mahoney's gaze, and then they were both off, running up the stairs.

As they reached the top, Miriam met them in the hall, the baby in her arms. Her face, blanched white, had no expression. She held Ava tight to her chest.

Michael approached slowly, not sure if she would drop the baby. He'd only stepped out for a few minutes after they both had fallen asleep. If something had happened to his daughter... Michael couldn't keep the tremble from his voice.

"Miriam?" he whispered, not wanting to shock her but hoping to see her eyes shift to meet his, to see the consciousness return. "Are you all right?"

Miriam moved to the side so that Michael could see into the room. He moved past her while Mrs. Maloney carefully coaxed the baby from Miriam's tight grasp. Nothing in the room had changed. The bed was as he left it, the furniture hadn't been disturbed. The curtains still blocked the sun. He turned back to Miriam, trying to keep the confusion from his face.

"What happened?" Michael approached Mrs. Maloney and took Ava from her. His daughter's blue eyes blinked open to stare at him. He brushed her cheek with the tip of his finger and breathed easier as she turned toward the movement.

"She wasn't right in the bed," Miriam accused Michael, pointing at him. "Did you move her?"

"What are you talking about?" Michael shifted his gaze to Mrs. Maloney, hoping she could illuminate the misunderstanding.

"Did you move her? What did you do before you left?" Miriam took a step nearer, reaching out for the baby.

But Michael took a step back. "I don't know what you are talking about. You were both sound asleep when I left. And I didn't move her."

"She was turned the other way," Miriam stated simply.

"How?"

Miriam pursed her lips and breathed out in frustration. "I laid her down with her head nearest to mine. When I woke, she looked exactly the same, but her head was at the other end of the crib."

Mrs. Maloney shrugged. "No one's been up here as far as I know." She reached out and brushed Ava's downy hair. "Maybe you just didn't remember?"

Michael could see Miriam studied the woman almost as if she didn't know her, searching for signs of deception, for ways in which she might be someone they couldn't trust. Michael sent a wordless apology to Mrs. Maloney.

"Why don't we go back into the room and rest a bit more." Ava punctuated Michael's statement with a well-timed yawn. He smiled down at his newborn. Miriam had to be mistaken; there was no other explanation. Besides, she'd been more and more withdrawn as the pregnancy had progressed. Michael hoped she would find her footing again. And quickly. But her shuttered expression, the way her eyes had blocked off access to her feelings, the way she looked at him as if he failed to support her, had him worried.

He handed Ava to Miriam, hoping the gesture would convince her that he had faith in her abilities. She took the baby and walked back to the bed, offering nothing else. No information. Nothing to try to convince him and Mrs. Maloney of the validity of her claims, and more importantly, nothing else to calm their minds as to Miriam's own health.

Michael nodded to Mrs. Maloney, wordlessly asking her to keep an eye on his wife. Then he followed her into the room and closed the door.

Ione opened the note again, read the message, and then tucked it into her pocket.

"Who's it from?" Grace called over her shoulder as she passed behind her with a new bolt of fabric Beatrice had wanted to examine.

The shop closed over an hour ago, but Ione always scheduled Beatrice for an after-hours appointment. It never worked to try to fit a friend into a time slot with a specific beginning and end, because the end was often difficult to find.

But she had tonight. They'd completed the fitting, picked out the fabric for the next dress, and finished design discussions for the Women's Pavilion uniforms in all under an hour. Thanks, in part, to the note she wanted to take out and read again.

Evan wanted to escort her to the Chicago Orchestra playing at the Auditorium Theater.

She'd sent a note back with the message boy that she would look forward to their evening.

Now her stomach had tied itself in knots, and she had only an hour to get ready.

"It's a note from Evan. Dr. Whitaker," she clarified. "We're going to the symphony this evening."

Grace dropped the bolt on the counter and spun around to grab Ione's arm. "What, in heaven's name, are you still doing down here?" She dragged her over to the door and opened it for her, giving her a small shove toward the stairs. "You get up there and get ready. I'll close up down here."

"But you've closed up often lately." Ione glanced back, apologizing for leaving the mess behind.

Grace huffed. "When I have a man who wants to take me to the symphony, you can pay me back. Now get out of here." She closed the door with a bit more emphasis than Ione had expected.

She stood in the dark of the stairwell for a moment before making her way up to her apartment to pull the cream-colored silk out. It had been ordered for another woman, but at the last minute the customer changed her mind about the color. Ione had tried to be upset over the loss, but truthfully, she couldn't. It had been a perfect fit for her, and she smiled every time she remembered Jenny's speechless reaction to the cream color against Ione's dark skin.

Ione opened the armoire, slid the hangers wide, and examined the gown. She lifted the cover that protected the bead work that ran at an angle from her right shoulder to her waist and checked for wrinkles. It had survived waiting relatively unscathed. Ione smiled, pulled the dress down, and spread it out over the bed.

The skirt hugged her hips and flared near her knees. Tiny cap sleeves were the narrow remnants of the wide pleats that wrapped tight against her ribs, cascading at an angle that accentuated her waist. Ione frowned in an attempt to fight back the vanity that threatened to swamp her, but she couldn't hold the expression for long. She gave up, made her way to the bath, and filled the sink basin. She avoided looking at the tub—it would have been nice, but she lacked the necessary time to wait for the water to warm and then sit there to enjoy it. She would have to make do with the basin and a cloth.

Ione scrubbed every inch and then dried off with a rough towel, rubbing her skin until it glowed. The ladies' magazines glorified the process, extorting the benefits of scratching away the dead skin. While sometimes she didn't look forward to the practice, tonight, the sting of it distracted her and kept her from questioning her sanity.

She tied on her robe and tested the curling rod she'd placed on the stove to heat up while she washed. The mirror she'd carried from the bathing room and placed on the kitchen table. She took a deep breath, grabbed her comb, and pulled her hair into a tight bun that took nearly twenty pins to secure. She frowned in the mirror, wishing again that her hair could be the kind that responded to the taming efforts of her combs.

She chose a few strands to separate from the rest of the mass and took the iron to them, waiting until she could smell her hair cook before pulling it out to examine the curl. She repeated the process again and again until tight ringlets brushed her shoulders and her reflection had taken on a sophisticated air. Or if she'd failed to arrive at sophistication, at least no one could argue that she'd made an obvious effort to get there.

The dress slid over her skin, the cool fabric gliding to rest over her curves and in the hollows of her figure. Ione tied on her shoes, pulled the matching shawl from the armoire, turned down the lamps and checked the stove, and then hurried down to her shop to turn back and forth in front of the full-length mirrors. The effect of the cream, the fit of the dress, the fall of the fabric was nothing short of stunning. She almost wished Jenny and Miriam and Beatrice were meeting with them so they could see her in the dress. She chided herself for the vanity but couldn't keep the smile off her face when she opened the door to the waiting carriage and Evan, standing speechless.

Michael loved her. That much, Miriam knew. And Mrs. Maloney cared deeply. Time had proven that. Why, then, did they not believe her?

She paced the floor, unable to stop thinking about her baby, blinking up at her from the wrong end of the bassinet as if nothing strange had happened. She shook her head and crossed her arms over her chest. Forgetting which way she set her baby down, forgetting the way she could caress the top of her head as she slumbered, forgetting the peek of her pink toes as she worked out of the swaddle—that was the impossible part.

She scowled at the door Michael had left through. He did care for her. He did.

He simply hadn't believed her.

Miriam crossed to her dressing table with the gilt-edged mirror and sat on the cushioned stool. She looked a wreck. Hair tousled, skin pale in some places and ruddy in others. She touched her cheek. It felt so different from the new skin of their baby. So worn and used, with marks and scars and the occasional freckle from childhood days in the sun.

A tear slipped out of the corner of her eye, and Miriam watched it travel down her cheek, pause, trembling near the corner of her mouth, and then slip to her chin. She wiped it away before it slid down her jaw and to her neck. She took a deep breath and pinched her hands together until her nails had become a deep purple at the beds and white near the tips of her fingers.

She hadn't imagined it. She couldn't have imagined it.

Ava's head had been near to hers. It would have never occurred to her to place her upside-down.

Unless she had lost her mind, it wouldn't have happened that way.

The thought nagged.

Could she have been that wrong? People were wrong all the time. She supposed at times she was too. But could she be that wrong about something so simple, so important? So natural. Placing her baby in the bed the wrong way was unnatural. Would she have done that?

And if she had, what else might she get wrong?

Miriam looked at Ava, nestled into the loose quilts on her bed. Placing her back in the bassinet hadn't been possible; the small white wicker basket with its filmy netting and ruffles now carried a sense of foreboding, of something not quite right.

But it was the worst kind of not right. Not the tenebrous kind that warned with black claws and hooks, but the kind that came on a cloud. The kind that floated over the sun, at first innocuous, but dangerous nonetheless. The feeling when she'd hovered over the soft, light bed had been the same one that came when someone evil smiled.

Suddenly, she could smell her paints. She closed her eyes, longing to circle the soft bristles of her brush in the palm of her hand, wishing for that clarity that came only when she drew paint across a clean canvas. If she were painting, the bassinet would be her character—a portrait of an inanimate object. Not a still life—she closed her eyes and felt the silken slide of the paint—but a portrait.

Her eyes flew open to rest on the small cradle that now held so much soul. Miriam clenched her teeth, rose, and made her way around the bed to grasp the edge of the bassinet. Each step dragging the frills across the floor felt better, lighter, as if she were unburdening the room and clearing the space for her and her baby.

Michael wouldn't like it, and no way existed that would make this choice appear the sensible one. But she would not abandon her baby back to the hollows of an unsafe bed. For now, she would sleep with Miriam. Michael was an adult. He could do what he wanted. He could believe her or not. It didn't matter. What did matter was that her baby stayed safe, and if that meant that Miriam kept her close, then that would be how things were done.

Miriam didn't need a nurse for her baby. Didn't need people telling her what to do. What she needed was a place away from people who looked at her like she was losing her mind.

Chapter 21

When Evan had been given two tickets for the evening's performance, he'd underestimated the gift. The box seats, tucked along the wall and overlooking the stage, offered a perfect view of the symphony.

But it wasn't the symphony that held his attention.

Ione sat to his right, and for that he sent a greedy prayer of thanksgiving toward the gilded ceiling. Every twitch of the corner of her mouth as the music swelled, each deep breath she took on heels of the closing strains of each piece, every flutter of her fingers and glance down at the rest of the audience—he witnessed it all without her noticing that his attention was fixed on her rather than the musicians.

The physician who had offered the tickets did so because his wife's sister had suddenly fallen ill. The guilt for being grateful for the turn of events gave him pause until he studied Ione's profile in the low light. Her small features spoke of strength and resilience, and, frankly, beauty. He took in a deep breath, catching a hint of her perfume. She smelled like roses and light ...she smelled so good.

Ione turned to him after the dying strains of a song that should have made him melancholy. He couldn't do it, though. He couldn't muster the strength to be anything but thrilled that she'd come with him. She flashed a brilliant smile in his direction, and his heart nearly stopped.

What was he doing?

She'd given him no hint that she had any interest in him outside of their budding friendship. In fact, when he tried to hint at it, her response led him to think that she had little room for anything but her work and friends. And here he sat, like an idiot, counting her breaths, watching the strong pulse at the base of her throat, and longing to move his chair another inch closer to hers.

"Thank you for coming tonight," he whispered over the introductory strains of a solo violin as he leaned in.

She shifted her head toward his, not so far that she couldn't watch the artist drag the bow across the strings, but close enough for his heart to race. He mentally frowned. It didn't take much.

He hadn't planned on meeting someone so soon. Of course he wanted a wife and a family, someday, but he had a practice to build, work to do. And when he did find a wife, he'd imagined she'd be one to play the role of a doctor's wife, someone who might help him in the office, someone who would spend her days caring for their children. He watched the dim light play with the curls of her hair. If she were his wife, she'd be anything but typical. With her successful business, and her network of society friends, their lives wouldn't be a bit like he'd imagined his future.

None of that mattered, though. He shifted in his seat, willing the final strains of the music to come so they could walk back to the carriage, so he could talk to her, so he could decide if he'd imagined the attraction between them or if she might somehow share the same obsession.

The final notes played, and Ione couldn't move. Although she'd made countless gowns for the symphony, she'd never had the opportunity to attend. And while she'd correctly imagined the power the music had to take her to other worlds, she hadn't anticipated the capacity for other elements to be just as influential over her assessment of the place.

Sitting above the majority of the crowd, at first Ione attempted to keep her attention to where it should be: the stage. Eventually she'd failed and, out of the corners of her eyes, scanned the busy crowd. While people were engaged with the performers, they were also making eye contact with others in their circle, wordlessly solidifying plans for the rest of the evening. Women, emboldened by the dark, slid their fingers into the warm hands of their escorts, and then men fought to keep their expressions passive, but the tense square of their shoulders communicated exactly the opposite. During intermission, those in the boxes to their left and right peered around the curtains and nodded politely when they realized that Ione and Evan were not who they'd expected.

Women visually took measure of one another's gowns. Men gripped hands in greeting, the strength of their handshake asserting their dominance or their submission to the other's status. Ione couldn't help but look down with pride, knowing that her gown would be the talk of the evening, not to mention their unexpected presence. Because of her service to a number of the major families in the city, people knew her name, her business. But very few knew her or would be able to connect her face with her name.

By the end of the night, that would change. She'd recognized many of her customers—in truth, she'd recognized their gowns first, and then the women in the gowns, but more importantly, they'd recognized her too, nodded politely, turned so she could get a look at the magic her dress had done for them that evening, and then whispered her identity to the women in their circles.

She hadn't anticipated it, but by tomorrow her mailbox would be filling with new appointment requests. She also hadn't considered the curious looks Evan received while standing at her side.

Ione knew the impression they'd made. He, in his black top hat and tailcoat, was the perfect contrast to the cream color of her gown. She met his gaze and smiled before accepting the offer of his hand to assist her in standing.

His eyes had been on her for most of the night, and while the movement and the obvious playing out of individual dramas during the performance held her attention, it was the feel of his gaze, hot at the back of her neck, that distracted her the most throughout the evening.

They had to talk.

Miriam woke with a start. It was dark outside, but the lamps still burned. They'd argued. Michael wanted to share her room, for Ava to sleep next to them in the bassinet, but she couldn't do it. He didn't have to believe her, that something had happened, or that someone in the house had moved their child while she'd slept, but she wasn't about to put the baby back into the insecurity of that cradle.

There were the kinds of risk one could take in hopes of a reward. This kind of risk, though, offered no such payoff at the end. It was risk simply for the sake of it, and Miriam wanted nothing to do with it.

With the tip of her finger, she reached out and touched her baby. The child's steady breathing reassured her. Pulling her closer, she closed her eyes and drifted off to sleep with the lamps' glowing comfort still pulsing into every corner.

"You look beautiful."

The words, whispered into the dark of the two-seat carriage, lodged in Ione's chest. She looked out the small window and watched the store windows reflect the lamp that hung on the corner of their carriage, and then melt into the blackness behind them. She had no idea how to respond to the gallant man sitting next to her, holding the reins. "Thank you. The evening, the symphony, was lovely."

Ione wrung her hands in her lap, weighing the need to be honest about who she was and what she had done before she had met this unsuspecting gentleman against the need to hold her secrets tight. She glanced at his profile. His flawless posture rivaled that of a mannequin. His black wool overcoat had not a speck of lint. And when he caught her looking and flashed a smile, his perfectly white straight teeth completed the picture of a man who came from better than she had. A man who deserved better.

She looked forward again, counting the lampposts as the horses clopped past them and wondering if her assessment of the man—that he hoped for more from her than simply her friendship—could possibly be correct. If it was, she needed to speak up. But if not, there was no need to seek out the humiliation that a revelation of her past would certainly provide.

He cleared his throat and dropped his gaze from the road ahead, slowing the horses and pulling to the side of the street. "I want to ask you something."

Ione held her breath and turned to better look up at him. The hat shadowed his eyes. "I can't see your eyes."

He didn't smile, but he pulled off his hat. He set it in his lap and looked up, locking his unwavering gaze with hers. "I think you are remarkable."

Ione had to fight to keep her eyes focused on his. Everything in her wanted to look away, to warn him that she wasn't what he thought she was. But part of her, a growing part, the same part that helped her build her business, clawed to the surface, screaming that she did deserve a chance at happiness. That she'd assumed happiness meant a business and friends and food on the table, but she was so wrong. That her definition of happiness had changed, expanded, and she wanted it. She wanted it.

"I'm not perfect." She risked everything.

"No one is." Evan picked his hat off his lap and hung it over the brake before taking her gloved hand in his.

"No. I mean, I'm really not who you think I am."

His eyes wouldn't release hers, and Ione fought to keep the tears that suddenly welled up at bay.

"I want to court you. I want to get to know you. I think you—what you have accomplished—is amazing, and I would be grateful if you shared my hope for more than a friendship between us."

How did she get here? Ione finally ripped her eyes from his and stared into her lap at their tightly joined hands.

"Are you cold?" He must be able to feel her trembling.

"No."

"Am I mistaken?"

Ione couldn't look at him. "No."

He dropped her fingers. The cool air rushed in even through her gloves. She felt his finger at her chin, forcing her to look up again.

"Why don't you tell me what I need to know, and we can go from there."

Chapter 22

Michael paced in his study. For the first time since they'd been married, last night, he had slept in his room alone. He stooped to pick up the fireplace poker and examined the blackened tip.

Women often had a bit of trouble adjusting to motherhood, Mrs. Maloney had assured him, but this, this protectiveness, this uncertainty, didn't feel right.

And it didn't feel right to sleep alone with his wife and newborn a room away.

Michael dropped the poker and sat down behind his desk. He leaned back, linked his fingers behind his head, and closed his eyes. He didn't have the right to be tired, he hadn't done the work of birthing their baby, but heaven help him, he was exhausted. And he missed his wife.

The stacks of correspondence had begun to build up. Letters of congratulations, gifts from business associates who had heard of their good fortune, notes of well wishes from the women who worked at the warehouse, unopened invitations, and requests to visit piled in by the hour. Miriam should be the one to respond, or at least the nurse she had let go could have responded with a quick note of gratitude on her behalf. Michael rifled through the pile, reading the senders' names without the benefit of comprehension.

She'd taken breakfast in her room with the baby, as well as the rest of her meals. And as far as he could tell, the child couldn't be any healthier. Of course, he kept slipping into the room to ask simplistic questions, or whenever he had the sudden urge to check on Ava, or when he missed how Miriam used to be in and out of every room he sat in. She had become part of him, and he felt her absence earnestly. Now she seemed satisfied to stay in her room with the babe in her arms.

At least she was good at the job. Ava had adapted to the outside world with ease, with the normal sounds of crying or fussing rarely escaping the room. She slept and nursed, and Miriam watched over her as if she were the only thing in the world.

Michael sat up. That was the concerning part. The rest of the world had faded away for her.

But how much of that was normal?

His arms felt empty. For Miriam, for Ava. He stood and made his way to the stairs, taking them two at a time. There was nothing for him in his office. All he had slept in the room at the top of the stairs, and if he needed to be there to be complete, then that was exactly where he would be.

"I'm not sure where to start." Ione hated to admit her weakness, but if things were going to go as she thought they might, it wouldn't be the worst thing she'd admit to that night. That he could be someone important to her went without saying; she knew it was a detail, a truth she couldn't keep from her gaze when he had forced their eyes to meet under the shadow and protection of the stopped carriage.

"How about how your sisters came to be adopted by my brother?"

Ione nodded. "My mother died." She glanced up at the circle of light that surrounded the next streetlamp. Its yellow orb unable to penetrate the dark all the way to where they sat, but still comforting and something on which she could focus. Her eyes darted back to his. His had never left her face.

Ione chewed her bottom lip, drawing his attention to her mouth. She turned away, breaking the spell. She had to tell him everything.

"I'd left, ran away, really. With a man." The last sentence had been quiet.

Evan stilled.

"He was older. He offered me things. I could sing well enough to make some money, so he decided I could make money for him. My mother tried to stop me, but I didn't listen."

Evan brought his other hand to where theirs already met and enclosed her fingers in the warmth of his palms. He nodded his encouragement.

Ione took a deep breath in and out and plowed ahead as quickly as she could, her eyes never leaving the sight of his hands on hers. "He decided I could make better money in other ways." She felt a tear quiver at the tip of an eyelash, and then splash down to her cheek, where it rested, trembling with the rest of her. "I ran back to my mother. By then it was too late. I didn't know she'd been ill. She was dying when I got back."

She met his eyes, surprised by the concern gathered in the lines around his mouth. "We had nothing. No money for food for my sisters, no money for medicine. I couldn't work during the day...I had to care for them." She looked back to that yellow flickering light and stared until it became a hazy orb, floating in and out of focus. It all seemed so far away. A lifetime ago. She wasn't the same person. "So I worked at night."

Her eyes snapped back to his, making sure he understood the meaning of her confession.

He pulled his hands back a fraction of an inch, loosening his grip, abandoning his previous post as protector. Ione nodded her understanding and turned away, shrinking into her side of the now too-small carriage.

Evan stared blankly at the horses. "I...I have to admit, I didn't expect that." He continued, keeping his attention focused on her. "Aaron told me there were things in your past that I, we, would have to deal with." He paused and looked up at the black sky. "He also said that sometimes the past isn't a predictor of the future." He let out a harsh sound somewhere between a breath and a laugh. "Now I understand he was trying to prepare me."

"I know," Ione whispered, closing her eyes against the truth of her words. She lifted a hand to her mouth and dropped it again before continuing. "You had a right to know. I didn't want to hurt you when, down the road, you discovered that I could never be a suitable wife." There. It was out. This last piece, done.

He took a deep breath.

"Maybe it would be best if you took me home now." She straightened her posture. Shame for her decisions burned deep, but so did the need to move on. Flirting with thoughts of a relationship, a real relationship, had been amusing, but deep down she'd known. Closed doors could be good, sometimes. Regret still swirled but thinking on it wouldn't change anything. Ione watched a couple—a woman in red and a well-dressed man—cross the street. By the way they were dressed, they were on their way home from some sort of celebration. She glanced down at her hands folded into her lap and frowned. It wasn't as if she didn't have a way forward. She had everything she needed, and what she didn't need was a man who would decide that her past mistakes had to devalue her for the rest of her life. Anger swirled in with the shame. He still hadn't picked up the reins. Hadn't moved. Maybe he wasn't the gentleman she'd thought.

"I can walk from here, if you prefer." Ione successfully made the suggestion in a tone that didn't betray the sick feeling that came along with her shame and the accompanying newfound anger. Picking up her skirts, she moved to climb down without his help.

He grabbed her arm, stopping her descent. "I didn't say that."

Ione hazarded a glance in his direction only to find him staring intently at her. "Didn't say what?"

"I didn't say who could or could not make a suitable wife."

She lifted her brows and leveled a lazy look. "I'm pretty sure 'woman of the night' was not on your list of desirable qualities. You do not have to play polite. I understand. There is nothing, has never been anything between us. You are not to blame for my mistakes." She glanced down to the edge of the road where the wet cobbles reflected the light in uneven wavers. It must have rained while they'd been at the symphony. How had she not noticed?

"You have no idea what is or is not on my list."

Emboldened by her confession and growing tired of the thought of a protracted rejection, Ione turned back to face him again. "You don't have to be kind. I know who I have been and who I am."

He ignored her last statement and lifted a hand between them, spreading out his fingers one at a time with each point he tried to make. "Things that are on my list are smart, loving, caring, and if I get lucky, beautiful." He fished her hands out of the folds of her skirt and squeezed her numb gloved fingers between his warm ones.

Ione met his expressionless gaze. He wasn't hurt, wasn't angry. If anything, he looked confused.

"You wouldn't be part of my brother's life if you were not special. But I don't need him to see that on my own. I'm a doctor. I know a lot of women are forced onto paths they would not normally have chosen."

Ione looked at their reflection in the store windows. The horse stood like a statue, and she with him, frozen by an inability to reason through the unexpected turn of their discussion. If he had thrown her out, she would have understood. But this acceptance. He simply didn't understand.

Ione needlessly dropped her voice, sensing the exposure of it all, even if no one was around to hear. "But I did choose. I left them. Everything that happened can be traced back to my poor decisions."

"You made your mother sick?" He raised his eyebrows and awaited her answer.

"Well—" Ione huffed. "Of course not."

"Then I don't see how you should be held solely accountable for it all."

"I left."

"You came back and took care of your sisters."

Ione had to look away again. "You should be courting a woman who doesn't have a past like mine."

"And who are you to tell me who I should and shouldn't spend time with?" He held up his hand to stop her from answering. "I told you what I am searching for in a woman?"

Ione nodded.

"But I didn't tell you what was not on my list." He paused. His eyes didn't read that he stopped to search for words. Rather, his soft brown eyes bored into Ione's, ensuring she truly listened. When she met his gaze, he continued. "My list didn't have a successful business owner. Or someone who is ambitious, brilliant, talented, and everything else you are."

Ione couldn't keep her own confusion from her face, but more importantly, she couldn't concentrate on anything but the entrancing way he looked down to watch as he pulled the gloves from her hand and wrapped his bare fingers around hers, lending warmth and security she had no right to want.

She found herself greedy for the contact, longing for the feel of another person's skin on hers. It was a need she never knew she had, and if she were to be honest, one she thought she would never know. Touch, for her, at least from a man, had never been about reassurance.

He continued, his soft voice and low tones coming to her in waves across the scant distance between their bodies. "Of all the things I could worry about making someone suitable or not, it wouldn't be things from their past. It would be things that could draw on our future." He shook his head and dropped a chaste kiss to the back of her knuckles.

Ione sucked in a shaky breath on the heels of the realization that she'd never actually been kissed before. Not by someone who cared. Numerous other lips had met her lips, her body, had urgently trailed across her repulsed skin, but it had been so different. There had always been a sense of an exchange. Even with Clarence. And now that she could look back, she'd known even before he'd admitted it that she had been with him because he could make money off her voice. This, though. This wasn't a trade. It wasn't a concession. It had nothing to do with what she could or could not do for him, or with the person he thought she could be. His lips, light and dry against her skin, lingering there for the briefest of moments, were there, tending to her fingers, simply because he wanted to offer comfort. Tears spilled over and ran to her chin. Touch, intimacy, had never been about comfort. It had been about needs and wants, supply and demand. He let go of one hand and shook out his handkerchief, handing it to her.

"With you..." He looked at the dark store windows. "Do you know what I thought?" He laughed, his eyes crinkling in the corners, and looked toward the moonless sky. "How in the world we would care for our children if we were both working."

Ione nearly snorted into the handkerchief.

"That's how ridiculous I am. You are sitting there, fearing my response to your past—which, by-the-by, how do you know I do not have a similar tale to tell?—and here I am, a grown man, having spent mere weeks with you, already planning our family."

They sat in silence, his hand intertwined with hers until another carriage rambled by, the drivers staring curiously behind as they moved past.

"I'd better get you home."

She nodded, unsure of what to think of the night.

When they pulled up to the store, he dropped down to the cobbles and lifted his hand to help her down. They had both slid their gloves back over their fingers, and much to her shock, Ione found she missed the feel of his skin against hers.

It was all so new. She never thought she could want a man in her life again.

But now she understood that really, this was the first time.

The morning light flooded the room. It shimmered along the edges of the glossy mahogany furniture, illuminating the room and obscuring any non-reflective surface. Miriam blinked against the onslaught and focused on her daughter. As expected, little Ava had woken every few hours to remind them both of her culinary demands. Michael rolled over onto his back, rubbed his face, and stretched out the kinks from a night of slumber, hard-earned in bits and pieces.

"Is she sleeping?" He whispered the question.

Miriam nodded. Her husband had taken up residence in her room despite her insistence on sleeping most of the night with the babe in her arms. That he thought her potentially off balance she didn't doubt. Frankly, if she were in his shoes, she might too. Equally, though, she didn't care. Nothing said he had to believe her. Nothing required more than the examination of the house that he and Mrs. Maloney had completed to make sure all was secure. And, while it irritated her that they didn't seem to think a turned baby was as much of an emergency as she did, her more reasonable side understood there were limits to the efforts one could take to ensure the safety of their family.

That didn't mean she would risk her daughter.

He turned so he could face them and reached to touch Ava's pink toes before yawning and sitting up. He dropped his feet to the floor and rubbed them against the soft carpet.

"What are your plans for the day?" He grabbed his trousers off the back of the chair and examined the ironed crease that ran down the front of the legs.

Miriam knew he waited for an answer. They never used to make up conversation where none needed to exist. What did he think she would be doing?

"I'll be here with Ava."

Michael paused. "Would you like someone to visit? I could send word to Jenny or Ione."

Miriam touched the edge of the white blanket wrapped around Ava. "We'll be fine here."

He frowned, his eyebrows coming together in soft lines of concern.

Miriam suddenly felt sorry. "Really. This is busy work. We will be fine, but for a while, don't you think Ava deserves all my attention?"

His answering glance suggested a hesitation, but the smile that didn't reach his eyes meant he would believe her or, at least, he would let them be. Swinging his jacket over his shoulder, he approached the door with hesitant steps. Hand on the knob, he turned again. "You mean everything to me. You and Ava. You know that, right?"

Miriam held her breath, the honesty of his admission harkening back to the days when she told him everything, when there were no secrets, and more importantly, no reason for secrets. And it wasn't that they had any now. She looked at her husband, at the honest blue of his eyes, knowing he examined the less-than-revealing depths of her gray gaze, and she couldn't help but feel a pang of guilt.

But then Ava squirmed in her arms. Miriam glanced down, and when she looked up again, Michael had closed the door softly behind him.

Chapter 23

With Ava in tow, Miriam closed the door to her room and walked toward the stairs. It had been days since she'd given birth, days since she'd seen the walls of a different room, and for the first time, she decided she'd grown tired of those four walls.

"What are you doing out of bed?" Sally rushed up behind her, appearing as if she were prepared to catch her when Miriam succumbed to the strains of walking.

"I can't stay in there forever," Miriam said, slowing to look at the clearly distressed maid.

"Mrs. Maloney said I was to bring whatever you needed, and you shouldn't feel like you had to get anything. She'll skin me if she knows I let you walk around without even a nurse here."

Miriam knew no one in the house had been delighted by her decision to send the nurse packing, but she simply didn't need the help. "I am perfectly capable of walking. And besides, if it's a new view I'm in search of, how exactly would you provide that?"

"I can bring you some picture books." The quick, matter-of-fact statement had the odor of desperation.

Miriam stopped and turned. Sally smiled down at Ava and reached out to let the baby's exposed fingers tighten around her own. "I'll tell Mrs. Maloney I didn't give you a choice in the matter. That you were only obeying my orders."

Sally tore her gaze away from the baby and glanced up at Miriam, clearly skeptical. "I don't think that will satisfy her. She was pretty specific."

"Well, it will just have to be, because I plan to go downstairs and at least sit by the garden windows and perhaps take a peek at some of the correspondence. It has to be building up by now."

Sally's silence only confirmed the need for her attention. She sucked in a deep, censorious breath and held it until the decision had been made. Clearly, she'd been learning the art of communication through breathing from Mrs. Maloney. "I will walk a step in front of you and hold your arm, or I'm going to call Mrs. Maloney before you can reach those stairs."

Although Miriam wasn't sure how happy she was with being parented by her maid, she capitulated with the nervous order if only to ease the distinct look of trepidation that had taken over Sally's features. "Okay. I'll follow you."

They walked toward the head of the stairs, Miriam intent on how the fountain of light from the far window played against the carpets, picking up the golds and shimmering against the reds, only to reflect off the edge of a gilt mirror and momentarily blind her. Miriam stopped, waiting for the shock of blue spots to swim out of her line of vision.

"I can take little Ava if you want." Sally reached out, and Miriam had to fight the urge not to snatch her baby to her chest. She knew offering to hold a baby was a courtesy, common amongst women, but it felt foreign, and although she knew it was ridiculous, invasive.

"I have her." Miriam blinked the last of the bright spots out of her vision and concentrated on the steps that stretched in front of them both.

A rustling at the foot of the stairs drew her attention to the men standing near the front door. Mr. Butler nodded and pointed, giving direction to the other man, Tamm.

Miriam swallowed, attempting to force the lump in her throat back down. She couldn't breathe. The dark light at the edges swam in, and

Miriam tried to shake the invasive force away, to keep it back. Ava squirmed in her tightened hold.

"Are you..."

Someone whisked her away, and the only thing Miriam could see was the red and gold as the colors rose to greet her.

The pins tucked into the corner of her mouth prevented Ione from answering the irritatingly astute question, and for that she was glad. So she hummed in agreement, partially concealed by the mannequin in front of her, and earned a knowing nod from Grace but thankfully nothing more.

Having forgotten to carry the program from the past night's symphony upstairs with her, Ione had been peppered with the inquiries for most of the morning, and so far, she'd been able to avoid answering most of them.

It wasn't that she wanted to exclude Grace from her personal life. Quite the contrary, standing next to Grace was almost as comfortable as standing next to one of her own sisters. The problem had more to do with her own lack of ability to even describe the previous night.

Yes, she'd accompanied Evan to the symphony, and yes, she'd enjoyed the time. But those broad strokes were almost untruthful in comparison to the personal disruption that had taken place. She felt the blood rush to her ears, remembering his gentle tone and the way he'd put her key into the store lock, opened the door, and bowed as he closed the door behind her, waiting outside to hear her secure the lock.

He knew. She'd told him. And he still wanted to see her. Her past, which had loomed large and ominous, barricading her own vision for her future, didn't seem to be an impediment for him. He simply stepped over the obstruction and held out a hand for her to join him on the other side.

Ione pulled a pin from between her lips and secured a scrap of fabric to the mannequin. She stood back, examined the angle of the addition, and then ripped it back off, only to miss it in the design again. Frowning, she dropped the fabric on the table next to her and sank onto the low stool.

"Guess who's here?" Grace's teasing, sing-song voice rang from around the corner.

Ione shot up, shaking the creases out of her skirts and smoothing her sleeves. She hurried to a small looking glass that hung in the back room, assessed the damage of the day, repositioned a few hair pins, and turned.

The lift of Grace's left eyebrow let Ione know she hadn't fooled her with the evasive answers. "I'll tell him you'll be right out."

Miriam fought her way out of the black sleep that had forced her to relinquish her hold on Ava and had pressed her to the hall floor. At first squeezing her eyes tightly, she then tried to open them but the sun fought back.

"Pull the drapes." Mrs. Maloney's voice whispered from far away.

A cool shade followed the shushing sound of the curtains being pulled across the heavy rods. Miriam forced her eyes open to the darkened room.

"What happened?" She tried to sit up, but hands on her shoulders held her down. "Where's Ava?"

"Right here," Michael said.

Miriam felt his weight sink against the mattress and opened her eyes to see him holding their daughter.

"Sally has been caring for her here in your room since you fainted."

"I fainted?" Miriam dragged her hand from the cocoon of blankets and rubbed her eyes. She struggled against the persistent haze, trying to piece together what had happened. "I didn't drop her?" This time she sat up too quickly for them to stop her. She took in the dark room, the brooding doctor, and the presence of an unknown face in a nurse's uniform.

Michael answered her questions before she could ask them. "You've been asleep for a couple hours now. You woke once, and the doctor recommended he give you something to help keep you calm. He also made it clear the nurse should stay this time."

She would have protested but decided it would be best to hold her tongue. What had happened anyway?

Miriam glanced at her baby, snuggled warmly in Michael's arms. She slept soundly, and Miriam fought back a pang of guilt that the one compulsion she couldn't shake was the nagging feeling that she needed to paint. Stretching her fingers against the fabric of the quilt, Miriam tried to concentrate on anything else, but the dark figure that dominated, that emerged in her dreams only to dissipate like the haze of fog when she opened her eyes, that overshadowed and threatened in a way only she seemed to notice... Miriam knew his form wouldn't emerge until she could mine the place between her wakeful hours and sleep with the colors that fell off her brush and onto her canvas.

The babe slept soundly. Could she risk it? The birth had taken place without complication. All had gone well. Her fears, the anticipation that had kept her from painting, had led her nowhere. She had a healthy child.

Miriam looked over to the disapproving expression of the doctor. His perpetually red jowls and narrow forehead did nothing to make his scowl any less obvious. The nurse he'd brought with him wasn't much of an improvement.

No. She wouldn't leave Ava in the nurse's care. And if that meant that Miriam didn't return to her studio for a while, then she would just have to think her way through the goading sense that, contrary to everything that had happened so far, something was wrong.

"I'll hold her." Miriam held out her arms and met Michael's doubtful gaze with one that communicated how little choice the rest of them had in the matter.

He surrendered Ava, earning a squeak of protest from the bundle at the momentary jumble of blankets and ruffling of her tiny world. Miriam tucked her hands into the folds and brought her close, earning a sigh from the contented child.

"The nurse is going to stay to make sure you are fine, though," Michael informed Miriam.

"But not in the room all the time." Miriam stated, never looking up from the round pink face of her daughter. "She can sit in the sitting room, and we will leave the door open, but she doesn't need to stand here staring at me the whole day long."

That the statement had been rude, Miriam knew. She could also feel the woman's frown from across the room. The grunt that emanated from the doctor communicated everything else that had been left unsaid. But Miriam didn't care. This was her baby and her house.

Michael cleared his throat and leaned in to rest his hand on his daughter's head. He let it stay there, as if he could share the warmth that flowed between Miriam and the child. Miriam hoped he could.

"We're a little nervous that you fainted…" The sentence trailed off, as if he expected Miriam to complete his thought.

She glanced up, and her resolve wavered in the heat of his blue stare over the rim of his spectacles. "I know." She whispered the words, suddenly feeling like a zoo-dwelling creature under the gaze of so many eyes in this, her bedroom, the most personal of spaces. "I think I simply stood up too quickly. I feel fine." She tried to reassure Michael the best she could. He had done nothing to earn her resentment, but keeping the baby safe was more important than any of their opinions.

One corner of Michael's mouth tucked back in a thoughtful frown, and he straightened, never taking his eyes of the pair.

"Everyone can clear out." Michael spoke quietly to Mrs. Maloney, who grunted in disagreement. "If you could make sure the nurse has everything she needs and set her up in the sitting room..." Again, the thought died away.

Mrs. Maloney offered a curt nod, avoiding the sputtering red gaze of the physician, and bustled everyone out of the room. "You call if you need anything." The pointed stare she sent to Miriam communicated she would comply, but only so far.

Miriam nodded her understanding and waited for the last person to leave before letting out the breath she'd been holding and allowing her head to fall back into the pile of pillows.

Think. She had to think. What had happened? Whatever the doctor had given her still infringed on her sense of time, and the faces of maids and nurses and servants floated in and out of memory.

But one face came to the top. Miriam clutched Ava tighter, and the baby wriggled against the violation of her space.

Tamm.

She had to think. The man had done nothing to her. He simply drove them from place to place. Why was it he unsettled her so?

Chapter 24

It had been a week since Ione had seen Evan. Only a week, and she couldn't help but wonder if he'd reconsidered.

If he had, it would only prove his intelligence, Ione reasoned, fighting back the stab of disappointment. She toyed with the idea of visiting the Whitakers, of fabricating some sort of excuse for needing to see her sisters, but decided against the notion. They would immediately see through even the most casual of questions.

He'd said he would be busy setting up the office. And he'd been excited, promising her a tour of the new practice once the cleaning and general spiffing up had been accomplished.

Ione walked in the nighttime darkness of her shop, remembering her first nights alone in the place. The opening had gone well, customers filled the store, cards and congratulations poured in for weeks—mostly from acquaintances borrowed from Miriam and Beatrice—but nonetheless, it had been a success to begin with and continued to grow. She hoped Evan would have such a welcome.

She glanced out to the dark street, to the lamp that burned in front of her shop. No one mulled about. And she hadn't heard from Clarence. The window had been fixed, and the rest of her life returned to normal. Except, of course, for Evan.

She turned back to the shop and closed her eyes, taking in the scent of fabric and paper and perfume. Of all the luxuries now at her disposal, the one that still surprised her was how a bit of money in her pocket made the world smell sweet.

The rustling of skirts alerted Miriam to the fact that she was not alone in her room. The nurse Michael and Mrs. Maloney had hired refused to leave, and even now, in the early morning hours, she bustled in and out of the room, dragging Miriam's resentment and appreciation from one side of the house to the other.

In some ways, Miriam couldn't help but marvel at the dour woman's efforts. Ava's needs came before anything else, including Miriam's wishes. If Ava required sleep, Miriam would be tasked with correspondence. If Ava squirmed as the result of a soggy bottom, the nurse whisked her away before Miriam could think of attending to her.

The help did allow for more sleep, but sometimes, in the night, Miriam simply wanted to hold the child. And that grew more impossible with each day.

"How are you feeling this morning? I think John is stopping by." Michael ducked his head into the room.

"I feel fine. Like I do every morning." Miriam threw off the blankets and didn't attempt to mask her irritation at the necessity of answering the same question multiple times every day. She sat up, taking in the pink light of early morning, and swung her legs over the edge of the bed, glancing around the room for the new cradle that Michael had ordered.

Nothing else had happened in the past week. Ava had woken the same way she'd slept, and Miriam couldn't help but consider the possibility that she might have imagined the entire incident. Mrs. Maloney had warned her that childbirth did strange things to a woman. But being wrong, when she'd been so convinced that she'd been right...well, the prospect was frightening.

Ava let out a soft mewling sound from her cradle, and the nurse popped into the room.

"You take your time and get ready for the day. I'll send Sally in to help." She reached down and plucked Ava from the tangle of blankets, holding her close. "I'll take Ava to the nursery and get her washed for the day."

Miriam nodded, trying not to be resentful of the woman for her obviously superior skill. "Will you bring her back?" Miriam asked, not really knowing how to say she wanted her baby without sounding like the weak person the rest of the household must think she'd already become.

"Certainly, dear." The nurse aimed a smile Miriam knew was intended to reassure her, but only succeeded in making her feel like a child herself.

And then Miriam stood there, alone.

She couldn't have been that wrong. She crossed to the still-closed curtains, grasped a fringed edge, and pulled them open. The people below rushed to accomplish their duties for the day, never considering that someone above them, someone with nothing pressing to do, watched them and wondered about their lives. Did the women have children at home? Had they also been so weak to have imagined threats around every corner?

She closed the curtain again, pulling it tight, making sure to fold one panel over the other so the line of light that tried to burn into her room had no path with which to do so. She blinked, waiting for her eyes to readjust to the dark, again leached of all color but the persistent pink hues won by the efforts of the sun through the drapes.

Deciding on her favorite pale green dress, Miriam wriggled into the garment and fastened the row of cloth-covered buttons that ran from just below her collar bone to the band that hugged her rib cage. In some ways, her body still thought it was with child; Miriam breathed easily in the style, grateful for the empire waist Ione had insisted she'd want even after the baby. Again, her friend had been right.

Her desk downstairs was heaped with correspondence. She looked at the closed door and considered how many people she would have to face simply to accomplish the task of getting to the parlor. Shoving her hands into the deep pockets of her skirt, Miriam troubled her bottom lip with the edge of her teeth before picking up her comb. While still standing, she ripped through the tangles, watching the door in case the nurse decided to return unexpectedly. First piling the mass atop her head and securing it with pins, Miriam finally turned to the hidden door that almost couldn't be made out from the patterned wallpaper. While keeping an eye out, she pushed against the opening until it eased back enough for her to feel for the hidden latch.

Then she disappeared into the passageway beyond.

Light wasn't necessary; she knew the tunnels and narrow halls with the roughhewn floors better than those that boasted plush rugs, marble, and warm, smooth wood in the main areas of the house.

But she only had to let the door close her into the dark space before the stench of death invaded her lungs. The still air of the empty space usually carried a hint of turpentine and the dusty reminder of an old library. Miriam gagged and lifted her sleeve to press against her nose. Had she known something was amiss, she wouldn't have filled her nostrils with anticipation of the familiar scent.

Now she stood, regretting the previous few seconds, and wondered what she should do.

After ducking back into her room to pull a wide scarf from the collection that hung at the back of her armoire, she filled her lungs and dove back into the rancid air.

She'd secured the fabric around her face with a bulging knot. Michael would have left already, and although Mrs. Maloney knew of the spaces, she didn't use them. If at the very least Miriam could find the poor creature, then she could have Mrs. Maloney send someone in to remove it. She frowned at the thought of allowing access to her private spaces, but this—she suppressed a gag at the hint of rot that made its way through her scarf—this, she couldn't manage on her own. Miriam felt for the candle and matchsticks she kept on a small wall-mounted shelf to the left of the door. Striking the match against the rough wall, she watched the flame swell against the blackness with trumpet-like indiscretion, and then concede to the gloom with a steady inch-long flame.

The first step was the most difficult. Miriam reminded herself of the phrase she used to repeat when she'd walked the night-fogged streets down by the docks. This was her own space. Her home. But her feet remained firmly planted as the tang of death worked through the weave of her scarf. It had to be a mouse nearby. The rooms had all been carefully constructed and sealed off from these areas. Nothing so big as a rat, or even a feline, could weasel into the passageways. A mouse, however, she could believe. It was a near impossibility to seal every crack that could be breached by one of those tiny creatures.

Fairy tales of mice who lived in the walls—of tiny homes, of sprites, and mythical tiny people—sprang up to make the first step a bit easier. She lifted a foot and eased it forward, choosing to focus on the less disturbing of the ridiculous childhood tales meant to explain the inexplicable occurrences that happened in every house. Miriam smiled and took another step. Maybe the things she'd noticed were the result of their own mouse folk. Maybe she wasn't overly sensitive due to the birth of her daughter and Michael hadn't been ignoring her concerns. Maybe the fairies had visited, had played with the new child, had lifted her and set her down the opposite way.

Miriam watched the line where the wall met the floor, hoping, in some ways, to spot a small door with a tiny knob and a rug the size of a postage stamp. Soon, though, the odor overpowered the abilities of even Miriam's imagination, and she dove forward, hand pressing the scarf tight to her face, warily scanning the hall that stretched into the blackness.

Michael skipped up the steps and ducked into the cool relief of the cathedral. Sun flooded through the stained glass, pooling and rippling against the dark stone floors. It wasn't the first time he wondered at the intentionality of the design. Sure, the space towered as expected, and the high wood beams of the ornate ceiling, nearly black with age, displayed the objects of the parishioner's devotion, but the truth of the place went beyond that of observation and fell into that of experience.

And that—Michael slid his hat off and brushed the dust from the crown—made sense. After all, one went to church to gain an expanded understanding of purpose and life. That a place should be designed with every sense in mind, that it should be pleasing to the eyes and the ears, that sound should move inexplicably, echoing whispers of adoration while absorbing cries of distress, that light turned to water, and with a blessing, water became holy, all made sense.

Michael sank into the last pew, listening for the footsteps he knew would eventually pass by. He concentrated on his own breathing, on taking in and expelling the still air of the place that smelled like restoration, if a thing like that were possible. He would have to ask John if even air could be blessed, and if so, could simply walking into the place of worship have the power to change the way a person felt? Could the involuntary movement of a man's lungs take a man a step closer to peace? A tiny reward for the sometime monumental humbling it took to enter a place where even the simple act of ascending the stairs meant something in their life needed to change.

And—Michael frowned and glanced down to his hands—that was precisely why he'd come. Something was not right with Miriam.

He steepled his fingers, measuring the distance from thumb to pinky. His shoes shined against the backdrop of the stone floor. Michael took a deep breath in and held it until familiar footsteps made their way down the aisle.

"What's the latest?" John slid into the pew next to Michael, not bothering to meet his gaze. They both stared straight ahead at the crucifix.

Michael slouched down, and looked at the paintings overhead. "Miriam is having difficulty adjusting."

"To what?"

Michael could now feel John's eyes bore into the side of his face, but he blinked away the feeling that he should return his gaze and continued to examine the play of colors overhead. "She stopped painting—a while ago, really, when the baby became a reality. She never said it, but I think she feared anything negative that her painting might reveal."

"That makes sense." John abandoned his attempt to have a face-to-face conversation and watched the slow path of an old woman who had entered behind Michael and now made her way to the front of the sanctuary.

"A while back, Miriam thought an intruder had somehow made it into our home and turned the baby." Michael now turned to his friend, waiting for him to acknowledge the strangeness of that day.

"You were telling me about that before."

Michael frowned and nodded. "I don't think she's been able to get past the feeling of someone watching her."

John's eyebrows pulled together, and concerned lines formed in the center.

"We had to insist she allow the nurse to stay, and if Ava is out of sight for more than a few minutes, she starts pacing around the room like a caged lion." Michael rubbed his face with both hands and sat up, leaning forward to continue. "It's as if she thinks we are all out to do the child harm and only she is capable of watching over her." Michael closed his eyes and then opened them to look directly into John's. "It's as if she no longer trusts anyone."

"Would you?" John shrugged, the movement barely visible under the shroud of robes.

"Of course I would believe her." Michael shook his head, no longer trying to lessen the display of frustration.

"I don't think you would."

Michael eyed his friend.

"Think about it. You found your child in a position you did not leave her in, and no one else admits to moving her. How patient would you be?"

Michael looked down at his folded hands and then back up at the stained glass. The setting sun had changed the colors that fell to the floor, darkened them, deepened the shadows, obscured the lines between the stones so that the floor looked like one dark pool. "But no one was there. No one saw anything. She's wrong."

John stood again, but stayed, letting his presence act as a mild accusation. He looked down at Michael. "What you mean is you *hope* she's wrong."

Chapter 25

Miriam leaned against the rough wall in the unfinished, hidden place behind the kitchen. The dried plaster, hardened after oozing between the lath, scraped through her sweat-dampened dress. Not every hall had been meant for her mother to use, not every passageway had been intended to cater to a wandering path. But the odor continued to intensify as the heat near the working part of the house swelled with the late-day summer sun.

She'd become accustomed to the stench and abandoned her scarf over a railing in hopes of finding a non-existent cool breeze. This, though, leaning against the wall, staring into the comfort of a single flame and wasting time, was getting her nowhere. And Ava was still in the care of the nurse, not her mother.

Miriam kicked up from her slouched position and continued forward into the one area of the house she typically avoided. The space between the kitchens and the hidden entrance to the basement also provided access to the garden, her garden, that tucked between the townhouses. That door, recessed into the brick wall and hidden from the outside by vines and the tangle of strategically placed plants, had never been intended for use. It was smaller than a typical door, and an entrance Miriam suspected her mother never knew about. She placed her hand against the rough barrier to the garden, felt the cool damp and mossy edges of brick against old wood. She dropped her gaze to the floor, to the indent where the door met the wall, and lowered the candle to examine the partial circle scraped into the dust and wood.

Someone had opened the door. Recently.

The flame flickered, and Miriam concentrated on not dropping the sweat-slicked candle holder. She took in a deep breath of the stagnant, death-laden air and examined the evidence that someone had gained access to the space. Miriam straightened, lifting the shaking flame, trying to remember where she'd left her keys, what doors she'd locked and which ones she'd left open. The flame leaned and grew. An imperfection in the wick made the light intensify and spark against the black tunnel that could now hold anything. She reached forward into the inky darkness, hoping to find nothing.

And then she saw it. The source of the heavy stench. The odor she knew would follow her for days. A cat, one of the kitchen cats, by the amber and black coloring of her rotting coat, hung, midair, from a tangle of cords. The lifeless head listed at an unnatural angle, its neck snapped and stretched. The small cat's tail hung straight, dropping between the extended hind legs. It was the gaze of the dead eye, though, that Miriam couldn't look away from. The clouded orb, sunken into the shrinking skull, white with time, stared nowhere. The once golden marble that peered around corners and hunted crickets and mice, was now shrouded with the haze of death.

Fear did not overwhelm Miriam, and as her heart slowed until its beat was almost imperceptible, she wondered at the justice of an organ that demonstrated its newfound lack of purpose, as if once the life leached from the body, someone closed the curtains of the window.

The odor faded, and Miriam had the sense of the single flame falling through the darkness, its light dimming with distance. And then the cool hard floor met her cheek, and for that, she was grateful.

Michael sat back, heedless of the rocking motion of the carriage, and considered his conversation with John.

She couldn't have been right. *Oh, God.* Michael pulled the brim of his hat down to cover his eyes. He hoped she wasn't.

But John had asked the simple question. The question Michael had ignored. When had she ever been wrong? Most of what they'd gone through, her paintings had predicted. They'd trusted that gift and followed her visions, and those paintings that made no sense had led them into and then out of some of the darkest places he'd ever seen. Together, they'd saved women at the mercy of a predator, and they'd followed Miriam's path through the labyrinthine Dunning basement. Now, because she'd simply had a child, because her body had performed the function it was intended to perform, he'd diminished her concerns.

What if John's question held warrant?

Michael pushed the brim of his hat back up and watched the other carriages speed past. He fought the urge to tap the roof and signal Tamm to pick up the pace a bit. At this time of morning, the city traffic accomplished little but frustration. Negligence was not at play. Michael tapped out an uncertain rhythm against the window ledge, hoping to reach Miriam in time. The blood drained from his face. He should never have left her. He closed his eyes, imagining Miriam lying in bed, holding their child, and how he would apologize to her for listening to the doctor and his incessant talk about the fragility of women.

The truth was, he wanted to believe what the doctor had said. He'd wanted the luxury of a nurse, of a rested wife. And he'd gone quite the distance to do everything he could to make sure their life stayed as simple as possible after the birth of their child.

But life with Miriam had never been simple. Instead it had been about trusting her, about believing her and having faith that if something didn't make sense now, it would soon. Michael's fingers froze an inch above the window ledge, hovering there, waiting. The carriage rocked and the street noise faded away. If she had been right all along, if someone had turned Ava, if...*if.*

Michael was left with the unease that came after waking from a disturbing dream whose details were still lost in the world of the sleeping. Like a sense of danger while standing in a sunny field.

Michael gave up and banged against the roof. He had to get home now.

Ione could do precisely nothing about the idiotic grin on her face. If she tried to control it, she looked dour at best. If she simply smiled, she appeared to be in need of psychiatric assistance. So she unlocked the door for Grace with smile fully ablaze and hoped for the best.

It lasted all of one second.

"Good heavens. Sent a note, did he?" Grace laughed and dropped her handbag behind the counter before pulling the pins out of her delicate hat and settling it on the sturdy, serviceable hat tree in the back room.

Ione couldn't even frown at her own transparency. So instead, she nodded and produced the note from the deep pocket of her working apron.

Grace read it, and Ione could tell when she reached the last sentence, the one that said he hoped she might agree to his picking her up this evening so he could show her the progress on his office. "Isn't tonight when you have dinner with your sisters?"

"Keep reading." The post script said they would go together, and Ione felt more secure about her ability to keep from crying if Grace read it instead of her relaying the information.

"Ah." Grace folded the note and held it back out for Ione to take. "I assume you are pleased?" she teased.

That earned a frown. But it was short lived, and Ione had to turn away to keep from being embarrassed by the brevity.

In truth, the evening before she'd thought she had come to terms with the possibility that he might never call again. And even though sleep had eluded her for most of the night, and she'd met the morning with a scowl, she'd still looked forward to opening her store and greeting her customers.

That, of course, all changed the second she'd walked downstairs and saw the envelope lying against the pink carpet. Her heart had pounded like it had no right to when she'd picked up the note and saw Evan's tiny neat script. And only now did she realize she hadn't even considered the possibility it might have been from Clarence.

Ione smiled up at Grace. "Do you want to rearrange the samples this morning or dust the cases?"

"I'll take the cases." Grace shook her head. "I know you and I are the only ones who typically pull the samples off the wall, but I can't figure out how they get to be such a mess. I'd rather dust hat pins, individually, than tackle that wall again."

Ione laughed, shocking herself at the unhindered sound.

Grace didn't comment and instead reached to remove the items from the uppermost shelves.

Ione turned, wondering what she would wear tonight.

Chapter 26

Michael jumped down from the carriage before it had stopped in front of their home. He took the steps two at a time and ran into Mrs. Maloney.

"We don't know where she is."

Michael towered over the woman, not even attempting to keep the fire from his eyes. "Miriam?"

She nodded. Strands of her typically secured gray hair clung to her neck. They had obviously been searching for a while.

"How long has she been gone?"

"I'm not sure." Mrs. Maloney lowered her voice. "Do you think she might have left?"

"Where's Ava?"

"With the nurse." The concrete in her tone spoke of conversations he'd not been part of, but could trust had happened, nonetheless. Without a doubt, the nurse had been given strict instructions to keep her eye on the baby at all times.

"Have you checked her studio? Her mother's library?" Michael shrugged out of his jacket and tossed it onto a chair, completely ignoring Mr. Butler, who had been holding out his arms to receive the garment. "The sun room at the top of the house? Sometimes she likes to be up there." His outer clothes slid off the chair and onto the floor, where they were left to fend for themselves while Mr. Butler informed the concerned cook of the latest news.

"Yes. Every place she typically disappears to." Mrs. Maloney looked near tears.

Michael leaned in close, wishing he could calm his voice but knowing he failed miserably at the attempt. "Did anyone check the attic or the basement?"

Mrs. Maloney and Mr. Butler exchanged glances and took off in opposite directions. Michael crossed to the phone they'd installed the previous year in the front hall and rang the operator to request a call be put in to the warehouse. Jenny would need to get a message to John. The priest needed to know of Miriam's disappearance.

John's eyes flicked to the hidden entrance to the left of the towering parlor fireplace. Had it been less than two years since he and Michael had first followed Miriam through the narrow corridors filled with oddities and unexpected turns? He felt decades older. "You're sure they've checked all the places?"

"All the ones I know about." Michael slammed the cover of Miriam's roll-top desk closed and paced to the glass doors that overlooked the garden tucked between their townhouse and the next.

John joined his friend and stood sentry next to him, waiting to see what his duty would be. When a parishioner came to him in pain or with a problem, his task was simple: comfort. But when it was a friend, family really, the act of comforting felt weak, insufficient, and pale. He clenched his hands to resist the urge to rest one on Michael's shoulder.

The brick walls outside the doors stretched up, the resulting box at once unsettling and indulgent in its pretense of safety. The thick green vines covered one wall in a lush carpet, while the gardener kept the others ripped clean as best he could. "It's hard to believe there's no door to this place other than this one." John craned his neck skyward. "It almost feels dangerous to build a brick room with only one way out."

Michael looked at him, and then back at the cascade of searching vines.

Wordlessly, they stepped out of the house and into the garden, Michael one pace ahead, and made their way to the obscured wall.

John watched his friend reach into the vines, his arm disappearing to the elbow. When Michael pushed his other hand into the mass, John duplicated the efforts and dove into the cool, damp cloak of vegetation.

It felt like night.

John fought the desire to take his hands away, to raise them to the sun, to warm them in the deep pockets of his robe, but one glance at the growing desperation on Michael's face, and instead, John closed his fingers around the tender growth and ripped.

Together, they tore at the wall, at the helplessness of a missing wife, at the hopelessness of insecurity and fear and the control that stayed just beyond their grasp. Leaves floated to the ground in a snow of desperation. Crushed and torn, they covered the grass in bruised mounds until both he and Michael stood in front of an unanticipated door, ankle deep in the waste.

The thick wood, narrow, blackened with age and damp couldn't have been more than five feet high.

"Who was this made for?" John bent his knees, estimating how much shorter he'd have to be in order to go through the opening.

Michael stood still, eyes wide, his breathing imperceptible.

"Where do you think this leads?" John lowered his voice to a whisper, trying to ease Michael back to a reality where his wife still existed, where the only bad things were still trapped in their minds. "This is good news. We now have another place to look."

Michael reached out to the ancient looking latch.

John knew the house wasn't that old. It had been built by Miriam's father. But the sense that they were about to step through to something else, into a wonderland, had John fighting the urge to pull his friend back into the patch of grass that still glowed with the warmth of the sun.

The rusted lock squealed in protest to Michael's efforts but finally gave way, and Michael pushed the door into a dark cavern, only to be greeted by the stench of rotting flesh and the damp, stagnant feel of an untended cellar.

"Let me go first." John put his hand on Michael's arm but was shrugged off as Michael pushed the swollen door farther into the space.

There was no telling who saw it first—Miriam's softly slippered foot, stretched out from her body, sprawled across the dirty floor.

A strangled sound escaped from Michael as he put his shoulder to the door and shoved and then stood back to make way for John's huge boot. They worked at the door, one after another for a few seconds until finally, Michael could squeeze through the opening.

"She's breathing," he called over his shoulder. "Go and get help. We have to get her out of here."

John heard the directions called out from behind. He'd already reached the glass doors and was shouting for Mr. Butler and anyone else who would listen.

Ione turned around in the middle of the newly decorated room. "It's amazing."

Evan smiled in response. His fisted hands were shoved deep in his trouser pockets, forcing his shoulders into a perpetual shrug. "I hoped you'd like it. Evangeline helped with the colors and things." He pulled his hands out and took a step nearer. "Hopefully, I'll open the doors in another week or so. I'm expecting some equipment from the old hospital, and by then my things from back east should be here."

"Have you spent any time at the hospital yet?" Ione hadn't been there, but she'd heard a lot about it. It had been largely furnished by donations from some of the wealthier families in town and had been a project that the ladies of Pastor Whitaker's congregation had taken on with alacrity.

"A bit. Just a tour of the place and a few meetings." Evan leaned against the newly installed desk and crossed one long leg over the other. Ione couldn't help but notice the shine on his black shoes. The man was always well groomed. She tried to make the detail unimportant but couldn't help but feel a jolt of pride that they would walk out the front door together.

There were two kinds of dressing up: the comfortable kind and the nervous kind. And she'd known both.

Ione smiled at Evan as he gestured for her to lead the way back out of the office. The comfortable kind of dressed up was how they were now. They could afford the clothes they wore. Looking nice hadn't involved sacrifice, and nothing rode on their success. With the uncomfortable kind, no amount of perfume could mask the mix of anticipation and quiet defiance that accompanied the task. Until her life had changed, it was the only kind she'd known. She'd dressed in her Sunday best and prayed no one knew of their family's poverty. She'd slipped on costume jewelry and sought out the shadowed corners of the room so Clarence would be esteemed at the tables. She'd sewn together scraps of cheap fabric with reused lining so when Clarence wanted her to sing, the patrons would assume the act was one of pleasure and not one born of the need to keep them at the bar for one more drink in hopes of a larger cut for the evening. And then she'd dressed up, covered the holes with ribbons, dyed the worn spots so when she wandered the dark streets, someone would still want her.

"Where are you?" The protective flutter of his touch on her elbow brought Ione back.

She smiled up at him. "I like your shoes."

Evan laughed. "Thank you. I like them too."

One of the church ladies, a portly woman in a dress and a corset that worked for its keep, winked as she passed the two of them. Ione fought the urge to grit her teeth. Evan, however, had the opposite response and let his smile shine on the woman so she preened like a peacock in a rare spot of sun.

Ione watched him until he turned back to her. "You really shouldn't encourage them."

"Why ever not?" Evan easily turned Ione so that they headed down the street to a waiting hack. "I wonder what's for dinner." He changed the subject but not the conspiratorial smile.

Ione let him get away with it. Besides, she didn't have an answer.

Chapter 27

Miriam woke, once again, surrounded by people who under normal circumstances would not be populating her bedroom. She supposed that was how one could gauge the severity of a situation, by how many people were in places where they didn't belong.

She suppressed the urge to moan and forced the puzzle pieces back into place before her keepers realized she'd roused.

She'd been walking with a candle in the dark. Miriam wiggled her toes; someone had removed her house slippers. It had been the tunnels, the places she never wandered. Everything flooded back as she became aware of the lingering scent of death. She scrambled up only to feel hands at her shoulders forcing her down. This time, she fought.

"There was a dead cat," she tried to explain to the wary pairs of eyes. "I could smell it. I went looking."

"We found you unconscious again." Michael eased down next to Miriam on the mattress.

She could feel his weight and wanted to turn to the warmth that she knew she would feel the second he held her, but she resisted the urge to sink her forehead into his shoulder, to find comfort when no one else knew that danger lurked.

"Where is Ava?" She sprang from the bed, clutching the coverlet to her chest and darting toward the door.

"You need to get back into that bed," the doctor commanded, his dour, pale expression looming in front of her. The nurse took a few steps to the side, hands on hips, effectively blocking her path to the hall.

Miriam looked down to where Michael's gentle hand wrapped around her forearm. She could see his strong fingers, sense the tension there, was subject to the restriction as he tugged her back to bed, but she couldn't feel him. She couldn't feel a thing. "Where is Ava?"

The doctor's frown deepened, if such a thing were even possible. The dark lines chiseled down from either side of his wet lips reached into his jowls, turning him into some sort of fat skeleton. If she painted him, if she were painting right now, the dominant color would be brown. But not the kind of brown that spoke of rich broth or fertile soil. No. The kind a well-fed, lazy spider wore as it waited for its dinner to wear itself out.

"She needs to be back in bed." He pointed. "And dear—"

The effect of the unwarranted pet name was immediate. Miriam shook free of Michael's grasp and swung around to face the doctor.

"Ahem. Yes. Mrs. Farling. I think it would be best if you had a few days away from the child."

Miriam laughed. Actually laughed. She could hear it coming from her at his absurd suggestion, and she knew she had made the sound, but the guttural, low chuckle was so unlike anything she'd ever before heard. She took a deep breath in and then a step nearer to the doctor, releasing her breath in a slow hiss. "You will remove yourself from this house immediately. I do not want you here. I do not want to see you again."

"Miriam," Michael warned.

She ignored his suggestion of civility. "And if you don't tell me where Ava is this minute..." She let the warning die off as he backed near the door, his pale skin now blotched with red welts that had risen from his collar nearly to his yellowed, bald scalp.

"She's resting in your sitting room." The nurse followed Miriam's gaze to the partially opened door.

"At least sit for a minute." Michael steered her toward the small round stool of her dressing table and forced her to sit.

Miriam avoided the mirror. She hadn't looked in days. Hadn't cared in days. The only thing that mattered was Ava. "Are you trying to keep me from seeing her?"

Michael took a step back, shaking his head. "No." He dropped to his knees onto the carpet next to Miriam's feet. "No." He waved the rest of the people out of the room.

Miriam watched her hands. Watched how they were gripped together until the nails turned white. Watched how her dress, still scuffed, still dirty, cradled them between her knees. "Then why isn't she here?"

"I'll get her for you in a minute." Michael eased his large hands over hers, slowly, like the first time they touched, when she would jump at the novel feel of his skin on hers.

The silence stretched. "What happened?" To her, to him, to them... how had they arrived here, together but equally alone? She couldn't find words for the bigger questions.

"I'm not sure."

Miriam could feel his eyes on her. She looked up to meet his gaze. The warm blue of his eyes melted the ice from her spine, and she sagged into the cushion. "I'm tired."

"I'm sorry."

Miriam nodded. She knew. He was sorry for not believing her, but she couldn't blame him. She wouldn't have believed her own story had she not been the one to experience it.

"I..." The setting sun reflected off the table top, and Miriam squinted, glancing over the mirror and the comb of her grooming set. She jerked away from the light, tipping the chair in a haste to get as far from the table as she could.

"What?" Michael caught her and lifted her to her feet.

But her knees wobbled. She couldn't stand. "Ava... Please..." She had to keep her safe from whomever had rummaged in the garbage bin and retrieved the brush, only to lay it back on her table.

This time, though, there was not one black hair. This time a thick mat of long black strands curled around the soft bristles. This time, there was no mistake.

Dark colors swirled in and out of Miriam's vision. First blocking Michael, then the bed. She wanted to paint this person, needed to find out who would kill cats and move babies, and why. Her fingers trembled with the realization that she'd rather risk seeing a pain-filled future than live without knowing who could so easily move in and out of their lives, wishing them evil.

Michael's concerned pale-blue eyes hovered over her. He lifted her, helped her back to the bed. She'd been a fool. She should have been braver, painted what she'd felt, or said something earlier and insisted she had not lost her mind like they'd all thought.

Michael barked orders as her room whirled and she was pushed into the warmth of the bed. His incomprehensible words swam about in the twisting, ringing mess of colors and darkness and sound as Miriam struggled to stay upright.

Then a pillow cushioned her head, cradled her neck, seduced her into that place without conflict, but at least this time she knew by his tone that finally, finally, he understood.

Miriam forced her eyes to meet Michael's. "Did you see the cat?"

Michael frowned, the lines between his brows deepening, and nodded.

Miriam breathed out, closing her eyes for the briefest of seconds before shaking off the black that hovered at the outside fringe of her vision. He believed her.

The tiny yard next to the parsonage, bursting with perennials and carefully placed pots of every kind of herb and vegetable one could think to use in a stew, had been lit by candles in glass jars, the ambient light from the lace-curtained kitchen window, and fireflies who had lost their way. The oak tree hung heavily with the dark wet of early summer green. The scent of brown-butter-glazed spice cake mingled with the fresh scent of growing things, frosting over the other city odors until the six who surrounded the little round garden table laughed and teased with an abandon and single-mindedness Ione had thought had been reserved for fairy tales and love stories.

She snuck a glance at Evan, seated at the place that had become his, and then at her sisters. Maggie had carried the white china from the kitchen, the dessert forks chiming against the plates and coffee cups. She sat next to Mrs. Whitaker, glowing with the lasting effects of Ione's praise for the whimsical table setting. Pastor Whitaker laughed lightly at one of Lucy's jokes and pulled her chair closer so he could rest his arm behind her. Lucy preened with the attention, correcting her posture and sitting as ladylike as possible for a child whose feet still dangled over the hard-packed gravel that made up the makeshift dining room floor.

And then she felt it. Pastor and Mrs. Whitaker had turned their heads to watch as a fine carriage with two well-groomed teams of horses ambled down the street, and Evan had made use of the distraction to slide his hand over hers and squeeze. He let go before the carriage disappeared and Pastor and Mrs. Whitaker returned their attentions to the table, but for those few seconds, Ione forgot how to breathe.

She looked up at the sky, at the early few stars that made it through the lavender and past the lights from the neighbor's windows and the lamps that were just now flickering to life. "I should walk you home soon." Evan had leaned in close enough for Ione to feel his warm breath against the exposed skin on the curve of her ear, and she had to fight the urge to turn into him, to forget that they sat at a table with their families, to let her head fall back to rest on his shoulder. Because until the past couple of weeks, she'd never expected that she might experience that delicious luxury of weakness, of leaning on another person. That she might have a chance to live the privileged life of a woman who didn't always have to be the strong one had been a desire long ago dismissed.

She looked back into his warm brown eyes and nodded that yes, she did need to get home soon. Her store opened early on Saturdays, by appointment only, but tomorrow was booked.

"I think we'll be on our way." Evan nodded to his brother and eased his chair back. Once standing, he held out his hand for Ione and nodded to Mrs. Whitaker with a few more niceties. A hug from Lucy and a smile from Maggie, and then the white gate snapped closed behind them and they made their way.

After they turned the corner, their pace slowed, and Evan tucked her hand into the crook of his arm. But instead of letting her fingers go, he held them there to soak in the warmth of his palm.

Ione looked up from where his hand covered hers and met his gaze. The street was empty, the sounds from the day had died into the cobbles, and they stood alone, listening to each other breathe, resisting the pull to be closer.

"I missed you this week," Evan whispered, his eyes rippling over every inch of her face.

Ione felt like she was being memorized. Nothing existed outside the two of them and the slow drip of a drainpipe trickling from someplace nearby. Her throat swelled and words failed her, so she nodded that yes, she'd missed him too.

He nodded again, the color of his eyes shifting to honey, and took a step to the side. "I should get you home." His voice had deepened, grown rough at the edges, and his hand, still resting protectively over Ione's, trembled slightly.

They walked in silence, an unspoken agreement to shield the tactile sensitivity that neither was ready to admit to feeling but both were unwilling to lose.

Rounding the final corner, their steps slowed almost to a stop until they were upon her doorstep and the only thing left to do was let go.

Evan shifted his hand over hers, but instead of pulling back, he lifted her palm and intertwined his fingers with hers. Ione could feel his pulse race against her own and, unable to lift her eyes to meet his, watched his chest expand against the sudden lack of air they both suffered. She knew he could see the same effects, mirrored by her own inability to breathe evenly.

And then he let go of her fingers, allowed the cool air to slip between their heated skin, and Ione fought the disappointment for the second it took him to run his thumb over the back of her hand, encircle the fine bones of her wrist, and slowly drag her hand so it rested against his pounding heart.

"I hope you will let me call on you tomorrow evening." He did nothing to mask the pleading tone, and Ione couldn't help but smile at the vocal evidence of the way she felt.

"Yes." She nodded.

And with that, he let go, holding out his hand for her key, turning it in the lock, opening the door for her, and then watching from the other side of the window as she locked it from the inside.

Safely behind glass, she met his gaze. It said everything she thought she'd never know.

"Bring her to me now." Miriam kept her voice low. She would not lose consciousness again. She would not let whomever this was destroy her family and convince everyone she'd lost her mind.

Michael nodded, stood, and with concern still troubling the corner of the small smile he offered, made his way to the other room. Miriam felt sorry—he knew nothing of the brush or of her feelings—but there was no time. She needed to get to the studio. She had to find out what was going on, and the only way she could work through it was with her paintbrush in hand. She knew that now.

And now that she'd decided to paint, she could hardly keep her mind from the task. Thoughts of bottles and rags and paint-splashed floors had her nearly giddy with anticipation. She could move Ava's cradle upstairs with her. Summer allowed for the windows to be open, so the odor of the paints shouldn't be overwhelming. She glanced to the windows. It had grown dark. Night approached, and she was ready.

"Mrs. Maloney?" Michael called from the other room.

Miriam paused. The tone of his voice raised the tiny hairs at the nape of her neck. Goose flesh started at her shoulders and spread down her arms like blooming lichen on a tree. Miriam stood stock still, waiting for Michael's next words.

"Mrs. Maloney?" This call rang louder, echoing down the hall and back into their room.

Miriam's feet grew roots. She couldn't move. Michael didn't have the same problem, though. His steps, fast and efficient, nearly ran to the top of the stairs, where he called Mrs. Maloney, John, and anyone else who might still be wandering the house.

Chapter 28

She knew what had happened even before Michael ran back into the room. "Has anyone left yet? The nurse or the doctor?"

Michael shook his head, the color leaching from his face.

"We need to search. Everywhere."

He nodded and unbuttoned the cuffs of his shirt, rolling up his sleeves. Miriam calmly picked up her already dirt-streaked slippers and tugged them over her feet. "We'll start at the top, in the attic, and work our way down."

"Do you think it will be faster if we have John and the others start in the basement?"

Miriam shook her head and struck a match under the lip of her dresser. She touched the flame to the lamp, turned the light up as far as she could without causing it to smoke in protest, and led the way into the hall.

That Ava was no longer in their home, she had no doubt. She didn't know how she knew it, and she wouldn't speak it out loud, but it was almost as if her decision to paint again had opened up her mind to what was really happening.

They still had to search, though. They had to cover every inch of the place, because the faster they could do so, the sooner they could send for the police and report her missing.

She fought the anger that accompanied the thought of the police moving through her house again. The last time, they'd not been welcome; when Ione and Jenny had most needed protection, they'd invaded. Unfortunately, Miriam knew that few options were available for a case like theirs. She led the way into the hall and toward the stairs that rose to the third story and eventually, the attic.

John, Mrs. Maloney, and the doctor and nurse, met them at the base of the stairs. Michael breathlessly described their plan to an audience of worried glances and the tear-stained face of the nurse, and they began the search.

Miriam heard Ava's cry everywhere—in the high-pitched disappointment of Mrs. Maloney's sighs, in the squeal of a seldom-used door in need of grease, in the whisper of a rushing maid, in the silence of her secret rooms. The sound would echo and Miriam would turn her head toward it, only to have it fade into nothing. She heard Ava's cry from every direction, and from nowhere she could reach.

What seemed like hours later, Miriam sat, her arms strangely light, and stared at the police officer as he spoke in hushed tones to her husband.

Ione rolled over under her covers and stretched in the still-warm cocoon. He said he'd call on her again today. She smiled even before her eyes were open.

After a luxuriously unhindered yawn—there were some benefits to living alone—she cracked one lid up and gauged the level of light in the room. Still early morning, still well before she would open the doors.

Kicking the blankets back, Ione considered bathing. She fumbled around for her house shoes, slipped them on, and then tied on her robe before making her way to the washroom.

Not everyone had indoor plumbing. Most of the country folks still used outhouses, and while they were growing more and more rare in the city as large numbers of families converted unused closets with the addition of toilets, warm and cold running water at the twist of a knob was still a luxury. Ione turned the cool metal and thrust her hands under the flow, suppressing an appreciative shiver.

The knock at the door interrupted her, and she lifted her head to stare into the mirror that hung over the basin, wondering if she'd imagined the sound.

At the series of staccato raps, this time louder, she scrubbed her face dry with a small hand towel and rushed to the front window to look down at the street for any sign of who it might be.

Jenny's plain carriage from the warehouse was parked in front of the store, with Jeremy, her husband, seated, reins in hand.

Ione rushed down the stairs and swung the door wide. "What's happened?"

"John asked that I stop by on my way to Miriam's. The baby is missing."

Ione heard the words but failed to understand. "What do you mean missing?"

"Missing." Jenny glanced down at Ione's state of undress and pushed her way into the shop, closing the door behind her.

"But how?"

Jenny shrugged and pointed to the stairs. "You need to get ready. You can ride with us."

Ione nodded and hurried toward the stairs. "Would you write a note for Grace? She'll have to reschedule my appointments today. Ask her to send messages out right away. Hopefully the ladies will see them before they leave their homes."

Jenny waved her toward the stairs and then grabbed a nearby paper and pencil and scrawled out the directions. "Hurry up." She hollered up the stairs.

Not wanting to take the time to choose an outfit, Ione slid into yesterday's gown, pinned the mass of her hair tight so it would fit under a hat, and rushed back down the stairs, through the shop, and outside.

She locked the door, and then took Jeremy's hand and climbed into the seat next to Jenny.

His somber expression matched Jenny's, and Ione sent up a prayer that everything would be resolved before they even arrived.

Nothing was resolved. Ione looked around the room, at the police, the servants, Michael and Miriam with their stone-like expressions, and John sitting on a footstool at the edge of the throng.

She lifted her skirts, squeezed through the crowd, and made her way to stand next to him. Placing her hand on his shoulder, Ione could feel the tension in his rippling muscles.

Ione bent to whisper. "What happened?"

John shook his head and turned to look up at her. "Ava is missing. No one here saw a thing."

"Have they checked all the passageways?"

John nodded toward Miriam. "She led the way. There were places even Michael had never seen, but we looked everywhere—every closet, cupboard, everywhere." His eyes followed the path of a police officer through the crowd. "She's not here."

Ione let her hand drop from John's shoulder and skirted the edge of the group until she reached Miriam. She knelt on the floor in front of her and waited for Miriam to meet her gaze with her gray stare. When she did, Ione rested her hand on her friend's trembling knee and willed the warmth of the insufficient touch to quell her fear.

The act of touch was something the three of them—Ione, Jenny, and Miriam—understood. It was the piece that stood in the place of words when none could be found, the element that grounded them when they most needed it.

Miriam's fingers flickered to rest on Ione's hand and then squeezed with an intensity Ione hadn't expected. "She's gone." She spoke plainly.

Her voice neither weak nor strong, and that absence of a reaction communicated more than a cry or a shout ever could.

"We'll find her."

"How will we find here when everyone is here?" Impatience, frustration, rage—the emotions Ione had expected—were removed from the tone of the question. Rather, it was spoken as a simple curiosity.

Ione glanced around the room and back to her friend. "I'll look. And I won't stop looking until she is back home." With that promise, she stood and walked a straight path to the police officer, who looked at Ione as if he could see right through her.

Ione narrowed her gaze and plowed into the gaggle of men. He could ignore her all he wanted, but it wasn't going to do him any good. Ione crossed her arms over her chest and refused a fluttering maid's suggestion of tea, instead planting her feet firmly in the center of the group of would-be searchers and waiting to learn where they intended to start.

She could play at demure. She could hide a smile behind a fan. She could speak incessantly about the weather. But she'd also survived far worse than most of these men could imagine. She knew the streets. She knew where to hide and where one went to be seen. And she wasn't about to be put off by anyone.

Ione clenched her jaw, met Michael's approving nod, and remembered why she loved her makeshift family so much.

Miriam interrupted the officer who seemed to love the sound of his own voice more than anything else in the world. When the conversation paused, and with the men looking down at her—some in expectation, some in resolution—Miriam took a breath and informed them of the basis for her fear. It seemed to be an element they wanted to ignore.

Miriam shifted from one foot to the other, finally resting her weight evenly between the two. "Someone has been here for a while. This... this... It was not new."

The doctor, who for some reason still lurked around the edges of the room, met the gaze of the officer and rolled his eyes enough to confirm what Miriam could see was still the doctor's conclusion: her mind was not sound. The officer smiled obligingly, jotted something in his note-book, and Miriam sighed in relief. The police officer was not siding with the doctor.

Gradually, their droning conversation buzzed again to life. Miriam walked over to Mr. Butler and leaned in close. "Will you please have him escorted out?" she said through clenched teeth, nodding once in the direction of the doctor she liked less every time she was stuck in the same room with the man.

Mr. Butler swallowed once, and then relaxed. He winked, and much to Miriam's satisfaction, did not confirm her command with Michael or any of the other men in the room. Instead, he ducked into the hall and back into the room with the man's jacket draped over his arm.

"It is getting rather late in the day, sir." Mr. Butler held the coat up in a manner that drew on the doctor's childhood urge to comply.

"But..." The doctor mumbled something while shoving one arm into his sleeve after the other. Eventually, he asked for his medical case and disappeared out the door, followed by the nurse who, for all her bossi-ness and fluster up until this day, Miriam could only feel sympathy for.

She turned back to the room. There was work to do.

Chapter 29

They planned late into the night. Miriam glanced around the room, at her friends' faces lit by the steady glow of the gas lamps. After a while, Michael had also turned the knobs for the electric lights he'd had installed—a completely unnecessary extravagance as far as Miriam was concerned—but as they clustered around a map illuminated enough to put the sun to shame, she reconsidered the wisdom in his decision. Those left in the room besides Miriam and Michael were John, Jenny and her husband, Jeremy, and Ione. Theo, Jenny's son, dozed on the chaise, and Mrs. Maloney and Mr. Butler were there, but dipped in and out of the room as necessary to see to messages or resupply the tea cart.

The police had tried to leave one man behind to fight sleep while seated in their foyer with the instructions to watch for a ransom note, but Miriam had refused. It had been hours since Ava had gone missing, and they all agreed they would rather the police be out looking in the few places they could think to search.

So far, there had been nothing. No messages. No real clue as to where her daughter was. Miriam shook her head and breathed deeply to quell the chill that had settled in hours ago and persisted even in their hot, overcrowded parlor.

"You'll begin here." Michael pointed to the blocks around the cathedral, and John nodded his understanding. "Jeremy, I think it would be best for you to help John. You know the docks better than most of us."

Jeremy scowled at the map. "House to house is going to be slow moving on a Sunday with folks in church and all."

"It's all we can do for now, and whoever took her probably knows of our interest in the warehouse. Until we get a ransom note, it's as good as any place to start." Michael stood, pulled out his pocket watch, and pressed the little button at the top. It flipped open. "Three o'clock."

"Well, we can't go yet." Jenny paced to stare at her wavering reflection in the glass door that overlooked the garden. Her arms were crossed over her chest, and her toe tapped a nervous rhythm against the wood floor. She glanced over to Theo, fast asleep on the chaise at the far end of the room where the lights didn't blaze so brightly. Face flushed with sleep, his white-blond curls stuck to the side of his neck. The conversation at the desk droned on.

Miriam walked over to her friend. "You should really get him home. There's nothing you can do here, and until we find out how they gained access to our house, well, I'm afraid for anyone to spend the night."

"What about you?"

Miriam shrugged. She'd been intent on keeping the sense of invasion, of violation, out of mind.

Jenny nodded, her eyes resting on her sleeping child. "I'm so sorry." Her impenetrable expression mirrored the helplessness Miriam felt. "I just can't imagine..."

"We're going to head back so we can get a start when the sun rises." Jeremy walked up behind Jenny and bent to speak the words into her ear before crossing to where Theo slept. He gathered him, cradling his soft, warm body, and Miriam had to look away from the dimpled elbows as they wound around Jeremy's neck.

Her body strained against the shackles of nothing to do, and her mind raced to useless details: the round curve of Ava's chin, the tiny brown birthmark on the top of her foot, the milky blue of her eyes. And then the emptiness of her own body. She'd grown used to not being alone.

A flash of anger, white hot, pierced her stomach. Miriam dropped her hands to the surface of her roll-top desk, sucked in a breath, and watched her fingers clench around the stacks of neglected correspondence, hopelessly creasing the delicate stationery. The letter opener rested, useless, on the gleaming wood surface, and Miriam knew, if the person who took her child entered the room at that moment, nothing would stop her from plunging the sharpened silver deep into their neck.

She trembled with the violence, the primal force of instinct that froze her knees and elbows and locked her into the hovering position.

Michael's gentle hand skimmed over her back. "Maybe you should sit."

Miriam looked down at her sweat-slicked hand, now clamped over the mother of pearl handle of the letter opener. She blinked as Michael ran his hand down the length of her arm until his fingers pried the weapon from her grasp. She didn't remember picking it up.

John appeared on her other side, and the two men walked, supporting her, until she eased onto the cushions of the davenport.

Ione had heard Miriam tell the men that this was not new, and the sick feeling of familiarity had poured down the veins of her arms and legs until her fingers tingled with apprehension. But it still hadn't seemed possible. The last time she'd stayed she'd found the note, except it had been for her, *only* for her. Of that, there had been no doubt.

But now that they were through searching the house, now that she could think, now that all the impossible pieces that shouldn't have fit together seemed to click into place, now, the sick feeling of certainty in the pit of her stomach swelled until she had to swallow back the bitter, aching bile. She should have told Miriam when it had happened. Ione breathed, feeling the air burn past the lump in her throat. She'd been so afraid Clarence would resurface, that he would destroy what she'd found, that the only thing she'd worried about was her own life. But the note had reached her here, in Miriam and Michael's home. They had been as exposed as she'd been. She'd been a fool not to see the possibilities earlier. Ione looked at the ceiling, willing her tears to dry before they escaped down her cheeks. This might be her fault. If she would have said something, even if she would have been a better friend to Miriam and visited more often, had taken the time to hear her say that other things had happened—Ione looked around the room at the anxious faces—if only she'd been less worried about losing her newfound life and more concerned about her friends, she would have realized the danger the note had posed to Miriam.

You will pay had been his last message to her. She clenched her fists until her nails bit into her palms, and she almost laughed at her failure. He'd always been smarter than she. Ione shook her head and took a step back to lean against a tall bookcase and press her forehead against the cool wood, willing her heart to slow. Clarence knew if he wanted to get back at her, all he would have to do is threaten those she loved. She pounded her fist silently into her thigh. It had been how he'd kept her singing so long—*you wouldn't want your mama to know where you been working.* And how he'd kept her away from her sisters even when she thought they might need her—*what do you think you have for them but humiliation? Just look at you.* The words echoed in her mind. She could still hear the tenor of his mocking tone, the scorn that scraped against her bare skin as her shame grew barbs and dug in.

It had been her fault. She had been an embarrassment to her family. They did suffer because of her decisions.

And now her new family faced the same.

Ione took a deep breath and crossed back to where Michael had left Miriam sitting, shoulders hunched, as if she tried hard enough, she could disappear into the same void that had carried her daughter away. Ione sat down and folded her hands. "I need to talk to you."

Miriam stopped breathing.

Ione looked around at the others, busy with either a task or with waiting until the sun came up. "I need to tell you something. I am so sorry."

Miriam lifted her face to Ione's, her brows knit in confusion, and Ione watched her friend struggle to find even the simplest of words. "What?"

"I need to talk to you. I should have said something sooner." She paused, glancing around the room again. "It happened to me too." Ione took a breath but forgot to release it when the bell at the front door interrupted her confession.

"It came for you." Grace shoved the envelope through the door as if it were about to burst into flame. Her eyes stood out in stark contrast to the skin tightly stretched over her moon-pale face.

Mr. Butler pulled her in out of the early morning black and took the thick, trembling paper from her hand. "Come in, dear," he said, pointing toward the parlor where they'd all spent the night planning, plotting, and hoping.

Of course, when the bell rang at the odd hour, no one had stayed in the parlor. They were desperate for news and well beyond the desire for a pretense of anything better to do.

Miriam watched Ione rush to Grace's side, ignoring the paper Mr. Butler held out for her. She shook her head, grasped Grace by the shoulders, and ushered her into the parlor, followed by the rest of the group.

Miriam met Michael's gaze, and he took the envelope from Mr. Butler.

They filed into the room and Mrs. Maloney closed the doors. No one had told her to. And there was no reason to think that whatever was in the letter to Ione would be anything but meant only for her. Miriam sat next to Ione on the cushioned surface of the davenport and waited. They all waited, but this time, the sense of expectation swelled.

They all knew what was in the letter. They only needed to know why it was sent to Ione.

Ione finally took the letter. Michael had slid it across the short table that usually acted as a resting place for teacups and small cakes. Choking on the bitter taste of how stupid she'd been, thinking she could move on, flirting with the notion that her past might simply flit away in the face of new love, Ione stifled a nervous sound—something between a laugh and a sob that had been stuck in her throat since she'd arrived.

And now Miriam fidgeted nervously next to her, waiting to hear if this letter had anything to do with her daughter, and Ione couldn't figure out how best to start.

Grace reached over and plucked the envelope from Ione's fingers. "I don't know what's happening, but this letter was delivered by messenger to my room at the boardinghouse in the middle of the night." She slid her finger in the slit of folded over paper and eased open the seal.

"Don't." Ione breathed the word out, at the same time taking the paper from Grace's steady fingers.

Grace nodded, once, wordlessly instructing Ione to read it.

Ione knew who it was from. The thick scrawl on the outside of the envelope, an echo of the previous messages, told her that much. She glanced at Miriam and shook her head. Where would she begin? "This is from Clarence," she said. Across from her, she saw Miriam shake her head, not recognizing the name. "The man I ran away with before my mother fell ill." The words fell like icicles from Ione's mouth, piercing the silence with precision and dread.

The color drained from Miriam's face. Michael took a step nearer.

They knew the story. Ione took a deep breath. She was with a group who all knew her story and still loved her.

And then she remembered. How easy it had been to forget when the subduing promise of a future with someone who cared loomed nearby. They all knew what she had done. They knew that she'd made the mistake, but they couldn't know what it meant that she'd chosen to go with him in the first place. That she hadn't been coerced, that she'd been the one to abandon. Tears sprung up, and Ione blinked them quickly away before tearing the envelope open. It had finally come full circle. She just hoped the cost wouldn't be more than the unfortunate people who called themselves her friends could bear.

Chapter 30

I made you who you are.

You would be nothing without me.

You can flaunt your success, and you can fool every-one around you, but you will never be more than the whore I know you are.

I followed you. I watched as you teased me, as you played with new men, as you paraded your stolen wealth about town, tricking your customers into thinking you are more than you were born to be.

But I know better.

And you owe me.

I used to think that I wanted you back, but now I see what you really are. So now I simply want what is due me.

I have her. Don't bother looking.

More importantly, I have what I need to make sure you are sent back to where you belong.

I can either sell the news about who you really are, or your friends can pay me to keep silent.

Your choice. I'm sure Mrs. Black would be glad for the chance to find out who you really are. I am sure her shop could use the boon in business that would come in the event of your downfall. Surely, she would pay any price I ask.

The price? It's difficult to place a price on betrayal, but this time, it is $5,000.00.

And I already know you don't have the money. Your friends will help. After all, it is their child that your actions have endangered.

You are, of course, familiar with the Women's Pavilion at the fair. Outside the building are two large, winged statues that hover over the entrance. One of the figures is supported by the three virtues of Love, Charity, and Sacrifice.

All the workers have left. Tomorrow is Sunday. Place the money in a bag under Sacrifice at midnight Sunday night, and then I will tell you where you can find her.

Michael passed the note to John, who handed it to Jeremy. He and Jenny still hadn't left.

"I don't think we should tell the police just yet." Michael waited for John's nod of agreement. The last thing Ione needed was a scandal. Five thousand was a large sum, but not so much that he didn't have it available. Michael looked over to where the three women, Miriam, Ione, and Jenny, huddled together. Five thousand was nothing if it would let air back into their house.

Jeremy finished reading and handed the note back to Michael, who looked for a place to set the menacing thing down. John took it and walked it back over to the desk, where the map they'd previously considered still sat, edges weighed down by paperweights, books, and knick-knacks.

John broke the silence. "I'm not about to let Ione deliver it."

"Agreed." Michael pushed his spectacles back up the bridge of his nose and moved the light over to the large, empty space that had become home to the World's Columbian Exposition. "We need a new map." He straightened and took in a deep breath. "Do we know who has plans for the fair?"

"Mrs. Penn had plans for the Women's Pavilion." Miriam had silently approached, and Michael had to fight to keep his startled reflexes under check. He had to admit the reality of someone stalking them in their home affected him more than he'd thought.

Michael glanced over to Mr. Butler and nodded. They would dispatch a messenger to the Penn mansion and see if they could get the plans. Mr. Butler ducked out of the room to rouse their driver, and Michael opened the center drawer of his desk and fished out a clean sheet of paper, decorated simply with their names embossed with gold near the top of the sheet. He dipped the pen in the already open ink well and scrawled a quick message, taking care to keep his lines light, easy—the opposite of those on the letter burned into his memory. He offered as little information as possible while still communicating their need for the plans.

"You said you had something to tell me before Grace brought the message," Miriam reminded Ione.

Ione tortured her bottom lip with her teeth, biting down until she tasted blood. "I do." She wanted to tell her everything, but so much had happened since they'd last spoken. "But I think I need to tell everyone everything."

The men, bent over the map, who she thought had been lost in discussion, turned to look at her. John, the first to make his way back toward the women, sat on the chair opposite her. Michael and John each took a ladder-back chair from next to a small table and joined their group.

They cared for her. They knew almost everything. She'd made a mistake not trusting them earlier, and now they'd paid—were paying—the price. Ione picked at the edge of her cuticle, punishing the bit of skin with the harsh edge of her chewed nail.

"Remember the last dinner we had here?"

Miriam nodded, encouraging her. Ione looked down. She didn't deserve the patient glances, the support, the comfort. "I spent the night." She stole a glance in Miriam's direction. Her friend's pale skin stretched tight over the tired bones of her cheeks and jaw. "I left early."

Mrs. Maloney, still standing on the outer edge of their circle, cleared her throat. "Yes, dear. I remember."

She had to get this over with. "Before the dinner, I received a message from Clarence." She met Jenny's worried gaze. "He'd sent a couple of them. I think he'd fallen on hard times, and at first it sounded like he wanted me back in his life."

"I should think not." The color rose in Miriam's face, burning through the pallor in two bright spots on her cheeks.

Ione shook her head. "Of course not. But I didn't want to say anything. I'd hoped he would lose interest."

"But he didn't." John frowned, his dark eyebrows bunching together in a frustrated line.

"No. He didn't. And somehow he found a way to place a message on my pillow as I spent the night here. It was next to me when I woke in the early hours."

"On your pillow, here?" Miriam asked. Ione nodded, but this time didn't look up.

"What did it say?" Michael shifted uneasily in the chair.

"Just one sentence. 'Do you miss me?'"

Collectively, the people around her took in a deep breath and held it, further emptying the room of oxygen.

Ione rushed to finish. "I left because he was so focused on me... I didn't want to put anyone else at risk." Ione stole a glance at Miriam. "I'm so sorry. I should have warned you."

Miriam placed her hand on Ione's arm and squeezed tightly. "You did what you thought was right. But I wish you would have let us help you."

"How can you say that?" Ione jumped up and turned toward the window. Night was losing its hold on the sky, and the garden had begun to remember its colors. She placed her forehead against the cool glass and wished it were all that simple. That she could let someone help her, and all would be fine. That her past didn't have enduring demands on her future. "At the time, I thought the risk was mine alone." Ione spoke into the glass, feeling the vibrations where the skin of her forehead touched the smooth surface. "He sent another note, later. That one was threatening, but only to me."

"What did you do?" John now stood next to her, his hands shoved through the slits of his robes and deep into his pockets. The posture made him appear benign, but Ione knew the opposite was true. It was the stance he took when he'd decided something needed to be done.

"I ignored it." Ione turned back to the room to face her friends again. "And they stopped. I thought everything was resolved, that maybe he'd won at the tables or something had taken him out of town."

"When was that?" Miriam asked, glancing toward Michael.

"A couple of weeks ago." Ione stared at the wary look that bounced between them.

"He broke the glass?" Grace piped up from behind the rest of the group. Ione had almost forgotten she'd been the one to bring the letter.

Ione nodded, pursing her lips to keep from frowning. Grace shouldn't have said anything about the window.

"What do you mean?" John turned to Grace and signaled for her to come closer into the circle of the group.

Ione interrupted. "The last note was delivered via rock. It said, 'You will pay.'"

That earned a shocked silence from everyone in the room. Jenny stared, mouth agape, shaking her head. "Why, in heavens name, wouldn't you have said anything?"

Ione thought about it for a moment. In retrospect, the decision had been foolish. If someone had threatened anyone else with a rock through their window, the first thing she would have expected would be to know about it. "I'm not sure." The childish reasoning mocked who she thought she'd become. "I mean, it is my problem from before I knew any of you...and it is my fault...and I wanted to stay away so none of you could be in danger. He knows me. Even then, he could have done anything he wanted to me, but he always used my family to get that last bit that I refused to give up. That's how he kept control."

"So you thought you'd let him still have that kind of control?" John's question shocked the room, and while Jenny had managed to close her mouth, the rest of them had lost the ability to do the same.

Ione felt angry heat rise to her cheeks. She clasped her hands and squeezed until the blood retreated from the tips of her fingers. "I didn't want him to involve anyone else."

"But he has." The color in John's face matched Ione's anger, and she took a step nearer.

"I was only trying to protect everyone."

"You were trying to protect yourself."

The truth stung, and Ione blinked back the tears.

"John." Miriam's low tone interrupted the standoff that had swelled between the two.

"It's true." One tear escaped and trailed down Ione's cheek.

John closed the distance and pulled her into his chest to rest there on the wide, muscled expanse. He felt solid, warm, like she could hide there, with him, forever. "There's nothing wrong with trying to protect yourself." He bent down to speak into her hair. "Your mistake was in thinking that you are alone, that what affects you happens in a bubble.

In a family, that's not the way it works. We all take the good and bad because that is the price for what we have here."

Ione nodded, not trusting her own voice, and buried her face against his chest.

"When something happens to you, it happens to all of us. If you are in danger, then so are we."

She sniffled and backed away so that she could look up at the man who had helped pull her from her last mistake. "It's embarrassing." She glanced over to Miriam and Jenny. "You worked so hard to give me a new start, and now here I am again, and now here you are, without your baby."

"It's not your fault." Miriam's tone had shifted to business, easily dismissing any kind of blame or hurt. It was time to work.

The bell rang again, and this time, like the last, they all went out to see who could possibly be standing there.

Pastor Whitaker stepped in and turned to face the crowd of people. "You haven't seen—"

"She's right here," Michael interrupted, and reached out to shake his hand.

"Aaron." John stepped up and embraced the other minister with a lot of back slapping and declarations about how long it had been.

"Come on in." Michael could see the confusion on the man's face and thought they'd best get to explaining the situation. Walking into a person's house in the wee hours of the morning, only to see a group of worried-looking friends, had to be disconcerting.

"We hadn't heard from Ione, and we were getting worried. Then Evan stopped by when he noticed her shop was closed..." Pastor Whitaker's words died off as he took in the number of people standing around looking at him.

Michael had mercy on the man and explained the situation, and Ione reassured him that she would be fine. Like the rest of them, Aaron lightly chastised Ione for her attempts to deal with Clarence on her own.

He glanced toward the clock on the hearth. Time had nearly stopped. Tonight. He, they, had to wait until tonight in order to see their baby. Michael sank into his desk chair, fighting the urge to pound his fist into something, anything, and then Miriam's hand covered his.

"She'll be fine. He wants the money, not our baby," she whispered next to his ear. Michael could feel her soft breath brush against his neck, the touch of her warm body as she leaned into him, lending her strength. God help him, he wanted to gather her up right here and bury his face in the soft hollow of her belly and breathe her in. And he'd thought she'd been the weak one.

The others, congregated at the windows that overlooked the gardens, left the two of them alone.

"I am sorry." Michael looked up into her gray eyes, searching for any hint that she blamed him. Not that he didn't deserve it.

"It's not your fault." Miriam slid her hands up to cradle his face. He felt the stubble of his night's growth of beard rasp against her soft skin.

"I should have believed you."

"Why would you have? What happened here made no sense. Still makes no sense. How did he get the message to Ione in our house?"

Michael frowned. "We haven't even begun to think of that yet."

"Mr. Farling?" Mr. Butler stood at the doorway and cleared his throat. "We can't find Tamm anywhere, sir."

"What do you mean?" Michael stood and crossed to where Mr. Butler stood.

While he might normally have lowered his voice when imparting information about a household employee, this time, under the watchful gaze and approaching footsteps of the rest of the group, Mr. Butler announced his findings to everyone. "You said to send word to Mrs. Penn to see if we could get plans for the Women's Pavilion."

Pastor Whitaker sent a questioning look to John, who waved the question back with a "later" gesture.

"We sent the kitchen boy to wake Tamm, and he said no one was there. All his things are gone."

"Tamm?" Ione's weak tone turned the room into a cavern.

Michael turned to face her. "Do you know him?"

Ione's eyes darted back and forth, as if she were searching for some sort of clue. She bit her bottom lip and took a step back. "It makes sense."

"What makes sense?" Michael took a step nearer.

"How he could do it. How he could get the message. How this all was possible."

"What?" John placed a hand on her elbow and steered her toward a chair. "What do you mean?"

"Tamm. Clarence Tamm. That's his name." Her gaze bored into Miriam's.

"He's been here the whole time." The cup of tea Miriam poured slipped from her fingers and shattered against the wood floor.

Chapter 31

Miriam paced across the floor of her studio, muttering under her breath. If only she hadn't stopped, hadn't given in, hadn't ignored her desire to paint for fear of what she might conjure. She stifled an ironic laugh. In trying to avoid seeing the worst, she was living it.

After the message, the pieces had slipped together, and then the faces all stared at her, measuring her reaction. She'd stayed only long enough to escape from the room, from the oppression of so many eyes, to make her way to the top of the stairs and lean against the still side of the locked door. All day to wait.

They were making plans, developing their strategies for who might be best to accompany Ione or if she shouldn't go at all. The police were to be avoided, that much they'd agreed on. No sense in opening up the possibility of others learning about Ione's past. News like that would spread like wildfire through society's matrons.

The money also didn't pose a challenge. Michael kept stashes of cash in their hidden safes. If only he would have asked—Michael would have given him anything he'd wanted.

Miriam crossed to the table where her paints still lay stacked and ready for use. It had been so long. She folded her hands together to keep them from trembling and sat on the paint-splattered wood table. Her paintings, the ones most recently completed, leaned against the brick wall. Miriam took a deep breath, settling into the weight of the painting that she knew would come.

He'd made her nervous from the start. But she'd been a fool. Ignored her instincts. Questioned her hesitation. And now her daughter was missing. Her breasts, full and painful, tingled with the thought of her baby. A familiar sweet stab of pain, and she felt the front of her shirt grow damp with the wasted milk. Miriam stood, grasped a dry brush, softened the bristles in the palm of her hand, and then put it in the pocket of the apron she didn't remember tying on.

The paints were next. Colors like old friends. She couldn't help but smile at the creases in the metal tubes. Opening one, she waited for the aroma to drift about her and lend the first hint as to the subject she should paint.

It was red. Miriam blanched at the bloody color, but squeezed a bit onto her palette. Next, a yellow. Color after color, the spots shifted hues, and the painting developed in her mind. She scooped white onto the wooden board, and breathed easier as the deep, serious tones took on a pastel ease.

Seizing the brush from her pocket, Miriam dipped it in the rich color and put paint to canvas.

She'd forgotten the feel. The drag of the brush against the rough texture as the paint dwindled, and the silky slide after she dipped her brush again. Miriam closed her eyes, letting the scents and the sounds fill the space where sight overruled, and then opened them again to a brighter light.

The colors on the canvas were not as she'd expected. Miriam's eyes filled with tears and she blinked them away, painting faster, learning what the painting wanted to tell her. A swipe of the brush, a curve, and a form without shadow emerged.

She'd expected fear. She'd braced for dark, for the figure of Tamm to come through with shadowed eyes and lurking hatred. But he was nowhere in her painting. The feeling of him, the apprehension, the questions, were gone, replaced by the soft contours of Ava's cheek and chin in the warm colors of the rising sun.

A knock on the door interrupted Miriam. She stepped back from the easel. "What is it?" she called, her eyes never leaving the canvas.

"It's Mrs. Maloney, dear. Would you like luncheon to be brought up for you?"

Miriam sucked in her lips to subdue the rising emotion. She hadn't realized before how the small, unspoken questions that came through in tone had hurt. She'd done her best to ignore the doctor's patronizing purse of his lips or the way John looked at her with concern etched across his face. Or worse, how Mrs. Maloney had gingerly asked permission, as if she couldn't trust Miriam's answers, and how in his more unguarded moments, fear would slip from Michael's posture to invade the room like an unwelcome shade.

Now, though, Mrs. Maloney's voice had returned to normal. Her clipped, business-like phrases had regained their confidence, and Miriam had to concentrate on keeping her breathing even in order to answer her question with a steady voice.

"Please have one of the maids leave the tray outside the room."

"Good. Good." Mrs. Maloney's footsteps receded down the hall, and Miriam turned back to the developing image of her child.

It might mean that all would be well, or it might mean that Miriam couldn't think of anything but her missing baby, but she chose to see it as a path to hope. After all, what was a gift if it couldn't be used to bring good? She'd expected darkness but had received only grace.

Evening sagged atop the city. It sank to cover the damp streets and tumbled into the alleys and through the gutters, nudging commuters into homes and pubs and every other available place of shelter.

Whether it was their purpose that drove them to see past the other pedestrians or the fog that rolled in from the lake, Ione felt like they were the only people in the city.

It had been a difficult decision that had involved a fair amount of debate, but eventually Ione had prevailed, winning a place in the evening's script. At first, Michael had insisted that she stay with Miriam and the rest of the household, allowing him and John to meet with the person they now knew as both the kidnapper of their daughter and Ione's tormentor. Ione appealed to their sense of logic in order to earn her role in the night's plan. After all, what would Clarence do to the baby if he had been expecting Ione and instead found his former employer and a priest?

Ione pulled the summer-weight cape she'd borrowed from Miriam closer around her face. It wouldn't have mattered if they had chosen not to listen to her reasoning, though. Short of locking her up, she wouldn't have given them much of an option. And no one else had been happy either. Pastor Whitaker, who had spent the day with them hunched over Mrs. Penn's maps, had put up quite the protest at the thought it would only be the three of them. But only so many people could walk the grounds, undetected by the guards posted here and there.

Sometimes the fog came in as a mist. This time it came in as a cloud, a wall of roiling, fishy haze. Ione glanced back to where their carriage, driven by Mr. Butler, had dropped them off. They had only crossed the street, and the fog had swallowed the vehicle whole.

Michael carried a lantern but kept it shuttered to avoid attracting any attention. "It's a long walk from here." He spoke over his shoulder as he flattened his body against a high stone pillar.

Ione nodded her understanding, and John followed behind, keeping an eye out for anyone who might follow. It wasn't the first time they'd spent an evening lurking about in the mist, and Ione frowned at the thought that without her, they'd be home safe in their beds. Miriam would have her baby, and the people she loved would not be in danger.

If the stupid clod had just told her what he planned—Ione kicked a stray rock to the side of the road, earning a disappointing small splash—she would have paid any price to keep it between the two of them. Ione clenched her fists to stop the shudder that began at the base of her spine and worked up to the delicate hairs at the back of her neck. He wasn't stupid, though. Calculating, vindictive, and dangerous when his ego faced bruising, but no one in their right mind would think he suffered a lack in mental acuity. Ione scooted closer to Michael. While she regretted that he'd become involved, the more selfish side of her nature wanted to close her eyes, huddle in a corner, and let him fix everything. Not for the first time, she missed Evan. But she'd made Pastor Whitaker promise to keep the truth of the situation from his brother. The whole thing was humiliating enough.

She frowned and inched the hood forward to cover more of her face. She would be honest with him, later, after they'd safely returned Ava. Clarence Tamm would never be completely out of her life. She knew that now. Evan had been a dream, a wish that might have had a chance if she weren't still paying the price for past mistakes.

Michael slipped around the light from a lone lamppost and signaled Ione and John to follow. She stepped into the thick black night. Some mistakes could never be forgotten, and their price was so high, no amount of money could satisfy.

She had only known Evan for a short time. Surely he would move on, and to him, her memory would be nothing more than a bump from a missing cobble in an otherwise clear stretch of road.

After memorizing the maps for the stretching white city that sprouted up, as if overnight, from the land many had thought unsuitable for such opulence, Michael had no need of direction. He led the way through makeshift alleys, behind the cover of tarps, scrambled around piles of lumber, and came up facing the sprawling Women's Pavilion. The massive building of white stone in various stages of construction didn't penetrate the fog so much as use it to make the towering facade appear more imposing than the architect had planned. Choosing whose drawings to use had been a contentious endeavor, with half the city griping over the fact that a woman designed the place and the other half proclaiming outrage, not because a woman had designed it, but because the woman they thought should win the contract didn't. All in all, it seemed to Michael that about ninety-nine percent of the city stood with bated breath, waiting for news of failure.

He didn't envy the woman.

But she'd done a remarkable job. Michael looked up through the mist, at the stories and the long white verandas that had suddenly taken shape since the last time he'd visited. The lantern he left closed, as it would be useless right now anyway, except as a method to give away their location. Tamm would be here, that much he knew. The advantage was his.

Michael signaled for Ione and John to stop and strained to hear a footstep, a cry, anything that might come through the blanket that suffocated the city.

But nothing pierced the fog.

They continued forward, inching toward the pillars and the smaller figure, Sacrifice, that held the angel aloft. *Sacrifice*. The place where they were to leave the offering had been intentionally chosen, but the absurdity of playing Tamm's game, of letting money define how much sacrifice a person was worth, chafed more than paying the amount he'd demanded. Michael opened one shutter of the lamp and aimed the beam toward the towering figures. The light pierced through the cloud and fell onto the impenetrable expression of Sacrifice.

Michael glanced back to where Ione and John stood but could only make out the outline of John's dark cloak. The silence, thicker than the fog, had a sound all its own. Feeling for the heavy envelope, Michael fished it out of his pocket, took one more glance around for anyone who might be prowling about, and tucked it under the ledge of stone.

The job done, he took a step back and waited for something to happen.

Nothing did.

The letter hadn't said when Tamm would exchange the child for the money, only made the demand and threats with the promise of returning her.

John walked up to join Michael, looking over his shoulder to where he and Ione had been waiting in the shadows. "I think we have to go back and wait now."

Michael nodded, frowning. If only he could have heard her cry or felt some sense that this was where Tamm had been keeping her, then his stomach might not be overwhelmed by the gut-twisting, acidic feel of something gone wrong.

He looked up to John and dropped the shutter over the light. "Where's Ione?"

"She was with me over there." John pointed to a pile of unopened crates.

Michael took hasty steps away from the building, but John pushed him aside and rushed to where he'd last seen Ione. "She's not here," he whispered loudly.

With John on his heels, Michael ran out of the space behind the stacks of boxes and rounded the corner in what he knew would prove a fruitless search. They scrambled around, darting here and there, searching, avoiding the guards, until daylight threatened to expose their efforts, and they were forced to retreat to the waiting carriage.

John climbed in first, pounding his fist into the cushioned seat. "We should have known better. We walked right into it." In his dark cloak and looking everything like a large, caged, and very unhappy bear, John's anger soothed Michael. Certain actions required a particular amount of outrage, and with John willing to feel the emotions of the situation, Michael felt free to puzzle over their next move without being plagued by guilt over his ability to function.

Michael stared, unseeing, out the window, and focused on blocking out the terror at the thought that both his daughter and his friend were at the mercy of a madman. "The only thing we can do is wait. We have to get back. Everyone will be worried."

John looked at his friend, accepting, with a transparent frown, the distance that Michael placed between him and the fear that threatened to overwhelm them both. "We'll get them back." John placed his hand on Michael's arm for a brief second.

Michael nodded and watched for his home to appear through the fog.

Chapter 32

He'd come from behind her, and Ione hadn't been in the least bit surprised. From the time she'd opened the letter—no, from the time Grace rang the bell—Ione had had that floating sensation of playing a part in a larger play. But this time, she hadn't had the privilege to read all the way to the end before being thrust onto the stage. This time, someone else had read the script, set the stage, and she was the marionette, hanging from the puppeteer's strings, responding as he would have her respond.

Nothing had changed.

Except one thing. He'd carelessly given her a reason to fight.

Ava squirmed in a young girl's arms at the other side of the room. A half-empty bottle sat on a rickety table next to her. Ione's head spun, and she tried to place the events in order.

Michael had been standing at the entrance of the building. John had joined him. That's when she felt the edge of a knife digging into the side of her ribs. The growled threat against her, the baby, and Michael had been enough to keep her lips clamped, despite the urge to scream and rail and kick and bite and hurt him in every way he'd hurt her. The stench of his hot breath on her neck brought the dirty rooms above the saloons back into full memory, and Ione gagged against the resurfacing visions.

It had been so easy to forget. She thought she'd remembered, that she had catalogued the horrors, but one simple smell brought back the reality of the pain of being used, not by the strangers, but by the man she thought had loved her. But he'd perverted love, made it something unrecognizable, something that she would have to work to relearn for the rest of her life.

Heavy boots now came into view, and he grabbed Ione by the back of the hair, yanking her up and forcing her to stare into his eyes.

"Look at me..." He spat the words into her face, only inches away from his, and then called her a string of names she'd forgotten could be linked together. All at once she wanted to laugh at the delicacy of the world that had been her new life, and then sob, mourning the loss of it.

He let go of her hair and crossed to the other side of the room, closer to the young girl with the baby. Using the knife to point at her, he introduced them. "Ione, Carrie. Carrie, Ione."

Ione looked at the dirty white girl who sat in a too-large dress cradling the baby the best she could. She couldn't have been much more than fourteen, but the way she looked at Clarence told Ione everything she needed to know about the role she played for him.

Her stringy hair had been pulled back from her face, revealing a fading bruise that shaded both eyes. Clarence never used to beat Ione—at least not at first. Ione glanced back to him, wondering how he had changed and what she would be dealing with, because, looking around the strange, quiet room, there was no sign that this would end soon.

Miriam had finished the painting and left it to dry on the easel. Back in her room, the hush of the night swelled to a hiss that filled the space a cry should occupy. He hadn't returned.

The black fog had grown lighter with the approaching dawn, but in doing so, illuminated the impenetrable curtain so nothing existed outside Miriam's window except the diminishing hope of holding her baby. Every so often the mist condensed, growing heavier, rounder, and plunged in minuscule, irregular paths down the glass to puddle ineffectively at the wood sill where, if the sun ever reappeared, it would evaporate, disappear again, and then attempt to fall to the earth once more, this time in hopes of accomplishing something.

The crunching narrow wheels of the carriage slowed against the cobbles, and Miriam strained to see more than a few feet past the cool windowpane, to catch a glance at what her ears confirmed. An impossible task, she shook her head and crossed the room without feeling the pile of the carpet beneath her feet.

Michael stomped into the foyer, shrugging off his jacket and ignoring it as it fell to the floor in a sodden heap. "He took Ione." He looked up as Miriam flew down the stairs, only steps ahead of the others who had all chosen to spend the night dozing in various bedrooms with their doors open so they could better hear the arrival of any important news.

"Did you see where they went?" Pastor Whitaker elbowed his way from the back of the crowd and walked with Michael to the parlor. Mrs. Whitaker and Ione's sisters, Maggie and Lucy, followed close at his heels, worry pulling the skin tight around their red-rimmed eyes. He had sent for the rest of his family after Ione had left.

Michael shook his head and again bent over the maps spread over the surface of his desk. "This is useless." He frowned at the tangles of roads and topographical notes. He slammed his fist against the hard surface of his desk, causing pictures and pens and the small statues that clung to the edges to tremble with the force of the impact. "Where do we go from here? He has the money, so why did he take her?"

"It wasn't about the money." Miriam stepped up and rested her hand over Michael's. Her husband, typically so unflappable, closed his eyes briefly. He straightened and pulled Miriam close into the hollow of his chest. Warmth radiated from his core, an anxious heat that Miriam wanted to soothe away.

The others milled about the room in impotent agitation while Miriam concentrated on the feel of her husband's muscles rippling under her cheek, the sounds of whispered conversations as they filled the empty spaces in the room, and the reassuring painting on her easel. She tightened her grip on Michael's lapels and squeezed her eyes against the emptiness that threatened to overwhelm her.

Ione woke to the slam of a door. She blinked a few times before realizing that the room lacked all source of light, and then she listened. Had the door slammed as someone exited, or was she not alone?

Her wrists and ankles, bound to the hard chair, throbbed against the chafing twine that held her. The muscles of her arms, unaccustomed to the restriction, burned with the effort to remain motionless, lest her bindings cut even deeper into the delicate skin exposed by the ruffled cuffs of her dress.

She was still wearing her dress. That, she supposed, was a good sign. She shifted to the right and the left, testing the give in the rope.

"Don't even try." Clarence's smooth low tones cut through the dark like lightning.

She heard a match strike, and weak light flooded the room. Ione's heart skipped beats, and her breathing, absurdly loud in the small space, quickened, responding to the jolt of his presence. But she wouldn't give him the pleasure of a scream or a cry.

"What do you want?" She stilled, waiting for his response

Three heavy footsteps, and his sticky breath razed the skin at the base of her neck. "You are mine." He spat the words at her, leaving no air in the room.

"Where's Ava?"

"You should probably be more concerned with your own skin." He grasped the hard armrest and spun the chair around. The legs grated against the wood floor, and the sudden movement threatened to topple Ione and the piece of furniture that held her upright.

She tightened her muscles against the impending fall, only to have his hand come down hard on her shoulder, steadying her and the chair. Her stomach heaved at the touch of his fingers on the bare place above the collar of her dress, and Ione swallowed convulsively, fighting back bile along with the memories of what it had been like to feel his hands cover other places of her body. Clamping her mouth closed, Ione concentrated on not angering him. "What do you want with me?" Ione kept her tone high, nonconfrontational, and earned the reward of his fingers dropping away. She breathed easier even though her situation had not improved.

Clarence circled the chair twice and then bent to face Ione. She'd forgotten how handsome he could appear, his nose long and straight, his high cheekbones smooth and angular. But what she had always remembered as wide, soft lips, were now a hard, resentful line. His looks had changed. The ease in how he carried himself, the fluidity of movement that distinguished him from other men in a crowd had disappeared, only to be replaced with simmering, twitching rage.

"I only want what is rightfully mine." The calm words stood at a contrast to the energy sparking behind his narrowed eyes.

Ione hesitated and took in a shallow breath before looking directly into his eyes. "You did get the money?"

The line of his mouth curved at the ends in a humorless smile. "That, dear, was only the down payment."

Ione nodded, not wanting to ask for anything he wasn't willing to give. Experience had taught her that would get her nothing, except possibly a beating.

One swift movement, and his huge hand cradled her chin in his vise-like grip, forcing her eyes back to his. "I thought you might come back to me, but I see that you have moved on. You forget our arrangement, though. I gave you your start—whatever you do, you owe to me."

Ione nodded stiffly, her chin still in the bruising prison of his fingers.

"The baby is fine. And everything in their life will be fine. It is not them that I want. It is you. You need to remember what you owe me."

Ione bit her bottom lip and immediately regretted the small movement that drew his attention down. Before she knew what was happening, he covered her mouth in a punishing kiss that tasted of onion and booze. She concentrated on remaining still. Fighting would do nothing but anger him.

Abruptly, he pulled back and studied her, frowning. "You are going to write down exactly what I tell you, and then we will send your letter to your new friends." The last word floated in a puddle of scorn.

Ione nodded, keeping her mouth shut.

Chapter 33

Breakfast hadn't occurred to any of them, despite the audible gurgling of stomachs and the general queasiness they shared. It was little Theo announcing his hunger that reminded Mrs. Maloney to offer food to the distracted crowd. Tray after tray appeared as if in apology for the imagined oversight, and Miriam, previously nodding her approval, finally vocalized their gratitude in hopes Mrs. Maloney would stop making amends with progressively intricate selections. No one wanted to take the time to sit down to a formal breakfast in the dining room, and after a polite pause, they fell onto the food with distracted abandon, forgetting napkins, utensils, or anything else that hindered the path from plate to mouth or slowed the sporadic progression of ideas regarding their now two missing family members.

Miriam frowned. All they could do was wait. Jenny picked nervously at the edge of a half-eaten pastry, and Jeremy studied the soft rain's lazy patterns as it dribbled down the windows.

John and Pastor Whitaker were huddled in a corner, discussing possibilities, and Michael had finally dozed off in an armchair, his head lolling to one side. Miriam bent, slipped off his glasses, and folding them, set them down on the small side table where a candle had burned most of the night. Now, with wax melted in a frozen fall, the flame had sputtered and died just as the wind outside gathered momentum and the first sheet of rain hissed against the large curtained window overlooking the street.

Theo's quiet conversation with Jenny echoed through the rich room. No one else had the energy to speak, let alone find anything pertinent that had not already been said.

It was Sunday morning.

John cleared his throat. "Pastor Whitaker and I will be leaving in a few minutes... It being Sunday."

"The girls and I will wait here." Mrs. Whitaker nodded toward Lucy, curled into the corner of a plush armchair in a darkened corner of the room. Maggie sat at her feet, flipping the pages of a book too quickly to read anything.

Michael roused, rubbing his eyes and reaching for his spectacles. He leaned forward, his knees stretching the fabric of the creased trousers he still wore, and adjusted the wires behind his ears. "Of course." He yawned. "I'd forgotten it was Sunday."

"I'll be back directly after service." John fastened the buttons of his overcoat against what would surely be a damp ride.

"I'll have the carriage brought around." Mr. Butler turned and disappeared into the dark hall without waiting for an answer.

A pounding at the door stopped all movement in the room. Miriam took one hesitant step and built momentum as the others gathered around. By the time they reached the door, they were nearly running.

The handle felt cold. She yanked it open to the spray of rain and a small hooded figure with a shaking envelope in her outstretched arm.

Collectively, and despite her objections, they pulled her out of the rain, through the foyer, and into the parlor, caring little for her dribbling overcoat or the mud on her boots. She shrugged, glancing from under her hood at the circle of faces. "H-he—here," she stuttered, thrusting the envelope past Miriam and toward the men.

Miriam stepped aside, making room for Michael to pluck it from the girl's thin fingers. A small streak of dirt or maybe a bruise spread from the back of her hand and up into the cuff of her worn sleeve. Miriam nodded toward Mrs. Maloney, wordlessly asking her to put together a plate of breakfast for the girl, or woman. Miriam studied the dingy skin that stretched across her pinched cheeks, unable to determine her age. She could have been twelve or forty. Unless they could get her to remove her hood, there would be no way to tell.

"Let me see that." Maggie touched Michael's arm. It was easy to forget the quiet girl was there, but as she elbowed her way into the crowd, no one could deny her likeness to Ione. She plucked the envelope from his fingers and studied the name scrawled across the front. "This is Ione's handwriting."

After a pause, she handed it back to Michael. He frowned and lifted the seal with the edge of a nail, smoothing the papers flat. "Same handwriting." He ran a finger over the dry ink.

They all followed him over to the desk, where he smoothed the paper against the flat surface of still unrolled maps and sketches of half-created plans.

Miriam leaned in, scanning quickly for news of Ava. Her breasts ached against the constraint of her dress, occasionally stabbing her with a jolt that nearly had her gasping. She'd expressed the milk, more than once, but her efforts to ease the pain were less efficient than her baby's. And while she'd done her best to distract herself from concerns over the safety of her little girl, it grew more difficult by the minute.

The letter, indeed, had been written by Ione. Michael cleared his throat as he read aloud:

> *Dear Friends,*
>
> *First, I would like to assure you the baby is doing well. She has not been harmed, and as long as you follow these directions, she will be returned to you in good health.*

Michael looked up, meeting Miriam's gaze with an emotionless expression that Miriam was sure matched her own.

> *I thank you for everything you have done for me,*
> *but I have come to the realization that I am still in love*
> *with Clarence. He helped me when my mother was ill,*
> *and he stood by me through tough times. Even though*
> *I have been unfaithful, he has forgiven me and would*
> *like a clean start with just the two of us.*
>
> *Not everything has to change. This week will be a*
> *test. I will be in the shop during normal working hours,*
> *and as long as you will let me move on and allow Clar-*
> *ence and me to move forward, your baby will be re-*
> *turned to you by the end of the week.*
>
> *I hope you understand I wish the best for you all, but*
> *I need to spend some time remembering who I am and*
> *what I should be doing in the future.*

John shook his head. "Ione didn't write this."

"Absolutely not." Maggie crossed her arms over her chest, sucking her lips as if she had to physically make an effort to keep from saying anything else.

"Of course not." Miriam reached out and rested her hand against Maggie's tense bicep. "She would never do something like this. We all know that."

Maggie nodded her understanding but remained tense with anger.

> *If you respect our wishes, the baby will be returned*
> *to you by the end of the week, and I will not bother you*
> *again.*
>> *Sincerely,*
>> *Ione*

Miriam looked around for the girl who had brought the letter. "Where'd she go?"

"Who?"

"The girl?"

They whirled in different directions, each of them looking around the room as if they'd lost something important.

"She's gone," Miriam muttered.

Michael crossed to the windows that faced the street. "She's going east." He pushed the curtain wider, the rings rattling against the rod hung near the ceiling.

"I'll follow," Mr. Butler called from the hall, not allowing for any time to argue or debate. In a matter of seconds, Miriam watched him jog down the street after the girl, sticking close to fences and trees so as to better slink behind them in case she turned to see if she had been followed.

"Ione didn't write that letter," Miriam said again, still watching Mr. Butler's progress.

"Of course not." Mrs. Whitaker stepped up. "She would never call Ava 'the baby.' What a fool. I thought he'd be a bit brighter than that."

"He is." Miriam worried her bottom lip with her teeth. "That's the part that worries me. In order to plan this, to wait and take his time, to place things around the house so that I had to question my own sanity... That much patience takes intelligence. There's something we are not seeing here."

"Do you think he might still love her? Could this be out of jealousy?" Pastor Whitaker grabbed his hat and drummed the top with the tips of his fingers. "If he is still in love with her, this might make sense—at least a bit. She has been seeing Evan."

"Who's Evan?" Everyone but Mrs. Whitaker and the girls asked at once, earning an eyebrow lift from Pastor Whitaker.

"My brother. We introduced them about a month back. He recently came from back east to work at Provident Hospital."

Miriam met Jenny's gaze with her own questions, and one look confirmed that she also had not heard of the man.

"She hasn't said anything?"

Miriam shook her head. "She can be like that sometimes. She tends to keep things to herself."

"I'm not going to let her get away with it this time." John shrugged into his overcoat and headed to the door, signaling for Pastor Whitaker to join him. "Sometimes silence is good. But sometimes it can only do harm. I know we want to keep this as quiet as possible, but I think we've crossed the line where that is possible." John shoved his hat onto his head and nodded at Michael. "Every woman in my congregation knows who Ione is and has the deepest respect for what you all have done for the women down by the docks, hiring them and helping their families and all. If I even drop a hint or two that her shop needs business, she will be flooded for weeks by women stopping in for everything from a button to a stray string. It's time Ione learns that she is part of this community for good."

"My thoughts exactly." Pastor Whitaker followed John into the front hall, the rest of the group trailing behind. "The ladies of our congregation would not take kindly if they thought Ione were being forced into anything she didn't want. And I think we can all agree that that letter was not from her, and that the last thing she wants back in her life is a man who would kidnap a baby."

"Stay here and be careful," John instructed, turning to Michael and everyone else who crowded the hall. "Send word if you learn anything, or if Mr. Butler learns anything, and we'll both be back as soon as we can."

Pastor Whitaker nodded, dropped a quick kiss on his wife's cheek, patted Lucy's head, and then, talking with heads close, he and John quietly clicked the door closed behind them.

"I wrote the letter like you asked." Ione pleaded with Clarence as he paced the dingy room. "What else do you want me to do?"

He turned, his flashing eyes snapping back to her face. "I want you to be quiet. Is that too much to ask?"

Ione shook her head as his steps neared. She remembered those boots. Large and black and faster that anyone could imagine. They'd met her ribs on numerous occasions.

She looked away, humiliated not by the things he had forced her to do, but mortified that she had been naive enough to think that she hadn't been abused, that she had deserved his actions, that she had been the stupid one, that she had known better, and that he had only been punishing her for mistakes as he had a right to do. Ione pursed her lips, concentrating on leveling her breathing, on being the person he thought she should be. At least for a little while longer. At least until Ava was safe again in Miriam's arms and that girl he had caring for her could escape from his clutches.

"Where is the baby?" Ione asked, flinching when he raised his arm in warning.

"She's fine. Some woman downstairs is looking after her."

"Not Carrie? The girl who was here before?"

His responding glare said he had no intention of answering.

Ione looked around the dingy room. They were in at least a two-story building. The noises that had escaped through the rough floorboards had made that apparent. But it wasn't a building she'd been to before, and it wasn't an area of town with which she was familiar. And the tangy odors that seeped between the cracks with the unfamiliar sounds let Ione know it was not a place she wanted to stay. Nor one whose inhabitants she wanted caring for little Ava.

"You know, if something happens to her, they will find us."

Clarence stopped the pacing that had him temporarily at the other side of the small room and turned, one side of his mouth cocked in a calculating smile. "Nothing will happen to her. We will be fine." He tested the bounds of her use of "us" by expanding the connection.

Ione fought to keep the calculation from her own eyes. He preferred his women simple and silent. That much she'd learned from experience, and luckily, it wasn't difficult to convince him he was right. He liked being right.

"If you let me care for her, then we know she is all right." Ione shrugged, allowing the tone of the sentence to uptick, so that her suggestion sounded more like a question than an actual idea.

He studied her face. His hot gaze traveled from her mouth to her forehead to the place on her neck where her pulse raced against the frail casing of skin. "When Carrie returns, I'll have her bring the baby up. Until then..." He scraped a wooden chair across the floor and, sitting down, faced her. "...you can tell me a bit more about how you have spent the last year."

Ione swallowed and then stilled as he sat, his knees on either side of hers, and reached for the spot on her neck where the frantic rhythm of her heart betrayed her feverish reaction to his nearness.

Chapter 34

"Why do you think she didn't tell us?" Jenny sat cross-legged on Miriam's bed, picking at a loose thread on her stocking.

It was nearly noon, and they still hadn't seen any sign of Mr. Butler, nor heard from anyone else. The clock on the mantel clicked slower than possible, resonating with each tick, sighing between each trembling jerk of the minute hand.

"I don't know." Miriam lay back against the pillows, staring at the coffered ceiling. "But I do know that if she thinks we or Ava is in any kind of danger, she will do anything it takes to protect us, including sacrificing herself or her business for whatever he demands."

Jenny nodded after a pause. It was almost as if their conversation had ground down to the tortured pacing of the clock, as if they measured their words, hoping that they alone had the power to propel the hands forward. "Why do you think she didn't mention Pastor Whitaker's brother?"

Miriam shrugged and looked back down to study her friend. She had dirty blond hair, blue eyes, and the kind of freckled skin that would make her look like a teenager well into her thirties. While Miriam had been isolated by her own choice, and Ione by a cascade of events and a bad string of calamities, Jenny had been alone in the world because her father used her body as a source of funds to support his drinking. She'd grown up in the upper rooms of various seedy taverns, and until John had found her, had never thought to want anything more from life than a warm bed she didn't have to share.

"Maybe she was too afraid to hope." Jenny frowned down at the floral pattern on the bedspread. "Ione is really good at being strong, and I've heard her say that she never wanted another man in her life, but if this Tamm is the only man she's ever had a relationship with, then I'm sure Pastor Whitaker's brother came as quite a surprise."

"Do you suppose he knows?" Miriam asked.

"About her past? I would imagine so, with Pastor as his brother."

"I wonder what he's like."

Jenny shrugged. "Probably not good enough for Ione."

"Mrs. Whitaker said he's a doctor. Finished his training and is opening up his own practice."

Jenny raised one eyebrow. "Being a doctor doesn't make someone special or better than anyone else. More than a few doctors visited the same taverns my dad brought me to." She sniffed, wiping her nose on the back of her hand, almost as if remembering the bad times put her right back to living there. Miriam handed Jenny her handkerchief, and she wordlessly wiped her nose and crushed the fabric in her palm. "Ione can't go back to that. We can't let that happen."

"We won't."

"But she's already there."

"So is my baby." Miriam chewed the cuticle of her nail and looked out at the gray sky. It had been two days. Two days since she'd held her baby, and the ache grew stronger every second that passed.

"I'm sorry," Jenny whispered.

Whether she was apologizing for not mentioning Ava, or apologizing for the world, Miriam wasn't sure. But it didn't matter because Jenny slid across the bed to sit next to her and then grasped Miriam's cold fingers in hers.

The girl walked through several areas of the city, around blocks more than once, past a theatre, where she stood and stared at the gilt carvings on the facade, and past the train station, where she sat for nearly an hour waiting. Instead of climbing on a train, though, she sighed, stood, and again turned east toward the misty lake rain that had persisted throughout the day.

Finally, she rounded a corner into a wide alley where people squatted, leaning against crumbling buildings that listed to and fro as if they, being bound by the land, still shared something in common with the vast body of water that could be seen from their upper floors.

With one quick glance back, she slipped down the dingy basement steps of what could be described as little more than a towering shack. Mr. Butler craned his neck looking for signage but only found a single sheet of faded red paper with oriental characters neatly inked in black.

He stepped nearer, and although he could not read the script, the odor of the place revealed his location. He frowned, turned to take in as much information as he could without revealing his presence, and quickly made his way back out of the alley.

She'd entered an opium den.

Everything told him he should barge in and take Ione and the baby back out, if that was even where they were being hidden, but he knew Tamm, had worked with Tamm, and had no doubt that the man could take him out in a single blow.

He rushed along, doing his best not to draw attention, until he all but fell into the street. He sucked in a deep breath and then broke out into a run. Father John's church wasn't far.

"We might have the advantage." Michael walked into the parlor, trailed by John and Mr. Butler. "Mr. Butler was able to follow the girl to what he thinks is her home."

Miriam stood. "When are we leaving?" An uneaten lunch had already come and gone, and the household moved quietly about preparing for the evening meal. The waning of the day had not gone unnoticed, and Miriam was not about to sit sleepless for another night while Ava was still missing.

"We're not," Michael said, crossing back to his desk. "Where did you say you were?" He spread his palms against the map, waiting for Mr. Butler to point at the path he'd taken when following the girl.

John frowned. "She is close to the cathedral."

"What do you mean, 'We're not'?" Miriam pushed in to stand at the edge of the desk where the men had once again congregated. Mrs. Whitaker, Jenny, and Mrs. Maloney were close behind, waiting to hear what their next move would be.

Michael stopped and looked up. "We can't just go into a building we have no familiarity with. We aren't even sure Ione or Ava is there. And if we go in now, it will be obvious that we followed that girl who delivered the message. We don't want to get another person hurt in all this."

Miriam took a deep breath and held it. "Then what do we do?"

"I could go in." Jenny elbowed her way to stand in the middle of the crowd. "I've been in places like that before. It's not nice." She looked down at her dress. "I would have to find something else to wear... Maybe I could sneak in..."

"Not a chance." John's typically accommodating tone darkened, leaving no room for argument.

"Agreed." Pastor Whitaker shed his jacket and rolled up the cuffs of his sleeves before leaning over the map. He'd arrived a little before John and Mr. Butler. "We can't risk losing anyone else."

"Should we let the police know?" Mrs. Maloney shrugged. "They should be able to help."

"Not if we want to protect Ione's reputation and her business." Michael pulled up his desk chair and sat heavily, never taking his eyes off the mass of streets and alleys and topographical obstacles. "He made it fairly clear that if he could not control Ione's business, then she wouldn't have one. We have to somehow rescue Ava and Ione and neutralize his ability to destroy Ione's life in the process."

"Well..." Pastor Whitaker shrugged. "One thing is certain. She won't be alone tomorrow." Half his mouth rose in a wry smile. "I mentioned that Ione was being bothered by someone from her past and that she could use a bit of extra attention. When she opens her doors tomorrow morning, it will probably be to a line of trussed-up women, loaded down with baked goods and preserves, requesting bits of ribbon or some other transparently unnecessary item."

"She's not going to like that much." Jenny smiled.

"Probably not. But we are not about to leave her alone either."

John cleared his throat. "Um... I did much the same with my congregation. I'm afraid her little shop is likely going to be overwhelmed by customers tomorrow."

"I'll send word to Grace," Jenny said, crossing to Miriam's roll-top desk and rooting around for a clean sheet of paper. "She's going to need a bit of warning."

"If he gets angry, though, he could still damage her reputation—revenge for the interference."

The room grew quiet, the sound of the clock that had been ticking away for days reminding them of every second Ava had been missing. "Not if we beat him to it." Miriam pushed Jenny out of the way at her desk and opened the drawer with the clean sheets of paper. She pulled out a blank card—one with the Farling name in gold relief on the top of the sheet—and uncorked the ink well. "Mrs. Penn loves Ione and adores her work. She wants to use her designs for the Women's Pavilion's uniforms. She'll know what to do."

"Do we want to bring anyone else into this?" John asked.

Michael nodded. "We can use her. If she shows up tomorrow, any gossip that Tamm is able to generate could not possibly win out over the news of her visit to Ione's shop."

"It will also publicly place Ione ahead of Mrs. Black as a contender for designing the Women's Pavilion uniforms. If Tamm expects to be able to stir trouble from that pot, he'll have a tough time doing it. No one is going to question Mrs. Penn's decisions. At least not anyone who wants to keep moving in her circles."

Michael sighed. "That leaves one more substantial problem."

All eyes turned to him.

"Where is Tamm going to be tomorrow...with Ava or with Ione?"

Ione turned to see Carrie finally enter the room, Ava squirming in her arms.

"I could take her." Ione risked the offer, holding her now unbound arms outstretched.

Clarence gave one curt nod of approval, and Carrie, relief etched in her tight closed-lipped smile, shuffled the wriggling bundle to Ione.

She appeared no worse for the wear. "You've done a good job." Ione looked up to Carrie and tried her best at a kind smile.

Carrie blushed and shrugged. "My mom had lots of kids."

Ignoring all the questions that sprang to mind, Ione wrapped the now dirty blanket tighter around Ava and held her close to her chest. The warmth and restriction instantly settled the baby. "I have little sisters too."

Ione glanced around the room. A small crate shoved into the corner must have served as a makeshift cradle, but the bottle Ione had earlier noticed no longer sat on the rickety table. "Where did her bottle go?"

"I borrowed it from a lady down the street. She needed it back right away."

"Do you think you could borrow it again?"

While for the moment Ava dozed contently and quietly, Ione knew it wouldn't last long. "And what have you used for diapering?"

"I think that's enough about the baby." Clarence, who hadn't moved from his seat facing Ione, scraped the chair back and stood abruptly. "The baby is fine."

"What"—Ione measured her words carefully—"What would you prefer I do?"

He glared down at her. "What do you typically do the day before your store opens?"

Ione shook her head. "It depends. I wasn't there on Saturday, so I am not sure what needs my attention. I would probably be in the store, checking appointments and sending out cards to reschedule any appointments I missed." She stretched her right arm while still holding onto Ava with her left, and then turned her neck to ease some of the stiffness from her bunched muscles. "I would be replacing fabric samples in the proper order, attending to any last-minute alterations before the next day's fittings. I'd be putting the finishing touches on any designs, adding touches of color here and there... There are a lot of things I'd be doing."

Clarence frowned down at her.

"I can't do them from here, though." Ione risked the addition. While she didn't want to make him angry, and while she would play his game for as long as necessary to keep Ava safe, if she could in some way direct his movements, then she would do her best.

Chapter 35

"That's the problem. We don't know where he's going to be." Pastor Whitaker rubbed his hands down his face and looked at Michael. "It seems like he would want to keep a close eye on Ione, so it would make sense that he would be at the shop with her. As strange as it is, he has done little to hide his identity. It's almost as if he wants to assert himself into her life, and he thinks we will simply accept his role over her."

"I think that's exactly what we are dealing with." Michael gestured for them to all move away from the desk, where more comfortable seating options were available for everyone. "He has no interest in hiding her away. He wants to cash in. I think, for as much time was spent writing about their relationship, the motivation behind this is money."

"And jealousy." Miriam scooched over on the chaise so Jenny and Theo could join her. He climbed into her lap, and Miriam took a deep breath of the baby smell that still hid in his hair. Blinking back tears, she hugged him closer. "He's jealous of her success."

"So what about Ava?" Jenny placed her hand on Miriam's arm. "Will he bring her to Ione's shop, or will he leave her behind?"

"I don't think he'll bring her with them." Mrs. Maloney's interjection had them all turning to face the woman holding yet another tea tray. "He's bound to know that we will be at the shop, and that if that baby shows up, nothing would stop the lot of us from barging in and taking her by force if necessary."

"It wouldn't take the lot of us." Miriam gritted her teeth against the sudden vision of Tamm, the one who had unsettled her since he'd begun working for them, holding her baby. If she would have only listened to her instincts and not given into her fear that she might see something she didn't like, she might have been able to paint who he truly was beneath his neat, innocuous appearance. She might have had some kind of warning.

Jenny reached over and cleared a few things out of the way so Mrs. Maloney could set the tray down.

"So we agree he is likely to bring Ione to the shop but unlikely to bring Ava." Michael glanced around the room at the heads nodding in unison. "And it is likely the girl who dropped off the letter led us to the place where he has Ava hidden?" Again, nods. "So how do we split up?"

"First, we have to keep the rest of the households, those closest to Ione, safe." Pastor Whitaker reached out as if by instinct to brush his wife's arm.

John cleared his throat. "It goes without saying that Ione's family"—he nodded to her sisters and Mrs. Whitaker—"need to stay here until everything is resolved."

"I think we would be—" Mrs. Whitaker's sentence was cut off by the swift cock of one of her husband's eyebrows. She took a deep breath in and looked down at Lucy's thick braids. Twisting one of the brightly colored ribbons between her fingers, she shrugged. "You're right. I don't like feeling useless, but the last thing we need is to have to find someone else."

"And Miriam," Michael said.

"How is it even possible for me to sit here while you all go searching for my baby?"

"Our baby," Michael said softly. "Our baby. I will be there."

Miriam squeezed her eyes closed and concentrated on the tiny details: the scent of Jenny's perfume, the sound of the clock, the feel of Theo's chest expanding with each breath, and the clinking of the cups and saucers as Mrs. Maloney prepared the tea. Slowly, she nodded. It was a promise she didn't want to make.

"I think we need to somehow verify the baby is there, though. I'm not sure how to do it, but if we swamp the shop with people in support of Ione, Tamm is bound to get angry." John stretched his legs out and crossed them at the ankles.

"That's where I can come in," Jenny spoke in hushed tones. Her fingers laced tightly against her skirt. "None of you could pass. You are all too neat, too..." She shrugged, struggling for the right words. "I've been one of them. I know how to talk, and how to act, and who will give information for a few coins."

Miriam stared at her. "You can't go in there."

"Yes, I can. If it will help end this, then yes, I can, and I will."

John sat forward, tucking his legs beneath him. "It would be dangerous."

"Wait." Michael took a step forward, closing in on the center of the group. "We aren't actually considering allowing Jenny to go into an opium den unaccompanied, are we?"

They all looked around the room, waiting for someone to offer another option.

"Not unaccompanied." Jeremy placed a hand on his wife's shoulder. "I'll go with her. We will pose as a...ahem...couple...in search of... amusement." He frowned, his distaste for the role evident in his posture. Although Jenny had told him of her past, Miriam knew playing a part in a similar situation, even if fictional, and seeing how she'd lived as a child would be far worse than hearing it. Some things grew in the imagination with the omission of details. But when things were truly awful, well, imagination didn't do justice to the reality of what he would see.

Jenny reached up and covered his hand with hers.

"Is that the plan then?" John looked from Jenny to Jeremy's faces, back and forth, waiting for a sign of hesitation.

Jenny nodded. "We'll get ready. I'll have to find different clothes—we both will." She bit her bottom lip and looked up at her husband. "You're not going to like this one bit."

He nodded. The grim set of his jaw shouted that he understood, and more importantly, that if she were going to walk into hell, then he'd be right there next to her.

Clarence struck a match, and the flame flashed to life. The flickering light played off his features for the few seconds it took to light the stubby candle that sat on a crooked shelf next to the door. The weak flame did a better job of illuminating the room than the sun had done for most of the day. With the heavy clouds and the rain, and a liberal amount of filth coating the small glass panes, not much light had been able to penetrate. For the first time in what felt like forever, Ione could take stock of her situation.

There were two chairs. She sat on one, and the chair Clarence had taken had been the same one Carrie had earlier used. The table she'd noticed that morning would have been proud of the designation of rickety. It leaned precariously against the wall, its four legs no longer up to the task. The crate for Ava, shoved up against the same wall, still provided a filthy, hopefully warm, cradle. But when Ione turned, she saw what she'd previously missed: a sagging bed with a straw mattress and rotting ropes slumped in the corner. Designed for one person, in this place, it likely held much more than intended, and Ione prayed that tonight it would not hold her and Clarence.

She prayed it also would not hold him and Carrie. Ione glanced up at the girl, huddled in the corner, and wondered if he had used her like he'd used Ione. And did he use her other ways? Did she sing? What other talent was he exploiting?

Jenny came down the stairs with Jeremy at her elbow. Miriam tried not to wince at the sight of her friend. Before heading upstairs to change, they'd gathered the clothes from the bins the kitchen maids used to store dresses and shirts and trousers beyond repair, clothes suitable for rags, and then Jenny and Jeremy put them on.

But it wasn't the worn and dirty clothes that made the transition back to poverty believable—it was how the lack of care and look of despondence infected Jenny's posture. She was incapable of looking Miriam in the eye. At Jenny's down-turned expression, so much an echo of the one she'd worn when they'd first met, Miriam's heart constricted in a strangled dive into a past that no one standing in the room wanted to relive.

"There has to be a better way," John leaned down and whispered into Miriam's ear. Miriam shrugged and clamped her trembling lips closed, not trusting her voice to answer.

"It's not as bad as it looks." Jenny protested what Miriam was sure were their shocked expressions. "I'll be back before you know it. I'll find her. If we can get her, we will. If not, at least we'll know for sure if she is there."

Miriam swallowed and nodded, her beleaguered heart sinking with guilt. She mouthed a thank you, and Jenny nodded her understanding.

Jeremy, his head adorned with a sagging hat complete with threadbare band, towered over Jenny like a lioness guarding a sickly cub. Miriam touched his arm as they paused on their way out the door. His muscles, like iron under the rough weave, neither rejected nor invited her touch, and she waited until she could feel the warmth of his skin seep through the fabric. It was as if their descent down the stairs and toward the front steps reminded them all of how frail life could be.

"It's getting late. I'll drive." Mr. Butler, no longer trusting anyone to drive or open doors or do anything he once relied on Tamm to do, shrugged into his overcoat and opened the door.

Jenny shivered but not from cold. Miriam knew that her shiver had nothing to do with temperature; rather, the humid night air cocooned the festering city heat. She shivered from exposure to the steady death of light, and her quickly approaching past.

Miriam closed the door and listened to the click of the metal as it latched. She leaned against the cool wood, breathing in the scent of her studio, resting in the black that enveloped her.

She hadn't bothered taking the passageways. Clarence Tamm had taken that away. Miriam reached up and turned the knob on the gas sconce. It swelled with smoky light, diffused by the aged and yellowed glass globe. Everyone had watched her exit, and no one had questioned when she climbed up to the attic levels. The feeling she had not disappeared to her studio unnoticed left her with a mixture of satisfaction and trepidation. Painting had always been a refuge, a place to be lost to the world, a place to lose herself. And the knowledge that she had indeed been lost to others had somehow stirred feelings of autonomy that she had grown to crave.

She kicked up from her leaning position and crossed the paint splotched boards. She wasn't autonomous anymore. She had a baby. And that baby would always need her, would always know where she was, would always be another human intimately connected to her.

Suddenly, being alone, being hidden, held less appeal, seemed reckless. Miriam took a deep breath, picked up a brush, softened the bristles against her palm, and examined the blank canvas.

So much hung there between her and what would be. A mixture of gift and ability and practice and wonder, an infinite space where everything was possible, until the tip of her brush, laden with color, stroked the canvas, nudging convictions from the back of her mind, and finding significance in the suggestions, meaning beyond her abilities, and forever stained the tight fabric with the future she couldn't see.

Miriam touched the canvas with her dry brush, feeling the pull of the texture, waiting for the colors to come to her. She longed to hold Ava, to nurse her, to know she was healthy and warm. Instead, Miriam stood in her studio, trapped by the dangerous impotence that came from knowing only bits and pieces. She glanced at the tubes of colors, at the angry reds and the deep- green despair that jumped out. Everything she'd done for the past day had been her second choice: she picked up the cup of tea when she wanted to throw the fragile china into the cold hearth; she forced kindness from her lips when she wanted to scream at everyone, blame them for not listening to her, for not believing her; she wanted to run out of the house and kick down the door of every home in the city, but instead she silently watched Jenny step into her past just so she could help find Ava.

And the colors she wanted to pick up, the ones that burst with frustration and spoke of sleeplessness and sacrifice and her racing pulse, would not be the ones she would touch to the white backdrop of the canvas. Miriam chewed the inside of her cheek. Painting was such a lie. Nothing in life began with a white canvas. There was no real beginning to anything. Everything, a continuation of some forgotten experience, shaded by what had come before. Yet, she began.

The soft blue that came off her brush wet the canvas with a hope she didn't, couldn't feel. Why did the painting always contradict her expectations? Miriam dipped her brush again, knowing the portrait that came would not be of the future. For the first time in as long as she could remember, the painting would be of what already existed. It would not be a warning, and it would not be a tool. The painting would not be an omen, nor would it be a gift of reassurance. It would simply be a reminder of what already existed.

Miriam smiled. The painting would be of Jenny. And in her eyes would be the sacrifice, the love, and the innocence that made her so dear. Her breath caught in her chest, and she ignored the sob that rose to the surface. She mixed colors of gratitude for everything Jenny meant to her and painted to the greatness beyond the gift of seeing what would be, instead choosing the gift of the present.

Chapter 36

Ione waited for the door to close and Clarence's footsteps to retreat down the hall before turning to Carrie.

"How old are you?" Ione shifted Ava in her arms. The weight of the baby grew, and her shoulders ached with the continued effort to keep her close, but Ione wasn't about to let her go.

"Fifteen."

Ione busied her eyes with the baby to hide her reaction. She'd been sixteen when Tamm had convinced her to follow him. It had only been a few years, but it felt like forever. "You said you have a bunch of brothers and sisters?"

Carrie nodded and took a step nearer. "You want me to take a turn holding her?"

Ione shook her head. "I'm fine," she lied.

The girl scratched her head and examined the lines between the floorboards.

"Where are we?" Ione looked out the window at the view of a brick wall.

"Not far from the lake. Clarence rented the rooms."

Ava squirmed and released a dissatisfied squeak. Ione shifted her and tightened the blanket around her dedicate arms. "I think she is going to need that bottle again soon."

Carrie turned her head to look at the closed door. "Clarence told me not to leave you alone."

Ione nodded. "But he also told us to keep the baby quiet. And that isn't going to be possible if she's hungry."

Panic blotched Carrie's delicate skin, and she brought the tips of her fingers to her lips to chew the last bit of a pink nail. Ava let out another squeal, this time more insistent than the last.

Carrie paced first to the door, then to the window to look down into the dark street, as if she might find help from somewhere outside the room. "I'll go get her the bottle, but you can't move. Clarence will find you, and that would be bad."

"I promise."

Carrie paused with her hand on the door, as if she might be able to divine Ione's honesty from the dismal surroundings. Eventually, after another squeak from Ava, she sighed loudly and disappeared down the hall.

Ione swung around, taking stock of the situation. She fought to stand, her cramped legs protesting under the rapid change of position, and crossed to the window to look down and try to gauge where in the city Clarence had taken them.

Ione backed away. Nothing looked familiar, in the sense that she'd never been to this part of town before, but that didn't mean she didn't know exactly where they were. He'd taken them into one of the alleys off Clark Street in Chinatown. Ione pressed her forehead against the dirty glass, trying to make out the people below. She hoped that someone she knew might be making a late-night clandestine visit to the purveyors who stocked the ladies with their morphine and the men with the popular dabs of opium they claimed flavored their tobacco. The police, while impatient with the area, had yet to close down the dens. Ione frowned. That had more to do with bribe money than any other difficulty.

Her shoulders sank, and she returned to the chair in the middle of the room. The chances someone would find them in this part of town were slim. On top of that, there was no place to run.

Ava twisted her face into what Ione could tell would be a mighty holler. She stood quickly, jostling the infant, cooing, doing what she could without the one thing she knew the baby wanted.

The door swung open, and Ione whirled around, readying for the blow that would undoubtedly land when he saw that Carrie had abandoned her post.

Carrie slid into the room and closed the door behind her, careful to press her palm tightly to the pocked wood surface to muffle any sound. "I got it." She sank her hand into a ratty apron pocket and pulled out a bottle.

The glass did not reflect the flickering light as Ione would have hoped—the bottle was less than clean, but it was something. "You did great." She waved Carrie over. "This will help."

Ione teased the infant's bottom lip with the brown nipple, hoping that, at least this once, prayers were sufficient sterilization. Ava jerked her head toward it and latched on as if her very life depended on it. Arms and legs pulled in tight with concentration, she gulped the milk, forcing Ione to fight the suction and pull the bottle from her lips every so often so that she wouldn't choke or fill her tiny belly too quickly.

"She's a good eater." Carrie nodded, a sense of pride in her tone.

"Miriam said as much, but I didn't give it much thought until now."

Carrie sat on the floor in front of Ione's chair and tucked her legs Indian style. She examined the dry, rough skin on her hands. "Is that her mother's name?" she said quietly.

Ione nodded, surprised that the girl had no idea where the babe had come from. "What did he tell you?"

Carrie shrugged, a movement that Ione realized to be a mix of habit, insecurity, and self-preservation.

"Don't worry about it. I know he doesn't like to tell you things he doesn't want to explain."

"He says it's his job to take care of me, and my job to do what he says, no questions."

Word for word. Ione paused, took a breath, and let the shock fall away. How many times had she heard the same directive from him? How easy it had been to let him make all the decisions, to delegate her happiness, her value, to him to be assigned, and then how easy it had been to forget. Ione closed her eyes for a moment, letting her own past wash by. How simple it had been to take a step out with Evan and come to a realization that a relationship did not mean dominance and subservience. She'd forgotten some relationships did mean exactly that.

"He told me that too." For the first time, Ione offered the truth without shame. It had not been her fault any more than she would blame this young girl for falling into the same trap.

Clarence was the one to blame.

"Carrie..." Ione cleared her throat and looked from Ava's suckling form to Carrie's childlike features. "Do you know why I am here?"

Carrie dropped her eyes to her lap. Her dirty hair fell in a concealing curtain of stringy waves around her face.

"He kidnapped the baby, and then me."

Carrie nodded without looking up.

"Do you know why?"

"He says you owe him. And you have rich friends, and now you're rich too."

Ione pulled the bottle from Ava's lips and hefted the milk-sedated baby to her shoulder to pat her back. "Do you believe him?"

Carrie shrugged, still not looking up.

"Once I thought I was in love with him." Ione looked up to the open rafters of the ceiling, and when she dropped her chin again, Carrie finally met her gaze.

"But you weren't?"

"No." Ione shifted Ava higher on her shoulder, earning an unladylike sound from the infant. One side of Carrie's mouth kicked up in an unavoidable half-smile.

"How did you know?"

"I didn't." Ione settled Ava back into the cradle of her arms and offered the bottle again, this time to a much less enthusiastic connoisseur. The babe halfheartedly took the nipple but failed to suckle. "I think she's done." Ione handed the bottle to Carrie.

Carrie didn't move. "But how did you know you weren't in love with him?"

"I didn't. At least not until later. I left because my mother and sisters needed me, and I grew tired of him not letting me see them."

"Is your mother happy that you came back?" The shame that radiated from Carrie's small form dredged up a sympathetic nausea.

Ione set the bottle on the floor. "She's dead now." Ione waited for the truth to sink in. "By the time I got back, she was too ill to worry where I had been, but yes, she was glad to see me again."

Carrie's shocked expression registered all the pain Ione had felt when she learned how much of her life she had wasted hoping to be loved by a man who could only love himself.

Jenny watched the view shift from stately townhouse mansions to more modest houses to business districts, industry, and finally, to the places with which she was most familiar. She brushed her hands down her skirt, smoothing it out of habit, even though in these clothes, it was unnecessary.

How quickly things changed.

Within a couple of years, she'd gone from working in the taverns at the demand of her father to running a business and helping employ the women who used to look away when she passed them on the street; honest women, who rightly feared if their husbands had spent the grocery money at the tavern...or for her services. Jenny pressed a cool, ungloved hand to her neck, hot with lingering humiliation.

And now she was back. She frowned at Jeremy, who was watching the buildings fly by as they neared the darker parts of town. He knew everything, but knowing and experiencing were different, and Jeremy, while having lived in Chicago for some time, had grown up on a farm. When they'd first married, Jenny had tried to imagine the kind of upbringing that could create a man who loved as deeply as the one next to her. Her efforts had been painfully inadequate. When she'd met his parents, and they'd welcomed her with the same openness that Jeremy had, understanding what had to take place in order to create such a man had been clear. She'd vowed then and there to do her best by Theo, and marrying Jeremy had been part of that vow.

He looked down at her with questions registering in his gaze.

Jenny shook her head. Nothing needed to be said. But she scooted over on the seat and tucked her hand into the crook of his elbow.

"We'll be there soon." He leaned down and kissed the top of her head. Instead of a hat, they'd decided to tie a rag around her hair to hold it back. For a moment, Jenny had forgotten the lack of decoration. She felt for stray hairs that had escaped from the loose scarf.

Approaching Chinatown, the colors changed from the cool grays that dominated in the dark to the seething orange that seeped up from basement rooms adorned with sagging red paper lanterns and lingering smoke. Well-dressed patrons slunk into the alleys, avoiding the approach of a carriage whose quality meant it might carry someone who could recognize them.

They turned a corner and slowed, and Mr. Butler climbed down. "This is a close as I dare take you." He reached up to help Jenny descend the carriage. Jeremy followed close behind. Jenny knew he wasn't about to get more than an arm's reach distance from her for the night.

Mr. Butler had explained the directions to the building where the girl who had brought the message had entered. Now, he silently nodded in the right direction and then turned back to the carriage. He would wait there for them.

Jenny took a deep breath of the stagnant, familiar air. The tang of fish hung heavily in the fog, and Jenny, acting on instinct, pulled Jeremy from the ambient yellow light of a window into the safety of the shadows. Skirting puddles of unknown origin and stepping over the sprawled legs of people who had resorted to making the street their bed that night, they found the entrance.

Jeremy frowned and looked down the street, checking for anyone who might be following before they stepped into the flickering hollow of the streetlamp, and then ducked down the filth-slick steps into the thick-sweet haze of opium.

"Where do you think he is?" Ione, growing more comfortable in the confined space with Carrie at her side, turned and paced back to the side of the room with the door.

"He's probably downstairs, or down the street a ways. There's no telling. He has money now, so he will be trying his luck."

"He left you in charge of me and Ava?" It seemed a reckless decision, even for Clarence.

"Oh no." Carrie shook her head. "He wouldn't do that. The lady downstairs makes sure we do what we are supposed to do." She frowned. "Or at least that I do. I have to check in with her every so often, or else she will be up here, and we don't want her up here."

Ione crossed back to the window. If she could get a message to Michael and Miriam—at least let them know where Ava was, so that they could come and get her—that would be the best. She glanced back to the sagging bed, where she'd laid the sleeping baby. "So he would know if you left?" Ione asked as casually as she could.

Carrie nodded and frowned. "You can't get out of here...I've tried."

Ione swung around and faced the girl. "I thought you wanted to be here."

"I did." Carrie didn't meet her gaze. "At first."

"And then..."

"And then I didn't have anything left to go back to. My mom won't want me now." Carrie's voice cracked, and she sank to sit on the bed next to Ava.

"Your mother will always want you. No matter what he says or what you've done. Even if you think that going back will only humiliate your family. It doesn't matter. Your mother wants you."

Carrie looked at the sleeping form. "I wish he hadn't taken her. It was wrong." She sniffled and rubbed her nose on her threadbare sleeve.

"But just because he does something wrong, and just because you may have done wrong things, it doesn't mean you have to keep doing them." Ione glanced down to the single circle of light that illuminated the corner of the building. A man and a woman had paused there, considering whether or not to enter. Ione wanted to bang on the window, to scream that if they'd made a mistake it wasn't too late to turn around, that one mistake didn't have to lead to another, that each decision could be measured alone. She pressed her palm against the glass, feeling the cool barrier, wishing the pair to stop, to think.

The woman reached up, tucking a strand of hair behind her ear with a delicate finger, and Ione held her breath with the familiarity. Without looking away, she reached for the sash, fumbling with the stuck lock, frantic to see the face of the woman.

And then the man looked up, unseeing, into the darkness above. Ione sucked in a breath and rattled the window that had swollen shut. It refused to budge.

"What is it?" Carrie jumped up and made her way to stand next to Ione.

"Those are my friends." Ione blinked fast. The gift of a familiar face made her voice tremble.

"What are they doing here?" The trepidation in Carrie's tone revealed her fears, that another person might become trapped, that someone else might end up lost in this dark place.

"They are looking for Ava."

"And you."

Ione shrugged. "How did they know to look here?"

Carrie shook her head. "We can't take the baby down. He might be down there, or if not, then he has people watching. There's no way we can get out without him knowing. And even if we do, he'll get us back."

Ione nodded. That much she knew to be true. Escape held risk not only to them, but to those they loved.

Carrie glanced around the room, her eyes falling to the bottle. "I haven't returned it yet."

Ione caught on. "Do you have a piece of paper, or can you get something to write...?"

"No...not in time, and if I ask, they will want to know why."

"But you have to return the bottle still, so you have to go downstairs at some point. Let's wait until they step in, and then you head downstairs. You could at least try to walk past them and let them know that Ava is here and safe with me."

Carrie nodded, watching out the window. "They're coming in."

"Then go." Ione handed the bottle to Carrie and gently shoved her toward the door. "All you have to do is tell them Ava is safe."

Carrie nodded, fear and determination marching in turn across her features and then stepped into the hall, careful to close the door behind her.

Chapter 37

Mrs. Penn's arrival had been expected, but simple expectation always failed to prepare for the flutter of activity and sheer force of personality that accompanied the woman. Miriam stepped back from the window and smoothed her skirts. After Mrs. Penn had received Miriam's letter, she'd sent word back to expect her early Monday morning.

And promptly at eight o'clock, her footman rang their bell.

Another sleepless night waiting for Jenny and Jeremy to return with news, and then the hours spent deep in creating plans after they did, had Miriam nearly giddy with exhaustion. She looked a fright, of that there was no doubt. But beyond caring, she raced down the stairs in yesterday's gown to greet her guest.

"Thank you for coming by." Miriam pulled Mrs. Penn past the others and into the parlor with none of the formality that usually accompanied such a visit.

"My dear, of course I would come." She tugged her white gloves off the tips of each finger and handed them to Mrs. Maloney. "Catch me up."

An hour later, Mrs. Penn stood at the door, stretching her gloves back over her bejeweled fingers. "I am going to make a couple more stops, and then I will be on my way to the shop."

Exactly as Miriam had hoped, Mrs. Penn had understood the risk to Ione and her business.

Mrs. Penn paused at the door. "I know nothing is going to help you until your baby is back safe with you, but I want you to know that I will do everything I can." She rested her gloved hand atop Miriam's. "In the meantime, we can make sure no one has the desire to spread any malicious gossip. Don't you worry, by the end of today, Ione will still have her business, and the respect of the community, and Ava will be safe in your arms."

Another knock at the door, and Mrs. Penn swooped out before the police officer ducked into the hive of activity. He'd stopped by to give them an update regarding the search for Ava. They were searching. They thought they might have a lead. Michael and Miriam should remain calm and at home in case someone contacted them.

Michael nodded, thanked the man, and closed the door once again.

"As soon as we can confirm Tamm is at the shop with Ione, we'll let the police know where we think Ava is." Michael unnecessarily restated their plans. His skin had taken on the gray tone of sleep deprivation. He took off his spectacles and rubbed his face.

Miriam took him by the arm. "Pastor Whitaker will send word as soon as he can. Until then, maybe you should sit down."

"I should sit down?" He shook his head. "Maybe it would be best if we both did."

He followed her into the parlor, and they collapsed together on the chaise, waiting, hearts racing, for any useful tidbit of information.

Ione and Carrie had shared the small bed, Carrie next to the wall and Ione at the edge. She'd placed the crate where Ava slept flush with the bed so that she could sleep with her hand dangling into the makeshift cradle. Not that her limp, sleeping hand could ward off evil, but it felt better than nothing. They'd hoped that if the three of them appeared to be sleeping, it would prove to be more than what Clarence would want to deal with when he returned.

They'd been right. He'd stumbled into the room in the wee hours of the morning, dragging a cloud of perfume and booze and smoke, and then left again, presumably to find an unoccupied bed somewhere else. Ione, eyes squeezed closed, had nearly cried with relief when the closing door echoed through the room. The thought of sleeping next to him, of her body dwarfed by the mass of his, of smelling his breath and feeling his skin against hers and waking the next morning in the same way she'd found morning years ago... Ione sucked in the stagnant air after he left, cool relief flooding her body and chasing the hot fear from her veins.

She woke again to the dark. Measuring time in the dirty room proved impossible, but the sounds coming from beneath the floorboards meant at least a few people were moving about. Ava squeaked, her eyes open in the dark. Swinging her feet off the bed, Ione scratched at what she hoped were flea bites rather than the brutal attentions of lice or any other kind of persistent vermin that would be hard to chase out of her thick hair.

It was Monday. The day she would open the store that Clarence had claimed as his own while holding her hostage with the sheer power of her own past.

None of that mattered, though. She had to get Ava back home.

Carrie moaned and stretched. She opened her eyes and sat upright in one swift motion. "What time is it?" she whispered.

"I'm not sure."

Tucking her knees beneath her body, Carrie crawled off the end of the bed and tested the door handle. It turned. "I'll be right back. I'm going to check the time."

Clarence pushed the door open from the other side. "No need." All evidence of his night erased, he stood in the middle of the room, clean shaven, dressed absurdly well, and preening for notice.

"You look very nice." Ione stood, careful to keep the attention off the baby. "Where should I go to get cleaned up?"

"The next room. Carrie will take you there."

Ione reached down for Ava. She would do what she could to keep her in sight for as long as possible.

"Leave her here. Carrie will attend to her while we are out."

"Don't you want to bring her with us?" Ione turned and faced him. While the message had been sent, and providing Jenny and Jeremy had made it safely back to Miriam's, leaving Ava still did not sit well. Ione touched her soft cheek, and the baby rooted toward the movement. "She's hungry."

Clarence grunted and waved dismissively. "Put it down. Carrie will get another bottle, and you will wash up. We need to be on our way."

Ione bit back the reply that wanted to be let out into the open, instead doing as he commanded. She placed Ava in the middle of the bed, tucked her now even filthier blanket tightly to keep her tiny arms and legs from flailing, and followed Carrie out of the room.

"I'll take good care of her," Carrie whispered before closing the door behind Ione.

Ione stood for a second, waiting for some brilliant idea to come, for some rescue, for some answer. But when nothing happened, no footsteps, no hero appeared, she plunged the already wet rag into the cloudy water and wrung it out. The water fell in drips, rippling the pool, spreading out in waves that begged to be stopped. She could do nothing. One foot in front of the other. Ione glanced up to her still-dark reflection in the tiny cracked mirror. Her hair stood wild on her scalp, her dark eyes appeared tiny in her swollen face. She almost laughed at the thought that in a few hours, she would be welcoming customers into her shop. Surely they would run at the first sight of her. Smoothing out the rag, Ione scrubbed her face with force enough to pinken her dark skin and erase the haunted look from her eyes.

The only way to ensure Ava's safety, and the security of her family and friends, was to do as directed. And that she would.

Ione plunged the cold rag back into the water and let it soak, taking the time to unbutton her wilting gown. She stood next to the door, see-ing as it lacked the comfort of a lock, and pulled her arms from the tight sleeves before attending to the top half of her body. After buttoning up, she finished the rest whilst leaning against the wood panel for securi-ty, shook her skirts in an attempt to free them from more than a day's worth of creases, and opened the door.

How long Clarence had been standing there, she couldn't tell.

"Are you ready, madam?" The last word, spoken with exaggerated hauteur, hung in the air between them like a challenge. If she said yes, then she accepted his veiled insult to her acceptability in polite society. If she deigned to answer, then she gave him the power he sought, the one that kept her quiet, accepting his low assessment of her abilities without him.

Ione straightened and inched her chin up enough to preserve her pride, but not so much as to challenge his. "Yes." Her answer rang clear.

He nodded and took her elbow, leading her down the stairs without first checking back in on Ava. Ione clenched her teeth. She wouldn't give him the satisfaction of knowing how much she worried for the child...or for Carrie. Instead, she would pander to him. She would be his puppet, the trick that earned him money. "Your jacket is very nice." She glanced his way out of the corner of her eye as they descended the sticky steps. "It looks expensive."

"It is."

Ione smiled. If there was one thing he couldn't resist, it was a com-pliment.

Chapter 38

Ione pressed her hands against her roiling stomach and waited behind the counter for Grace to unlock the front door. Regretting the decision to wear her tightest corset, Ione tried to breathe deeply, to forget that Clarence waited mere inches from where she stood, on the other side of the curtain, listening to every word, every breath.

They'd already arrived by the time Grace entered through the service door, and Clarence had been quick to introduce himself to her. He had also been quick to make it clear that she now worked for him. Wisely, Grace nodded without glancing in Ione's direction and then set to preparing the shop for their typically busy Monday.

But by the looks of the traffic—the familiar faces who darted in and out of the cafe across the street and the pedestrians who crossed in front of the windows, not-so-casually squinting into the dark glass—this day would be anything but typical.

Ione chewed her bottom lip nervously and then stopped herself. No. She had to play, had to act as if nothing were amiss. If they were not able to get to Ava, then Clarence continuing to think everything was progressing according to his plan would be essential for her safety. Beyond that, Ione didn't care. She would work here the rest of her life, subject to his whims, as long as he left the rest of her friends alone.

"Go ahead and unlock the door, please," Ione said, her voice steadier than she felt.

Grace flipped the modest sign to open and turned the key in the lock.

She opened the door, and a woman Ione recognized from Pastor Whitaker's church stepped across the threshold.

"There you are, dear." She waved with her one free hand to Ione, standing behind the counter. A basket dangled from the crook of her other arm. "I need a couple of ribbons for my granddaughter's hair."

The woman waddled over to the counter, which for her, stood chest height. Despite the situation—Clarence waiting behind the curtain listening to every interaction and threatening ruin—Ione had to smile at her customer. She pushed the basket up to the dark stained surface and pulled back an embroidered flour sack. "These are for you, dear. Thought you might need a little something extra today."

Ione looked down into the basket at the heap of still-warm cinnamon buns. "You...you didn't have to bring anything to me...but thank you..." Ione sent a questioning look toward Grace, who was too busy with the next customer to notice.

In fact, women were piling in.

Another woman, this one also a member of Pastor Whitaker's congregation, hefted a ceramic bowl next to the basket. "Breakfast..."—she pointed to the buns— "...and lunch for you and Grace here." Uncovering the bowl instantly filled the room with the aroma of chicken soup.

"Don't forget dessert." A woman Ione never remembered seeing lifted a cloth off a pie that looked like it might have been baked as an advertisement for perfection. "Apple," she said proudly.

"Grace?" Ione called for her assistant, but the growing throng of women prevented any kind of sound other than those of a happy reunion. "Excuse me, please," she said to the smiling women lining her counter. They obviously knew something she did not.

Grace, busy cutting ribbons and counting out buttons and pinning on hats and taking orders, looked in five minutes the way they tried not to look at the end of the day. One side of her hair had let loose its pins, and small circles of sweat had gathered under her arms. But her conspiratorial smile informed Ione this had not been a surprise. She'd also played a role.

Ione reached the door and stuck her head past the women waiting to gain access to her remarkably small shop. The line stretched near the end of the block.

"How are you?" A woman with bright red hair offered a crooked smile and held out a bundle of bluebells.

"Ruby?" Ione reached out and hugged the woman, more because greeting her in any other way with the crowded conditions would have been nearly impossible. "Why are you here? Is everything all right at the warehouse?"

Ruby had been one of the first women they'd hired. She'd become faster than anyone else on the largest of their sewing machines. "No problems." She smiled. "Father John mentioned to some of the women that you were in a situation where being surrounded by your friends might be helpful." She smiled and blinked against the build-up of tears that threatened to spill out of her warm blue eyes. She leaned in closer to whisper, "Jenny said I could have the day to come down here and help. I'm here for whatever you need."

Ione hugged her again, tighter this time, and pulled her into the shop. "If you could stand at this counter and cut ribbons..." Ione pointed to Grace. "I don't think she has time."

"Of course." Ruby smiled, her countenance shifting from that of concerned friend to one of business associate. She brushed her hands together and looked around. "I'll go in back and grab an apron."

Ione tried to stop her before she could reach the door, but Ruby's formidable gait carried her through the crowd and to the curtain that concealed Clarence's presence before Ione could do anything but stare.

"Oh." Ruby, nearly running into Clarence as he pushed aside the curtain, stood her ground, frowning at him. "I'm Ruby. I'm here to help Ione," she said, crossing her arms over her chest.

Ione bit back a smile.

Ruby, having a dock worker for a husband, was no stranger to bullying her way past any man who might stand in her way. Even Clarence stepped to the side for her before realizing he had lost the battle. Her sweet smile, contrasting with the icy blue glare she leveled at him, announced her victory.

Clarence looked around the room. Ione waited for him to see her standing amidst the women. He took a step forward onto the pink carpets, and instantly a gaggle of old women surrounded him, feeling his silk vest, commenting on the fine fabric, and in essence making further progression into the room impossible.

Ione shrugged innocently and turned, not waiting to see his reaction to the blockade.

John and Pastor Whitaker walked side by side down the one road in the city least likely to appreciate the presence of clerical collars and long black robes. They'd been sure to make no secret about their presence, instead relying on the authority often afforded a minister to help them gain access into places typically unpopulated by churchgoers. The fact that their presence would usually indicate a death worked only in their favor, as those raised with religious mothers crossed themselves and moved out of their path.

"I think it's the next door down." John didn't turn his head to speak; instead, he kept his chin higher than typical, hoping to carry an air of intimidation. He didn't like it much. A few doors back he'd had to nearly step over a man, still passed out in the street from the previous night's drinking.

"Do you get the feeling we should spend more time here?" Pastor Whitaker frowned at John.

"Undoubtedly."

Pastor Whitaker made a guttural sound that communicated both agreement and regret.

Slowing, they stopped in front of a sagging, three-story wood building. After the Chicago fire, housing had become a crisis, and wood structures were raised with abandon. Of course, they had been intended to serve as temporary buildings, only to be used until more permanent, and fire resistant, brick structures could be constructed. And in most places, the plan had been complete, with many neighborhoods now lined with stone facades. But here, in the poorer areas, near the docks and the meat packers and other industries that filled the skies with thick smoke and stuffed the pockets of the elite with money, the temporary housing had become anything but temporary.

"Should we begin with the basement or start on the first floor?" John craned his neck to look up to the drooping roof peaks.

"I think the basement is the main entrance." Pastor Whitaker shook his head. "The first floor looks like an entrance to a brothel."

John's eyebrows shot up, and he looked for the telltale lantern in the window that advertised the services that could be found within the thin walls. He took a deep breath and frowned. "Maybe we should have called the police first." It wasn't that he'd led a perfectly clean life before he'd taken his vows. As a boy, he'd done his fair share of sneaking into places he shouldn't have been. But this place, this stood out. Avoiding another sticky puddle, John came to the conclusion that his life had been much more sheltered than he'd previously thought.

"Why do you think this place is here? Even the police avoid it." Pastor Whitaker took the first step down to the basement entrance. "Or, maybe"—he lifted one eyebrow—"they come here to partake of the spoils."

John exhaled loudly. "Let's get this over with." He pushed ahead, holding his robes to keep them from dragging against the filth of the stairs, and opened the door to a cloud of stench that had them both backing up a step.

A shared cringing frown, and they dove in from the street.

The countertop next to her appointment book, now stacked high with various gifts of canned goods, fresh baked breads, flowers, a hand-made length of lace, notes of encouragement, and anything else the women could carry in, looked dangerously close to toppling.

Ruby elbowed through the crowd. "Why don't we carry some of these things upstairs for you?"

Ione glanced across the room to where Grace leaned around a woman, measuring her waist for a sash she wanted to order as a way to update an old gown. She looked back to Ruby. "We?"

Ruby nodded toward the women congregated in front of the fabric samples, handing them out, cataloguing who wanted to order what and how much. "Put some others to work too. Too much to do today."

Ione nodded, dumbly.

"Should we then? Carry it all up?"

"Oh." Ione swung around again and examined the counter. "Of course. I'm afraid I'm a bit..."

"Distracted?" Ruby laughed. It was a cheerful, rich sound that expanded the walls of the room. "Don't worry about it. I'll take care of things. I think that gentleman over there could use some assistance."

Ione twisted her neck. The only man in the place had been Clarence, but he had retreated to his place in the back room, no doubt calculating the profits earned from the packed store.

"Over there." Ruby pointed toward the window at the front of the store.

Her heart skipped at the sight of Evan. Outside, peering in through the glass, he stood, waving in her direction.

Ione gasped and turned to make sure Clarence hadn't seen him. He couldn't be here, now. He had to leave. As far as she knew, he'd not joined the list of people Clarence had threatened, the list of people who stood to lose so much simply because of their relationship with her, the long list of friends and family who could suffer because of even an imagined slight. Clarence considered Ione his, and in reality, she was. She had to be. At least she had to act like it, to make him believe.

And Evan, showing up now, could only put everything in danger.

Ione shook her head, and Evan responded not with the confused glance she might have expected, or with a hurt expression, or in any other way that might make sense. Instead, he smiled, shrugged, and cocked an eyebrow. He was in on whatever all these people had planned. Ione turned to face the rest of the room. Suddenly, the orchestration in it all was plainly evident. They were here to protect her from Clarence.

From the time they opened, it had been apparent that some kind of news had gotten out, but Ione had been so busy, she hadn't taken stock of the scale of what had obviously become a mission on the part of her friends. The women in her store had gathered from every corner of her life: the warehouse, John's congregation, her customers, Pastor Whitaker's parishioners, and—she turned back around to find Evan now in her shop, towering over her like some protective sentry—him. Even he had come to her rescue.

An unchecked tear fell from Ione's lashes as she took in the smiles of the women who surrounded her. Even with the tragedy of a missing baby, her friends had still taken care to make sure she, the one to blame for the entire situation, was safe.

Evan reached for her hand, and Ione, too stunned to resist, didn't pull away.

Chapter 39

They took the creaking steps two at a time, John in the lead, Pastor Whitaker close on his heels.

The house, passed out from a night of debauchery, had offered little resistance. Doors had been left unlocked and gaped open with opium-induced shamelessness. A stench rose from the basement rooms where pallets full of people, who looked like they hadn't moved in days, ignored them as they walked around, or, when necessary, over them. The wrinkled madam on the main floor shrugged when she learned they were not customers in search of companionship.

John clenched his fists against the desire to throttle his brothers who had opened that possibility in the ancient woman's mind.

The second floor melted in a haze of peeling wallpaper, grungy, cluttered floors, and sagging ceilings. An arguing couple pierced the silence with a burst of profanities that died as quickly as it began.

"This place needs to be condemned." The disdain in Pastor Whitaker's tone matched nicely with the snarl John knew had taken over his own face.

A closed door at the end of the dark hallway was the only one they hadn't opened.

"Attic entrance?" Pastor Whitaker pointed to it.

"Let's." John stepped ahead of him again, careful not to brush up against the filth that dripped down the crumbling plaster walls. He pushed open the door and climbed up into another hallway, this one lined with closely packed doors.

No longer bothering to knock, John opened the first one to an empty room. The next and the next sparsely furnished rooms were also empty.

"It's cold up here." Pastor Whitaker reached for the handle on the third door. He rattled the knob. "Locked."

John closed the door he'd opened and walked over to where Pastor Whitaker stood, testing the knob again. He leaned in, pressing his ear against the dry wood. He heard whispering.

John knocked. "Anyone in there?"

Nothing.

"I'm looking for a baby. Does anyone here have a baby?"

Again, silence. John looked at Pastor Whitaker and then at the door, shrugging.

"It's not like it hasn't been done a hundred times before." Pastor Whitaker pointed to the splintered and nailed doorjamb and then moved out of the way.

John backed up, lifted his robes past his knees, and with one swift kick and a loud crack, the door lay on the floor of the room.

The girl who had delivered the note crouched in the corner, a crying, squirming bundle in her arms. John took a step closer, and she shrank even further into the dank room.

"You'll be fine now. We've come to get you." John again approached her, slower this time.

She touched Ava's face, stroking her soft cheek. "She's a good baby."

"That she is." John nodded. "And you've done a good job caring for her. What's your name?"

She looked past John and into the hall, no doubt searching for any-one who might be listening and report back to Clarence. "You have to take her fast. Before he comes back." She struggled to a standing po-sition, Ava clutched to her chest, before they could reach her to help.

Thrusting Ava into John's arms, she pushed them out the entrance of the room.

Surprised by her strength, John let her herd him for a moment but stopped before he reached the broken door. He turned. "You need to come with us. And I still don't know your name."

She sighed with exasperation. "Carrie. I'm Carrie, but I can't come with you. He will be angry the way it is."

Pastor Whitaker nodded. "I imagine he will be, but I don't think he'll be able to do much from jail."

"He's in jail?"

"Not yet, but we know where his is, and he will be soon."

Clarence watched the events unfold from his post behind the curtain. The shop, filled to the brim with twittering biddies and their plumed hats, had taken in a considerable sum so far.

He frowned and crossed his arms over his chest. Without a doubt, word had gotten out that Ione had been missing. And these women were the reaction. One of them, the insufferable redhead, barged into the back room, ignoring him, grabbed a bolt of fabric, and ducked back into the crowd. Clarence smiled coldly. They might think they were here supporting Ione, but they obviously had no idea that he held the Farling's child as security against any foolishness on the part of her friends.

And if that failed, he could always call on the competing dressmaker. Clarence leaned against the stool and crossed one well-dressed ankle over the other, examining the shine of his new shoes. He'd missed expensive clothes. Yawning, he reached up to cover his mouth and then sat up on the stool. It had been a long night, but he hadn't lost too much. And besides, now that he had Ione working for him again, his income would be more reliable.

Clarence glanced up to the ceiling. He hadn't been up there to see what kind of luxuries she'd hidden in her apartment. It wouldn't be a bad idea for him to get some sense of where he would be sleeping from now on.

The curtain parted again, and Grace stepped into the room. Like Ruby, she chose not to acknowledge his presence; instead, she walked past him, picked up a pair of scissors, and turned to walk back out.

He dropped a foot in her path. "Everything going well out there?"

"Yes, sir." She hunched her shoulders, waiting for his permission to leave.

"You may go." Clarence moved his foot and stood to follow her out.

The room was even more crowded than it had been a few minutes ago. Clarence skirted the wall, trying to make it to Ione's apartment entrance. Maybe her bed was comfortable. Of course it would be. Clarence stifled another yawn and decided that it might be a good time to take a short nap.

Then, over Ione's head, his eyes locked with another man's.

Ione followed the direction of Evan's stare. Clarence.

He had seen them. How long had he been watching?

Clarence took a step nearer, and Ione backed into Evan's chest. His hands wrapped around her waist in a protective net, and Ione knew she shouldn't be seen allowing a man to touch her, that her heart shouldn't be racing at the feel of his fingers burning through her corset, that the very fact that Evan's touch was a relief instead of an intrusion made all the names Clarence was bound to call her true.

Evan pulled her back against the warm muscles of his chest, and in one swift motion turned her, placing himself between her and the dead stare Clarence had leveled at her.

Ione pulled at Evan's jacket, trying to fight her way back around. He didn't understand. His actions would make him a target. The crowd pressed in, and Ione gulped air into her constricted lungs. They had to leave. She had to empty the store. Maybe she could talk Clarence into taking her to a new city, talk him into a new start. What had they all been thinking?

Clarence pushed one woman out of the way in an attempt to reach Ione, but stopped short as the door bells sounded and a new ruckus started up.

Ione stretched to see who it could be, who she would have to beg Clarence to forgive, the identity of the next victim, but all she could make out was a crowd of tall pastel-colored hats, festooned with feathers and nests and ribbons, and every other kind of decoration one ever thought to put on a hat.

"Where are you, dear?" Mrs. Penn's voice called out over the crowd.

Ione stopped short. Mrs. Penn was in her store. *The* Mrs. Penn.

Her eyes locked with Clarence's, and everything became clear. He knew who the Penns were, and he knew with her support, nothing he could say, no rumor he could spread, would have more power than her acceptance. Ione smiled, enjoying Clarence's suddenly ashen expression.

Miriam had thought of everything.

"Dear? Dear? Where are you?" Mrs. Penn's church-bell voice rang out over the other noise of the room, and the women hushed. "I'm here to discuss the uniforms for the Women's Pavilion."

The blood rushed back into Ione's numb extremities. Her fingers tingled with the suddenness of it all. "I'm over here." She raised her arms and waved them over the heads of the other women.

"Oh good." Mrs. Penn, all smiles despite the crowd, made her way to stand in front of Ione. She leaned in close. "Ava is back home."

"Oh..." Ione covered her face with both hands and dropped to her knees.

Evan knelt down next to her. "It's okay. Everything is going to be fine. It's over."

Stunned, Ione looked up, meeting his warm gaze. "Where's Clarence?"

"He snuck out when Mrs. Penn came in. The police were waiting out back to take him away."

Ione struggled to get back to her feet. "What about Carrie?"

"Who's Carrie?"

"She's the girl Clarence made watch Ava."

Evan looked around the room, pulling Ione to lean against his chest until she was steady on her own feet. He waved toward the door. "You can ask Father John what happened to her."

Ione rubbed her face. Everything happened so quickly. Groups of women were waving and stepping out of the store into the street, and after waiting for an opening, John made his way behind the counter to where Ione and Evan stood, flanked by Grace and Ruby.

"Did you help Carrie?" Ione asked John even before he stopped.

"Yes." He smiled. "She's at the Farlings'. Last I knew, Mrs. Maloney and Theo were dragging her down to the kitchen to feed the poor thing."

"And Ava is healthy? She's fine?"

John nodded. "Everything is back to normal."

Ione glanced back to Evan. The last two days had thrust her into the past she'd feared, the one she'd tried to conquer on her own, and the results of her efforts placed the people she should have trusted to help into harm's way.

"Do you think Miriam will forgive me?" Ione chewed the inside of her bottom lip and stared at the things still piled on the counter.

"There's nothing to forgive." John reached out and covered her hands with his.

"I want to see her." Ione looked around the room at the few close friends who remained. "I need to go see her."

"Let's give them some time." John released her hand and looked around the room. "I think right now we should clean up this place, and then maybe go see the Whitakers. Your sisters were worried."

"Oh my goodness." Ione looked around. "I was so worried about Ava..."

"As you should have been." Evan nodded, smiling down at Ione. "But Evangeline is planning dinner tonight, and I think we should probably not miss it."

Chapter 40

Miriam watched Ava, bathed and safely tucked into their bed, as she dozed contentedly. Her daughter's fingers, pink and plump, wrapped around Miriam's pinky, and Miriam couldn't stop watching how her sleeping face twitched and smiled and moved even in her sleep.

"I can't believe it's over," Miriam said to Michael, sitting at the edge of the bed. "He's in jail."

Michael took his spectacles off and folded them before tucking them into his vest pocket. "I'm so sorry I didn't believe you."

Miriam shrugged. "I might not have believed me either." She looked up at her husband. So much had changed in such a short time. She'd gone from avoiding contact with anyone to craving it. Miriam wiggled her finger out of Ava's grasp and moved so she could sit next to Michael.

"What should we do about the passageways?"

Miriam looked to where she knew the opening for the hidden door rested, and then held her hand out for Michael to enclose in his warm fingers. "I don't think we need them anymore."

Michael stilled. "You're sure?"

Miriam closed her eyes, considering life without being able to hide. "There's no one here who doesn't care for us." Miriam paused, searching for the right words. "If I'm avoiding them, then isn't that rejecting them in a way?"

Michael lifted his arm and draped it across her shoulders, pulling her close. "Should I have the things moved out of the rooms and the doors sealed?" His husky words ruffled Miriam's hair, and she tucked her head in deeper into the strength of his chest.

She nodded. "We'll have to find space for a few things, but...well, things have changed. I think I will feel more secure being around everyone than alone."

Michael nodded. "We'll get started on it tomorrow."

The summer evening promised to stay warm for hours. Ione looked around the garden table at her sisters and Pastor and Mrs. Whitaker and finally at the man sitting next to her.

"It's time for you to be off to bed." Mrs. Whitaker stood, gathering the plates in one hand and the silverware in the other.

"Do I have to?" Lucy pleaded with Pastor Whitaker.

Ione hid a smile. Not only had she stopped asking Ione for permission when she was there, but Ione had noticed that when Lucy called him *Dad*, it was without hesitation.

"Listen to your mother, sweetie. But I bet there's a cookie inside on your way."

Lucy jumped down out of the chair, followed by Maggie. "I'll help her." Maggie trailed closely behind her sister but paused to send a knowing look in Ione's direction.

Ione frowned. Her overly perceptive little sister could use lessons in subtlety.

Evan chuckled after the screen door slapped closed behind the pair. "I should be getting you home too."

They stood, and Mrs. Whitaker wrapped Ione in a tight hug. "We were so worried. Thank God you are back."

Ione blinked back the tears that had been either flowing or threatening to flow for most of the day. "I'm glad too," she whispered to the woman who, although too young to be her mother, had partially filled the hole left by her mother's passing.

The night, so much like the last time she and Evan had walked together, echoed with the summer sounds of crickets and scurrying things, of birds finally settling in, and houses alive with quiet chatter.

Evan cleared his throat and stopped once they'd passed out of sight of his brother's house. Ione looked up, expecting to see the familiar laugh lines at the corner of his eyes or the teasing half-smile he sometimes wore when they were together. Instead, she looked up to his eyes roaming her face, finally resting to search the depths of hers. "I don't know what I would have done if he had taken you away."

Ione looked down but felt his hands under her chin, lifting her back into the intensity of his gaze. "I'm serious. When I heard that you had been taken, I nearly panicked. Seeing you in your shop, healthy and moving around and talking, was the best gift I've ever received."

Ione tried again to look away, only to be dragged back in. "You need to understand," he pleaded. "We haven't known each other for long. I know that. And you may not feel the same way I do, yet. But I need you in my life. I don't care what has happened in the past. I don't care if you feel like there is no future or that the future would be difficult. I don't care because I need you in my life."

Ione swallowed and nodded, not trusting her voice to make any kind of coherent words.

"I need you to know that I intend for us to be together. That this is not a game for me, this is not me trying to control you, that I would never treat you like he treated you. I need you to know that my intentions toward you are honorable and that there is not a thing in your past that you could tell me that would change that."

Ione chewed her bottom lip, again nodding.

"And you shouldn't do that." Evan brought his thumb up and tugged on the tender place under her lip. Ione released the skin, entranced by the feel of his fingers and how his eyes changed color the closer his face came to hers.

"I..."

He paused.

"I don't think there's anything you don't know." The words came out in a rush and Ione closed her eyes, first feeling their breath mingle, and then the pressure of his lips as they took hers.

How many other men? The question raced through her mind as every one of her senses turned inward, contracted to concentrate on the feel of his lips covering hers. How many other men had done the same thing?

None. The answer was simple. This kiss...his...was her first.

Epilogue

Jenny and Ione poked their heads into the open door of Miriam's studio. "What are you painting?" Jenny was the first to step in.

"Nothing yet." Miriam dropped her brush and waved her friends in. "You both have some time today?"

"Why?" The hesitation in Ione's voice meant she knew what was going to happen next.

"I'm going to paint us." Miriam pointed to the brick wall where she'd hung a green velvet backdrop.

A squeal from the other side of the room alerted Jenny and Ione that they were not alone. They both rushed to the side of the cradle Miriam had placed close to the window to allow for fresh air. Ava, now nearly four months old, giggled as Ione reached in and tickled her toes.

"I think she gets bigger every time I see her." Jenny turned back to the easel and the determined look Miriam leveled at her. "So you want to paint us." Jenny raised a brow and twisted up her face in a mock scowl. "That means I have to sit still."

"You'll manage." Miriam pointed to the chair in front of the fabric drape. "And Ione, you'll stand behind and a little to the side."

The women walked over. Miriam adjusted the angles, turned up one lamp and down another, and closed the shade on one window. "There."

"You'll add yourself later?" Ione asked, trying not to move her face while speaking.

Miriam frowned at her. "Yes. Later. But right now I need to capture you both."

"Why now?" Jenny asked.

Miriam paused, brush in midair. Then she lowered it to the brown and then the white and mixed the colors on her palette until they blended to the perfect shade. "I suppose because it is now," Miriam said, her eyes drifting over the curves of her friends' faces, studying the lines, the proportions, the shadows and highlights. She dipped her brush again and then brought it to the canvas. "And now is the greatest gift."

PORTRAITS OF GRACE SERIES

SOUL PAINTER
Miriam can paint the future...but can she change it?

SOUL'S PRISONER
She will fight for her future...but can she escape her past?

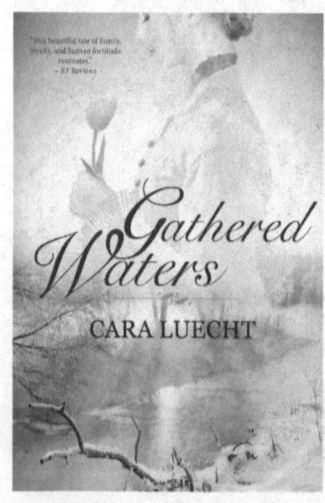